ABOUT THE AUTHOR

Maggie Allder was born and brought up in Gamlingay in Cambridgeshire, the second daughter of a village police officer. She studied at King Alfred's College, Winchester (now the University of Winchester), in Richmond, Virginia, and later at Reading University. She taught for thirty-six years in a Hampshire comprehensive school. After exploring more orthodox forms of Christianity, Maggie became a Quaker, and is happy and settled in the Quaker community in Winchester. She has previously written three novels that form a trilogy of sorts: *Courting Rendition*, *Living with the Leopard* and *A Vision Softly Creeping*. The fourth and fifth novels, *The Song of the Lost Boy* and *Beyond the Water Meadows*, both stand alone. All these first five novels take place in and around Winchester, where Maggie still lives. This is the third book in her 'Lonely Island' series following *Dark Waters* and *Marigold's Tale*. Maggie volunteers for a not-for-profit organisation, Human Writes, which aims to provide friendship to prisoners on death row in the USA.

THE RECLAMATION OF JARVIS

BOOK THREE OF
THE LONELY ISLAND SERIES

MAGGIE ALLDER

Copyright © 2024 Maggie Allder

The moral right of the author has been asserted.

Apart from any fair dealing for the purposes of research or private study, or criticism or review, as permitted under the Copyright, Designs and Patents Act 1988, this publication may only be reproduced, stored or transmitted, in any form or by any means, with the prior permission in writing of the publishers, or in the case of reprographic reproduction in accordance with the terms of licences issued by the Copyright Licensing Agency. Enquiries concerning reproduction outside those terms should be sent to the publishers.

This is a work of fiction. Names, characters, businesses, places, events and incidents are either the products of the author's imagination or used in a fictitious manner. Any resemblance to actual persons, living or dead, or actual events is purely coincidental.

Matador
Unit E2 Airfield Business Park,
Harrison Road, Market Harborough,
Leicestershire. LE16 7UL
Tel: 0116 2792299
Email: books@troubador.co.uk
Web: www.troubador.co.uk/matador
Twitter: @matadorbooks

ISBN 978 1805142 980

British Library Cataloguing in Publication Data.
A catalogue record for this book is available from the British Library.

Printed and bound in Great Britain by 4edge Limited
Typeset in 11pt Aldine401 BT by Troubador Publishing Ltd, Leicester, UK

Matador is an imprint of Troubador Publishing Ltd

To refugees everywhere
and to all who work to improve their lot.

PROLOGUE

It was a bitterly cold, dark day. On the cliffs a man was standing looking down from his vantage post, where he could see my bothy and my beach. He was wearing a long, dark coat and a football scarf, and his feet were bare. Jarvis. I would have been uneasy, alarmed even, if I had been aware of his presence. His hair was long and dishevelled and his face, I am sure, was inscrutable. I had no idea that he was watching us, that he knew just who we were entertaining, who came and went from my little home, where the door was never locked, where anybody could wait until we were all out and come in for any nefarious purpose…

Inside, of course, it was warm and bright, with no sense of foreboding.

"We'll have to eat off our laps!" Malcolm was saying. "There's only room for three at the most at the table, and Marie will need to move her tablet and all that clutter!"

"It's not clutter!" I objected, laughing. "It's my Christmas present list! The ferries are so unreliable nowadays that we have to put in our orders at least a month in advance if we want things to arrive on time!"

"You should have done as Dad did!" Beth was sitting on the settle nursing a glass of whisky. "He emailed me two sides of A4 paper with all the things he wanted me to bring over. It took me two full days in Edinburgh to do all the shopping!"

I had never thought of my bothy as being small. Even when Malcolm, my partner, was there, and my son Duncan with his group of friends sitting round the range or taking over the kitchen area, there always seemed to be plenty of room. But the day I am thinking of now, the eve of *Huldufolk* Day in the year that Lyle and Verity married, my home seemed seriously crowded. Malcolm's youngest daughter, Beth, was there, and Angus, his son. They were over from the mainland, visiting their paps for the first time since he had returned to the island a little over a year earlier. Travel between the island and the mainland was really precarious by then, although still possible. You probably know that there are no timetabled services at all now, all these years later as I tell this tale.

Duncan and his good friend Marigold were sitting on his bed at the north end of the room, putting the final touches to their wee house, the cardboard model that would be taken in procession the following day and finally burnt on a special fire, or *brenni*, down at the summer harbour. Sigrid had delivered some wool that Freda Sinclair had dyed ready for my next knitting project, but she had left by dinner time. My phone kept pinging in messages about plans for the celebrations. It was a busy, happy scene, but not quiet!

If you have seen the documentary that the young BBC Alba crew made about our island, En-Somi, which means 'Lonely Island', you will have seen shots of our village, Gamla Hus. You will even have seen some scenes from inside typical bothies or crofters' cottages, but not any pictures of my home. I live west of the village, with a stunning view over the North Atlantic looking towards the uninhabited island of Liten Stein, which is always just beyond the horizon.

You might remember the year that all this happened. It was the year of Storm Fyodor, the storm that seemed to affect the whole of the northern hemisphere. The big news was that the last of the Florida Keys went underwater, the Palace of Westminster was completely flooded and they closed the Tate Modern – the clean-ups had become just too expensive. Those things all seemed a long way away for us, living on our tiny island in the North Atlantic.

But it was a tough summer for us too in more ways than one, although it had started well enough, especially in and around our little community of Gamla Hus, west of Fyrtarn Fjell, which is the highest hill on the island of En-Somi. We had welcomed into our midst a group of climate refugees, people who had been used and abused for years. Some of us – Lyle, the local *nasyoni*, or police officer Verity his new wife, my partner, Malcolm, and I, had been able to free them from those who had trapped them in modern-day slavery, and the wider community had rallied round, doing all that we could to enable them to stay, to settle and to flourish. By the autumn of that year, we had one family living in their newly renovated home next to the shop, and another household in a new-build bothy just round the hill from the Kullanders' place, a little exposed but with an impressive view of the summer harbour.

We had been exceptionally busy all through the long summer days; building, fishing, tending our gardens and looking after our animals. When the older bairns came home from school in Lerwick, Shetland, for the long summer holidays they had joined in with the work, as is our custom. We made jams and chutneys, froze cuts of lamb, and dried and smoked fish. We took a day off from our labours for the summer solstice, picnicking on the beach at the head of Loch Innsjen, where the young ones swam in the bitter cold water, and my son Duncan and young Shawn raced to the mooring rock and back, and Duncan only won by the length of an oar.

But in many ways we were up against it, struggling with high taxes and ever-worsening weather, so that we felt more and more cut off from the mainland and even from the Shetland Islands. Malcolm and I were really thankful, I remember, that one of his daughters and his only son were able to come over for the traditional *Huldufolk* Day celebrations, and that the ferry had made it from Lerwick to the island in time for the bairns in school on Shetland to come home. It was 31 November, we were well into the dark days, the days of wild winds and driving sleet, of grey skies and long, black nights. These were the days of huge, rolling waves crashing onto the shore, of plumes of spray as high as the Stacks of Seamus, of closed shutters, of fur-lined winter jackets, broken internet connections, of isolation.

It was easy to see why the *En-Som-in-Fedii*, or islanders of days gone by, had felt the need to please the hidden folk and to keep them on their side when faced with such a winter. And it was easy to see why the tradition had remained, despite a veneer of Christianity and more than a veneer of rationality. We all need protection against the darkness.

CHAPTER 1

*H**uldufolk* Day was, by the time I am remembering, pretty much a children's festival, but there is still, I think, a sort of lurking belief in the wee hidden folk among some adults. We share these beliefs – or perhaps I should call them instincts – with Icelanders and the people of the Faroe Islands, and some of the tales we tell are not dissimilar, I have heard, from Irish stories about leprechauns. To keep the *Huldufolk* friendly towards us and to celebrate that they live among us, once a year we make miniature *hus*, or houses, and process with them around the island we all share. At the end of the day we burn these wee houses on bonfires close to the sea, and this brings us, so we say, good fortune on land and water.

Malcolm had raised his family on the mainland, and they hadn't grown up with our island traditions but Beth, especially, had discovered a new sense of identity and wanted to experience our traditions for herself. My son Duncan, of course, had grown up immersed in island lore, and had attended the village school and taken part in *Huldufolk* Day every year since he was quite small. Marigold was still learning our island customs, but she was lapping up everything to do with life on En-Somi. The wee house that she had started to make at school was a beautifully coloured little cardboard construction. It seemed a shame that it would be burnt.

That year, I seem to remember, 1 December fell on a Sunday. That was why Marigold had brought her *hus* home to make the final touches, but we were all to meet up at the school just as we always did. Each year we followed a different route. The bothies that were hardest to reach, if you started from the village, are to the south of Gamla Hus where Jamie MacLoughlan works quite a lot of land, mostly used for sheep but with a couple of fields where he grew oats – and where oats are still grown to this present day. Since we were planning to visit his croft, it had been decided to include Malcolm's bothy and then to follow the clifftop path over to Hunger Moor, and to include the almost-completed new home west of the Sinclair property, where the newcomers, Mandy and Harry and Mandy's two youngsters, were already camping out.

Tradition stipulates that at each dwelling the procession will stop and call for food for the *huldufolk*. If refreshment is forthcoming and is generous and of a good quality the inhabitants will be blessed, but if the food on offer is sparse or stale it bodes badly for the year to come. Since the *huldufolk* are normally invisible, it falls on the islanders to taste the food. Malcolm and I had been preparing for a couple of days before his son and daughter arrived. The wee folk should be happy enough with what was on offer at his place. However, both Malcolm and I were comparatively well-off among the *bondii*, or common people, Malcolm because he had a pension from his employment as a social worker, and me because Bjorn was still generous, despite having a new family in Norway. Other *En-Som-in-Fedii*, or islanders, were struggling, but of course they would do their best.

Beth and Angus met us at the school around noon, where an excited procession of bairns of various ages were lining up with helpful parents and Sigrid, the schoolteacher. It was a crisp, cold December day, the wind blowing from the north, so that by the time Duncan and I had walked up from my bothy to the village my lips were chapped and I needed more of Lyle's mother's amazing home-made lip salve. We all visited the village shop first, just a stone's throw up the track from the school, where Marigold's mother Rose and Shona, one of the owners of the shop back then, gave us shortbread and hot herbal tea. Everyone seemed cheerful. The children were just getting into the swing of things, banging on their home-made drums and a selection of saucepan lids that served for cymbals, while their parents – usually the fathers, as custom dictated – held their *hus* aloft.

Duncan, of course, considered himself too old to have made his own wee house, but he and his friend Andy were in among the younger school children, helping where they were needed and allowing themselves to enjoy the general excitement and hubbub. Beth and Angus walked alongside me – at least, they did where the path was wide enough.

"Paps brought us back to En-Somi for *Huldufolk* Day once," Beth told me. "I don't remember it very well; I was quite small. And we were on the other side of the island, because that's where he had grown up." She looked around at the moors and the rough, stony track, at the dark blue sea glistening beyond where the blades of Malcolm's turbine were circling gracefully in the wind. "It's very beautiful," she added. "I'm not sure kids notice such things."

Angus chuckled. He had a laugh that was an echo of Malcolm's, deep and hearty. "I remember that," he said. "It rained all day, and you sulked, and Bonnie said that she didn't believe in fairies, so Mam told her off for saying such things in front of wee bairns. It was all a bit of a disaster!"

"How old was I?" Beth wondered.

"Oh – five or six, I suppose. Mam wasn't ill then – or, if she was, we didn't know it. Paps wanted to bring us over again after she died, but we all vetoed it. Looking back, I think that Bonnie and I were horrible teenagers!"

"You were all right," encouraged Beth, stepping across a small burn that crossed the track and gurgled down between two huge, grey rocks. "You looked after me. Do you remember meeting me from school on the last day of term, so that I could carry everything I needed for the holidays?"

"*Nei.*" Angus grinned. "Are you sure that was me?"

3

★★★

It was hard work, climbing up to the MacLoughlans'. Their bothy and quite a lot of their acreage is on a spur of land, almost a peninsula, and under normal circumstances the only people to use their track were the MacLoughlan family themselves. They had done their best to keep the pathway in working order, not least because they had bairns at the school, coming and going every day. There is an ancient stone bridge across the burn just where it empties into Oden's Inlet, and huge rocks planted across the lower part of the moor where it becomes marshy, to act as stepping stones. Even so, the children had to stop their drumming and hand over their makeshift instruments to the adults in order to balance as they crossed the most difficult terrain, and some of the fathers ended up carrying the wee ones. I remember Shirley, one of the newcomers, riding on Eric's shoulders, and Elin holding Olaf's hand as she hopped from one wet stone to the next.

When the bothy came into sight as we came over the ridge, the ragged procession became noisier. The bairns set up their traditional cry, "Food for the *huldufolk*! Food for the *huldufolk*!" Saucepan lids and home-made drums were restored to their small percussionists, and everyone seemed to walk faster.

Well, not quite. Just there the track is wide, and Beth was right beside me. As the bothy came into sight, she stopped, and gave a sort of sigh.

"Talk about remote!" she exclaimed. "Do you think they would mind if I took a photo? It's amazing!"

And she was right: the view was pretty stunning. From where we were standing it looked as if the bothy was right on the edge of the land – a small, squat building with the usual two chimneys, though, like the rest of us, the MacLoughlans were using home-harvested electricity by then. Oden's Inlet is to the north of the bothy, and another inlet skirts round to the south. Straight ahead, beyond the cottage, we could see only sea, with white caps on the water mirroring the gulls wheeling and diving in the sky. Three or four sheep, frightened by our approach, were scuttling down the slope towards a drystone wall.

Just at that moment, Jamie and his wife came round the corner, smiling.

"Come on up!" invited the crofter. "There's food for a whole tribe of *huldufolk* here!" Then his grin broadened. "And a dram or two for the adults as well!"

From the front of the bothy it was evident that it was not, after all, built on the very edge of a cliff. There was a steady slope down towards a bay a long way below. The MacLoughlans had a series of outbuildings, as I had, dating, no doubt, from the days of storing coal or peat, and still providing stabling for animals. There was a sizeable area of cultivated land, bare now that it was winter, and a polytunnel with something green still growing within it.

We tucked into toasted cheese on home-made scones, and made a serious dent in a bottle of good Scotch whisky. Beth and Angus went off with Sigrid and her daughter, who had her youngest in a sling and a toddler holding her hand, and Jamie came over to me, offering to top up my glass.

"Isn't Lyle here?" he wanted to know, his eyes searching among the small crowd for our tall, Viking-looking *nasyoni*, or police officer.

"*Nei*, he stayed back at Hus," I told the crofter. "He and Verity are looking after the old people in the school, so that Sigrid could join us, for once."

Then I noticed a worried frown on Jamie's face. "What's up?" I asked.

Jamie reached out and caught one of his sons by the collar. "Be a good lad and offer everyone top-ups!" he told him, giving him the whisky bottle. "Adults only, mind!" Then, to me, he said, "We've had some stuff stolen. Not a huge amount, but some, and we can't afford to lose anything, not this year, not with the taxes so high. I thought Lyle ought to know."

"Theft? Here?" It was hard to believe. "Who comes out here? I mean, you're on the edge of nowhere! You hardly have passing traffic!"

He sipped his whisky, and stood staring west out to sea, his eyes screwed up against the low winter sunlight. "So you would have thought," he agreed.

"What's been taken?" I asked.

"Well… we thought the chickens had stopped laying earlier than usual. They do that sometimes, you know. The old folk used to say it was the sign of a bad winter to come. But then we lost two hens. And…" he gave a sort of crooked grin, "I really don't think the wee hidden people took them!"

I smiled back, in sympathy rather than amusement. Jamie had a family to feed through the winter and times were hard. "What's worse," the man added, still looking out to sea, "a lot of our smoked fish has gone. A whole barrel of it. We have our permitted harvest of salmon in the freezer, and some crab that Malchi dressed for us, and the one remaining barrel, but that's all." Then he did look at me. "With no cash to top up our provisions, I'm not sure how we're going to cope," he said.

★★★

From the MacLoughlans' we moved on to Malcolm's home. He had renovated it scarcely a year earlier and it looked very trim and neat after the more ramshackle establishment we had just left. By then it was already after two in the afternoon and we had a wonderful view of the sun, hovering just above the horizon and then dipping down, making a golden pathway that seemed to lead from the skyline to the foot of the slope, where Malcolm's bothy was built. We ate cold lamb and kale baps and drank more whisky if we wanted it, or hot tea sweetened with honey and cinnamon. We didn't stay long. Dusk is a long-drawn-out business on En-Somi, and we didn't want to walk the cliff path by night, especially with wee ones among us.

Malcolm joined me for that leg of the journey, his job as host done. Duncan was way ahead of us with his friends Andy and Marigold. The fourth member of their friendship group, Alana, had stayed in Shetland. Malcolm's two adult offspring were engaged in lively conversation with Sigrid's daughter, so I could talk in confidence to Malcolm.

I told him what Jamie had told me about the thefts and his worries about feeding his family through the winter. "He said he had only lost small stuff," I commented, "but it sounds like quite a significant amount to me. I wouldn't want to go into winter with half my provisions gone."

Malcolm was quiet for a minute or two. Then, "Well, we won't let them go hungry, of course. But who on the earth would trek all the way over there to steal a few eggs and a couple of chickens?"

"And half a winter's supply of smoked fish," I added. "I think that's the worst thing. Who would do that?"

Again, he was quiet. Ahead we could hear wee Shirley saying, "But I *want* to walk!" and her Uncle Eric saying something quietly, to calm the bairn.

"There'll be a few families struggling this winter," he mused. "I dare say none of them would mind extra fish or chicken...."

I looked around at the long-drawn-out line of *En-Som-in-Fedii*, islanders, just approaching the unfinished bothy where four of the newcomers were already camping out, before beginning the slippery descent down to the summer harbour. Here and there people had turned on torches, although it was gloomy rather than dark. "I can't believe anyone here would steal another family's food!" I exclaimed. "I mean – have you ever heard of such a thing happening on our side of the island?"

"*Nei... Nei*, I haven't," agreed Malcolm. "But have we ever been taxed like this, or lived so close to the breadline? Not in our lifetimes – you and me. There's no knowing what people will do when they're under stress."

I knew he was right but I just didn't believe any of my friends or neighbours would do such a thing.

We didn't stay long with the four newcomers, although they had been told about our customs and had cake and tea for anyone who wanted it. We set off again, weary but with the long trek almost over. Then the first people in the procession reached the place where the bonfire had been built. Adults helped bairns to position their wee houses here and there on the sticks and planks that were arranged in a rough pyramid. Marigold's, I saw, was placed at the top – a rare honour, which, judging by her face, she fully appreciated. Then the fire was lit and we watched the flames licking round the children's constructions, and more food was brought out of backpacks and pockets, and Olaf and wee Elin sang a song together in honour of the hidden people.

As we walked back up to the village, Malcolm reminded me, "Do you remember, this time last year, when we saw the Northern Lights?"

"*Aja.*" Of course I did. It had been a very romantic moment. We had just been beginning to fall in love.

I looked back over my shoulder, down towards the summer harbour. There were dark clouds tumbling in on the cold north wind. "No Northern Lights this year," I said.

Malcolm looked back too. "*Nei*," he agreed. "No Northern Lights. It looks to me as if a storm is brewing."

Did I see someone down there, by the burnt-out bonfire? A dark shadow, a long dark coat? Or was it just my imagination, a trick of the dying light, the growing darkness. Why did I feel a sudden discomfort, a feeling that someone I loved was in danger? I know I shivered and Malcolm, thinking I was cold, put his welcoming arm round my shoulders.

CHAPTER 2

It must have been almost a week later. Angus and Beth were still with us. I seem to remember that they were becoming anxious about getting back to the mainland. The Norwegian ferry company that had brought them to the island had cancelled their next two scheduled trips because of the storms, and the only way home seemed to be to island-hop, going first to the Shetlands and south from there. Duncan was perfectly happy to stay on En-Somi until after solstice and by then there was always some sort of provision for online learning, although it was never ideal. Malcolm and I had taken Beth and Angus up to the *fi'ilsted* for a midday meal after several days of hurricane force winds and driving rain had kept us all in our respective bothies.

There weren't many people there when we arrived. All across the island storm damage was being repaired and folk were catching up on outdoor tasks. A driftwood fire was burning in the hearth, and over in the far corner there was an array of small lights decorating a macramé hammock, lighting an area of the low-ceilinged room which had always seemed a little gloomy until recently. There was a delicious smell issuing from the kitchen behind the bar, and Petter was engrossed in some sort of retro puzzle, chewing the stub of a pencil and frowning at his phone.

"*Morgoni!*" he greeted us, as we took off our soaking jackets at the entrance. "Can you think of a five-letter word with an 'h' and an 'n' in it, but no 's', 't', 'p' or 'f'?"

"Hunch?" suggested Angus. "Something smells good."

Petter tapped the letters into his phone. "Oh, nearly!" he exclaimed.

"Punch? Lunch?" contributed Malcolm.

Petter tapped some more. "Lunch it is!" he responded. "And I'm guessing lunch is on the menu for you, too?" He put his phone down on the bar, and peered round into the kitchen. "Are we ready to serve, Malchi?" he wanted to know.

"*Aja!*" Malchi's voice responded. "How many people?"

"All four of us," Malcolm told Petter, and we moved across to the round table by the hearth.

"So, you survived the storm?" Petter asked, as he put cutlery on the table. "Yanni told me that the waves finally destroyed the old jetty down in the summer harbour. We'll need to build a new one, come the spring."

"Everything was fine with me," I answered.

"Us too," affirmed Malcolm.

"And have you checked your store rooms?" Petter queried.

"I checked the ponies, of course," Malcolm replied. "And I bet Marie checked her chickens! But I don't usually find that storms affect canned goods or potatoes!"

"Are you thinking of the MacLoughlans?" I asked Petter.

"*Aja*," he replied. "And Sigrid. She heard a door banging early on the second morning of the storm and thought the latch to her storehouse must be broken. But, when she went out to check, the door was closed. She had the sense to check her provisions while she was there. You know, she keeps all those preserves in that building. She's sure the top shelf was full, but half the jars had gone. Missing. Stolen."

"I always thought you had a really low crime rate?" Angus chipped in. "I've watched the documentary about En-Somi half a dozen times. I'm sure the commentator says that there had only been one or two cases of drunk and disorderly in the last twelve months, and no other offences."

Beth giggled. "*Aja*," she agreed. "And wasn't there a boundary dispute and a fight? I love that documentary. I made all my friends watch it. It's one of the reasons that I asked Paps if I could come over now, instead of waiting for next summer, when it ought to be less stormy."

"I read on social media that the video was made by a group of students. Is that right?" Angus wanted to know.

"*Aja*," Petter told him, as he placed bowls of steaming lamb stew in front of Malcolm's two visitors. Then, over his shoulder as he went to fetch the other two portions, he added, "She's coming back, you know. Elise. The lassie on the BBC Alba crew. Malchi had a text from her yesterday, as soon as the internet was restored. She wants to be here for solstice."

I was surprised. It had been lovely having the three young people from the mainland with us recording all that happened during the previous winter, and the documentary that they had made had been a huge success. But their year's placement with the BBC had finished in July, and they should have been studying for their finals by now.

Petter pulled up a round stool to sit with us as we ate. "She promised Olaf, you know. That she would record our struggle with the *harkrav* on film, and he would record it in song. So, she's coming back to do just that."

"Trouble with the *harkrav*?" Beth queried. "Is there trouble with the *harkrav*? Paps, you haven't mentioned it!" She sounded almost accusing.

"It's to do with the refugees." I tried to explain, as succinctly as I could. "The *bondii*, the ordinary people of the island, are happy for them to stay—"

"We *want* them to stay!" interrupted Petter.

"*Aja*," I agreed. "But the *harkrav*, the people the newcomers call 'the bosses', they don't. They've got their eyes on their bank accounts. You know, more island children to educate, folk needing health care – it all costs money. And they're rich, compared with us, so the expense would fall on them."

"*Would have* fallen on them!" Malcolm corrected, and took over the explanation. "So, they changed the tax laws on the island. It used to be that we were all taxed according to our incomes, but now we're taxed according to the amount of land we farm."

"Which means," I took up the thread again, "that all the crofters on the island, the *bondii*, will have huge increases in our tax bills, but the *harkrav*, who own stocks and shares, and expensive houses in Oslo and Edinburgh, but who don't farm on En-Somi, get away scot-free."

Beth looked shocked. "Can they do that?" she wanted to know. "Is it even legal?"

"Oh, *aja*, it's legal enough," her paps told her. "But we're going to fight it. We *are* fighting it. We've set up a relief fund. Marie's ex has made us a huge, interest-free loan and we're getting support from communities on other islands. We'll pay the taxes for two years, then we'll vote the *harkrav* out of office. That's the plan."

"Will you be okay, Paps?" Angus was looking worried. "Jo and I were thinking of buying a place together, but we could put it off for a couple of years."

"*Nei!*" Malcolm was laughing. "I only work a moderate amount of land, and I've got a good income through my pension – well, good enough for island life! It's people like the MacLoughlans who'll suffer. Which is why it's such a worry if their supplies are stolen."

"Who would do something like that?" Beth wondered. "It doesn't sound like the sort of thing that would happen here."

Petter was looking worried. "It isn't the sort of thing that would normally happen among us," he agreed. "But it *is* happening. And it's already making people suspicious of each other."

"If we're not careful," Malcolm suggested, wiping his empty dish with a piece of bread, "we'll start finding scapegoats."

"It's started already," Petter told us. He stood, and started collecting up the plates. "Robert told me this morning that the newcomers are being blamed. After all, they come from a very different background from us…"

I thought about the refugees I knew best: Si and Rose and their two children, Frankie, Eric and wee Shirley, even Harry and Mandy with her two, over by the Sinclairs on Hunger Moor. I was sure they wouldn't steal from us – from anyone. But there were others I didn't know. Would they feel desperate enough to start taking what didn't belong to them? And then there was Jarvis, the strangest of all the erstwhile slaves, still camping out at the old airport. Would he steal from the *bondii*? He had stolen before…

"Well, we couldn't expect to get through the winter without some trouble," Malcolm said, sitting back and looking content despite our uncomfortable conversation. "But I think I'll go over and visit Jamie MacLoughlan this afternoon, just to see if we can help."

I looked out of the small window of the *fi'ilsted*. "You haven't got long," I pointed out. "It's sunset in less than an hour."

CHAPTER 3

I remember that more storms were threatened for December. All across Western Europe, governments were putting emergency procedures into effect. Climate change specialists reminded us that we had known for years that these floods and hurricanes would come if we didn't take stronger measures, and different nations were blaming each other. India was still producing massive carbon emissions, but they were way down the league if you calculated per head of the population. The UK had made some important reductions, but were still benefiting from all those years since the beginning of the Industrial Revolution, and from colonialism. There remained climate deniers too, claiming that all these disasters were manufactured deliberately in order to subjugate all the nations of the world, ready for the Beast to come and reign over us. It all seemed a long way away from En-Somi.

The secondary school in Lerwick allowed the island children to come home while they still could. The ferry that took Beth and Angus off En-Somi also brought Shona's youngest, Alana, so the little gang of four bairns that had formed in the spring and been so supportive of each other all through the summer, was reunited. My son Duncan was one of them, Alana and Andy were about the same age, but wee Marigold was a key member of the group despite being so much younger, and she loved having the older bairns around. They would wait for her in the afternoons in the early En-Somi dusk as she came out of school, and they usually bundled down to my place, or sometimes up to the Kullanders'. When the internet was working they played some game involving Viking invasions. It seemed to me to be extraordinarily unrealistic, but they loved it. One afternoon they built a fire of driftwood down on my beach, and invited Malcolm and me to a barbecue. Alana had music on her device and the kids danced around the fire, teaching Andy and Marigold some steps that were all the rage on Shetland, while Malcolm and I sat on rocks and watched them, and laughed.

Andy was teaching Marigold the local dialect, and Duncan and Alana taught her a few words of Norwegian, which they were learning at school. Once Malcolm took the four of them on his pony and trap over Fyrtarn Fjell and beyond the little town of Storhaven, to visit Marigold's sister's grave up on Aeloff's Hill, and they took photos for Si and Rose, so that they could see for themselves where their daughter was buried.

I know that it was a good time for the bairns. Marigold, Duncan and I have talked about it often since. For the rest of the *bondii* things were not so good. Well, Sigrid did her best to shield the younger ones in the school from the troubles that we were all facing, but there was an air of anxiety when people met in the *fi'ilsted* and it was true, as we had been threatened by one of the *harkrav* during a public meeting at the end of the previous winter: families were having to cut back on gifts for their children during the much-loved holiday season.

The first of the new tax bills came in about ten days after *Huldufolk* Day, on the day that Angus and Beth left the island. Since Malcolm was over at the ferry port seeing his son and daughter safely onto the boat, he was given the thick packet of brown envelopes to deliver to our side of the island. Thus it was that a number of us were together when we opened up those very unwelcome communications.

Yanni Sinclair and the refugee Harry, who was living on Yanni's land, had become quite close. Harry was a quiet man, perhaps the oldest of the refugees, with a mop of grey-black hair and an air of stillness about him. He and Yanni had fished together through the summer, and they were over in Gamla Hus picking up some furniture made by Petter and Si for Harry's almost-completed bothy.

"Look at this! *Nei*, this can't be right!" Yanni was looking in shock and amazement at the printed sheet in front of him. "They say I owe as much for this quarter as I paid for the whole of last year!"

Robert was scrutinising his bill. "Same here," he grumbled. "I can't believe this is right! How can I possibly owe so much tax?"

Malcolm looked at me and wrinkled up his face in an expression that said, "Don't say anything!" He only owned a small patch of land, enough to grow some vegetables, to graze his goats and to let his ponies out, so – like the *harkrav* – his bill had remained low. Quite a lot of acreage belonged with my bothy, but it was technically Bjorn's land, and he had long ago arranged for the taxes to be paid by his bank in Norway. Few other *bondii* were as secure as us.

Olaf, our bard, wandered in, and Malcolm delivered his brown envelope to him. The old man opened it, glanced at it and tucked it into the inside pocket of his coat.

"Is it bad?" Yanni wanted to know.

"As expected," Olaf responded, and he had a twinkle in his eye. "So now the battle begins!"

★★★

By common consent most of us who lived west of Fyrtarn Fjell met the following evening. Sigrid's daughter, Kenna, was there, pondering a document on her device while Sigrid held the sleeping baby. Three of my little gang of four had turned up, although Marigold was at home in their little bothy just up the track. Rose had become a stickler about bedtimes – one of the reasons, Sigrid had suggested to me over our knitting, for the bairn being so lively and enquiring during the day. Petter was serving drinks and Malchi was doing something on his phone. The room was crowded, and there was a sense of grim determination coupled with real worry among us all.

Petter called us to order. "Kenna's been doing the maths," he said. "One or two of you haven't told her yet what you owe. Of course, it's up to you, but we really need to know the full extent of the damage before we can make any reliable plans."

A few people stood up and went over to Kenna, some holding their official letters. The rest of us broke into conversation again. I could see Kenna inputting the details, tapping on some keys, passing her device across to her mother to show her the outcome. Sigrid nodded slowly. The baby stirred. Kenna passed her device up to Petter.

Once again, Petter called us to order. "*En-Som-in-Fedii*," he said, addressing us formally, "Kenna knows, now, how much we, on this side of the island, owe in total. It's not insignificant."

"Never thought it would be!" grumbled Robert.

"It's a disaster, that's what it is!" called out someone else.

"It's criminal!"

"I never thought I'd see the day…"

"No, it's not a disaster!" Malcolm was on his feet. "We knew this was going to happen. *Nei*, we weren't expecting quite such huge bills, but we knew they would go up. Remember, we've planned for this! We set up a fund. Kenna, how much have we got in our community account?"

Kenna smiled up at Malcolm. "More than enough to pay this quarter's bills," she told us.

A few people looked relieved, but by no means everyone.

"*Aja*, that's as may be," somebody called out. "But this is just one quarter. Have we got enough to pay the next quarter, or the one after that? Aren't we just putting off the inevitable? And building up debts?"

"Well…" Kenna was hesitant.

Malcolm spoke again. "*Nei*," he said, clearly and calmly. "We haven't got enough to pay the next quarter, but then we don't owe the next quarter yet! We need to take this one step at a time. If you can, we ask everyone to give Kenna the amount you paid this time last year, when the tax rate was normal. And give her your bills. The community fund will pay all our debts, and we'll start at once – tomorrow, if possible – raising the money we'll need in April."

"It won't be so easy next time," grumbled a woman in the far corner, the corner lit by the fairy lights in the hammock. "People get tired of endless appeals."

"*Aja*," someone else agreed. "Charity fatigue."

"But we've got to try!" Yanni Sinclair called out. "Our whole island way of life is at stake!"

Then Olaf stood. He spoke formally, our bard speaking with the authority of his role. "*En-Som-in-Fedii*," he began, then paused and started again. "Noble *En-Som-in-Fedii*," he said, his voice taking on a sing-song tone as if he were telling a story. "We are facing some problems. Have we not faced problems before? Did not our ancestors brave the rolling oceans to find this lonely island? Did they not build *hussi* and cultivate fields? Were not our forefathers the ones who fished this wild Atlantic in the days when we called it the Vestrsear? Did we not send our young men to fight in wars, and our young women to nurse them? Have we not known times of hunger, and times of plenty, and survived them both? Are we not strong, and bold, and faithful? Noble *En-Som-in-Fedii*, we are facing grave problems but we have the blood of our ancestors flowing through our veins. We are not among those who give up, who go home with our tails between our legs! We are of the stock of those who fight, who struggle against the odds. And we are in the bloodline of those who win!"

I almost stood and cheered when Olaf sat down again. There were murmurs of approval. Nobody clapped or called out; it was almost as if the situation was too serious for that. Nevertheless, the atmosphere had changed completely. People were smiling. They seemed to sit up straighter, to stand taller.

Then Malchi stood, holding his phone in the air. "And, *En-Som-in-Fedii*," he announced, smiling. "Our struggles will be recorded on film. Elise is coming back. She'll be here on the next ferry!"

Olaf remained seated, but I heard him say, as he had said once before, "Then I'll record our struggles in song, and Elise can record them on film."

CHAPTER 4

Ingrid and Dougie Fraser, Malcolm's friends who lived across the island in Storhaven, brought Elise over in a small trap pulled by a beautiful pure-blood Shetland pony. They wanted to see Lyle and Verity, whose wedding they had missed for reasons I can't now recall. Ingrid had been quite close to Verity when Verity was the minister in the kirk, and had, by all accounts, held things together when Verity resigned.

We all met up in the *nasyonihuss* – the house where the newlyweds lived. It consisted of a traditional bothy with a small additional room built on some time back in the previous century, which was supposed to serve as Lyle's office, but which at various times had been a workshop, a storeroom for school supplies and, more recently, a temporary home for the first of the refugee families to come over to our side of the island.

Before Lyle married, I didn't call in at his place often. He was always out and about, visiting outlying bothies, doing cursory checks to make sure that we all abided by our fishing limits, advising crofters on Agriculture and Fisheries forms that always seemed more complicated than they first appeared, and generally keeping an eye on us all. In the last twelve months he had spent a lot of time on the other side of the island. His sergeant had been arrested along with the alms dealers and slavers who caused such a scandal, and for a while Lyle served as the only representative of law and order on En-Somi. By the time Elise returned to us a new *nasyoni* had been appointed – not to be a sergeant but to serve out of Storhaven as an equal to Lyle. She was a middle-aged woman, her family had come from somewhere in eastern Europe but she had grown up on Hoy, one of the Orkney islands, and seemed ideally suited to her new posting.

I suppose the last time I had visited Lyle at home had been almost a year earlier. I remember that some of us had gathered there for breakfast at the beginning of the winter solstice celebrations.

I seem to remember that Malcolm and I arrived, on the occasion I am telling you about now, at around eleven in the morning. It was one of those grey, blustery days that are not uncommon on En-Somi. Sunrise is just after nine in the morning at that time of year but we could go whole days when we needed electric light in our bothies. We blessed the wind, which gave us a constant supply of power.

My first impression, when Verity welcomed us in, was that it was a different bothy. The one room looked, at the same time, larger and more homely. Lyle's free-standing bed, which had rather dominated the space, had been replaced by a high platform with a seating area beneath, and they had managed to find room for a round wooden table between the sofa and the kitchen area. I suppose that Lyle had always used the ceiling light that hung close to the cooking space, but now there were several small lamps with red shades, and a cluster of empty whisky bottles with tiny lights sparkling within them.

Verity looked wonderful. Her eyes were shining, her hair reflected the red glow from the lamps, and in her jeans and cable-knit jumper she looked ridiculously youthful.

"Lyle's just popped out," she told us. "He won't be long. Robert came round after breakfast. Someone broke into his outside store last night and took a couple of sacks of oats that he was planning to feed his ponies with. He was pretty upset, so Lyle thought he should go down there at once."

"More theft!" Malcolm frowned. "I don't know what's going on!"

"We definitely have a problem," Verity agreed. "It's making people very edgy. Lyle's mam phoned a couple of days ago to say that her purse had been taken. It had all the cash they needed for December in it. She was really upset. Lyle was all set to go over to Fremdes Haven to investigate, when his paps phoned back. The purse wasn't missing at all. It was in the kitchen drawer, where it was always kept. People are panicking. They don't feel safe anymore. Coffee? I've made scones, using Sigrid's recipe."

Lyle came in at that moment. "*Hei!*" he greeted us, and kissed his new wife. "Ingrid, Dougie and Elise are on their way. They're just finishing their breakfast at the *fi'ilsted*."

"How's Robert?" Verity asked, taking mugs from hooks under the wall-mounted kitchen cupboards, which I'm pretty sure were new, and pouring water into the cafetière I had last seen in Verity's flat over in Storhaven. "If they've been eating Malchi's breakfast, there's no way they'll want my scones!" Verity had stayed at the *fi'ilsted* the night before her 'religious' marriage ceremony in the ruined bothy in Gamla Hus. She was speaking from experience.

Lyle hung his jacket up and put his outdoor shoes neatly by the door. "He's quite philosophical about the theft of his oats," Lyle told us. "But some of the harnessing for his ponies was taken too, and that's weird."

"*Aja*, really weird!" Malcolm agreed.

"But what use would harnessing be to anyone, unless they owned ponies? And everyone with ponies on En-Somi already has that sort of thing!" Verity sounded upset. "And Robert needs to be able to use his ponies. They're his only source of actual cash."

"Exactly!" Lyle squeezed onto the sofa next to Malcolm and me. It wasn't really designed for three people when one of them was as big as him. "So, I'm wondering whether the thief is planning to steal some ponies, too!"

I thought about that. "*Nei*," I responded. "People would recognise stolen ponies – and probably someone would recognise the kit, too."

"So, just a troublemaker, then?" Verity wondered. "Someone with a grudge against Robert?"

"That's hard to believe!" Malcolm and I had borrowed Robert's ponies in the past, before Malcolm had bought his own. "He's what my paps used to call 'one of nature's gentlemen'!"

Elise arrived before the Frasers. "Ingrid and Dougie are discussing some word game Petter plays," she told us. "They said they'd be along as soon as the problem's solved."

I stood up and went over to the pretty lassie, giving her a hug. "It's great to see you again!" I told her. "But shouldn't you be studying hard for your finals?"

She hugged me back. "Marie! I've deferred for a year. With my tutor's blessing. And my parents'."

"And are you still working for the BBC?" Malcolm wanted to know.

"No – I'm freelance this time." She grinned. "Actually, Dad's subbing me, bless him! He was really impressed with our documentary. He says there might be a future for me in the media after all!"

We all laughed, and were still chuckling when Ingrid and Dougie arrived. "It isn't even a real word!" Ingrid was saying. "The past tense of 'to shake' is 'shaken', not 'shook'!"

"Oh, that game!" groaned Lyle. "Every time I go into the *fi'ilsted* Petter bothers me with it!"

"So, what's been happening since I was last here?" Elise wanted to know. "Yes, Verity, I could eat a scone. Thanks."

"Well, we got married!" Verity reminded her.

"Aye – congratulations!" Elise was tucking into her food as if she hadn't eaten for a week.

"That's the best thing," said Lyle. "The worst thing is the thefts. Have you heard about them?"

"I have! Ingrid was telling me on the way over. Holti had a sack of potatoes taken. Who would steal from an old man?"

"And Jeanie had a break-in," added Dougie. "They didn't take anything, but they trashed the place. It'll cost her a pretty penny to set it to rights. Just when her income is so reduced! People can't afford to go out for tea while the taxes are so high."

"Kids?" queried Elise. "Sounds like the sort of thing teenagers would do."

"On En-Somi?" Lyle was almost dismissive of the idea. "*Nei*! I mean, which kids? Andy Kullander? Young Christian? That brood that live in Frigg Alley and took part in last year's Celtic music finals? It's a ridiculous idea!"

Dougie was making good inroads into his scone too. "The new *nasyoni* told me that some folk are blaming the newcomers. There's no evidence it's them. They're quite disbursed now, only that young couple Quincy and Mo sleep regularly in the kirk. She's visited all of them on her side of the island. She told me that they don't have much at all – and absolutely nothing suspicious."

It isn't a pleasant characteristic of human beings, I've noticed, to want to blame people who are different from ourselves in some way. I was wondering about the refugees too. "Has she been out to the old airport?" I asked. "Isn't that guy, Jarvis, still squatting out there?"

"Ah! Now that I don't know!" Dougie told me.

Elise was intrigued. "I thought all the refugees came into town? I'm sure most of them were sleeping in the kirk by the time we left."

"*Aja*," Lyle agreed. "But not Jarvis. As far as I know he's never even been into Storhaven. He's a bit of an odd one, that guy."

"He's all right," Verity chipped in.

"Oh, of course!" I had temporarily forgotten. "You spent some time out there, with him. Do you think he could be our thief?"

Verity screwed up her face. "*Aja – nei* – oh, I don't know. There *is* something odd about him. But he's got a kind heart."

Lyle laughed and stood to hug her. "Verity, my love!" he said. "You think everyone's got a kind heart!"

Verity laughed and pushed him away. "Well, they usually have!" she insisted, looking a little pink.

From beyond the *fi'ilsted* came the noise of children, a sure sign that Sigrid had taken the bairns outside for a break. Our youngsters get lots of exercise. Even walking to school across the moors or via well-worn tracks must supply them with more than the ten thousand steps a day that used to be recommended. However, many of them live in quite isolated places. The one thing they don't get at home, and which Sigrid feels is really important, is the experience of playing together, of mixing with people outside their own immediate family. For that reason she organised some sort of game every day. That was partly why the custom of holding birthday parties at the school had evolved, too.

Verity went across to the bothy door, opened it and looked out. The *nasyonihuss* is almost opposite the grassy area that counts as the school playground.

"Oh, they have a new student!" she exclaimed. Then, over her shoulder she said, "I love watching the bairns play. But, Lyle, who is that wee girl?"

Lyle walked over to join her, casually putting his arm round her shoulders. Malcolm caught my eye and winked at me.

"Ah!" Lyle looked pleased. "That's Mandy's little one. Yanni was telling me, she's just turned five. You know – from over beyond the Sinclair's place? Harry will have brought her down."

"They're settling well, then – your *En-Som-fly-Kninger?*" Dougie wanted to know. He meant the refugees of course.

"*Aja.*" Verity closed the door and squeezed in beside Malcolm and me on the sofa, leaving Lyle leaning against a kitchen cabinet. "It's a joy to see Marigold and Shirley out with the other bairns.

Wee Shirley is picking up the local dialect so quickly – it makes me laugh, sometimes, hearing her calling out as they play! But I worry about the teenagers. We have Mandy's son over on our side of the island, and you've got the lad, Shawn, over beyond Aeloff's Hill, haven't you? I don't suppose either have had any education."

Ingrid was reaching out for a second scone. "We hardly ever see Charlie and his family. Shawn came into Storhaven with his paps to collect the small piping they needed for the renovation – and they all came over to this side of the island for the summer solstice barbecue, didn't they? But we don't see them around the town much at all."

"They're quite remote out there," Malcolm agreed. He had spent a lot of time over the last six months or so, helping to renovate a bothy that had, in its ruined state, been home to us for a few nights the winter before. "Charlie has a younger lad too, ten or eleven years old, I would say. Very quiet. Charlie never brings him into town. He could probably do with some of Sigrid's wise help."

"So, you don't have any refugee children in the school over in Storhaven?" Verity asked.

"*Nei*, and I think that's a pity," Ingrid told us. "There's not much contact at all between the locals and the newcomers. Even that young couple, Mo and Quincy – people see them around, sitting on the wall outside the kirk or down on the quay, but they don't talk to them. Well, maybe young Harris does – but he has a bit of a reputation too!"

"And now, with all these thefts…" Dougie was picking up the story. "People think it's bound to be the *En-Som-fly-Kninger*. Well, who else could it be? Jeanie, at the Copper Kettle, told me that she has heard murmurings that some folk want the refugees gone. Thanks to them we have these sky-high taxes, and because of them we have a rising crime rate."

CHAPTER 5

Malcolm and Duncan were sitting at the small table by my west-facing window, deep in conversation about the royal families of Norway and Britain, and the different attitudes of those with republican tendencies in the two countries. With his own son and daughter back on the mainland but Duncan still home with me, Malcolm was more or less living at my place. He and Duncan went over to Malcolm's bothy most days to care for his ponies and goats, and Malcolm was teaching Duncan to drive the traditional long, slim cart that Malcolm had ordered at the end of the previous winter, to use on our narrow tracks.

Duncan was studying at home via the internet, but he and his three friends usually met up when Marigold came out of school. Like most of the bairns on the island, they were busy building *brennii* – the bonfires we would light on the shortest day of the year for our winter solstice celebrations. As with *Huldufolk* Day, it is our custom to visit several bothies, but starting at the top of Fyrtarn Fjell at sunrise. Much to the delight of Duncan and Marigold, my bothy had been chosen to be one of the venues. They were, therefore, happily engaged in the dusk of every afternoon, in collecting driftwood from my beach and dragging it up to a flattish area north of my home, beyond the chicken run.

I can't remember the exact details – all this is a long time ago now – but I expect that Alana, Andy and Marigold must have been coming down to join Duncan for further beach-combing. What I do remember, very clearly, is Duncan's phone pinging, and him checking it, then saying, "Wow! Mam! Malcolm! Look at this!"

I went over from the kitchen area, and Malcolm peered over my son's shoulder. Duncan was looking at a short piece of video, obviously filmed on a phone. For a moment I couldn't work out what I was looking at. Then I realised. It was a fight. It was not well filmed, the camera was jumping about, and the sound told more, initially, than the picture. Someone was saying, "Leave them alone, can't you? Get away from them!"

Another voice called out, "Peasants! I'll teach you to answer back!"

I could hear some heavy breathing, almost gasping, close to the phone. A voice I recognised – I later realised it was the refugee, Mo – called out, "It's all right, Harris! Leave 'im alone. 'E 'asn't done us no 'arm. Not really."

We could hear more scuffling, then Harris's voice: "Why don't you just go back to the mainland? We don't need any *harkrav* telling us what to do!"

"Oh, don't you?" we heard, then more scuffling and panting. In the background Mo was calling out, "Stop it! Stop it!"

Then the camera seemed to turn wildly to the grey sky, and back down to the ground. We could clearly see Harris, the young islander from beyond Fyrtarn Fjell, lying on the ground. The camera whirled around and showed a figure running away.

Then came a woman's voice. "Better turn that off, and hand it to me," came an authoritative instruction.

"Ah, the arrival of the *nasyoni*!" proclaimed Malcolm.

★★★

We watched that short piece of video a couple more times, then Duncan's three friends arrived and they watched it again.

"That's Mo!" exclaimed Marigold, who, of course, knew the refugees better than any of us, having lived among them for so long.

"And that's Harris," Andy added. "My paps says he's a bit wild."

"*Nei!*" Alana corrected him. "Mam says he's just young. He dropped out of uni. Mam reckons he'll find his feet soon enough."

Duncan was looking at his phone, frozen to a still where Harris was lying on the ground. "Well, he didn't find his feet today!" he remarked. Then, "I think he might be injured!"

"Who was he fighting?" Andy wanted to know.

None of us knew. "Some *harkrav* kid," Duncan answered. "It looks as if he ran away when that new *nasyoni* arrived."

"It's horrible!" Alana said, and shuddered.

"It's just a fight!" Marigold remarked, full of worldly wisdom. "I seen lots of fights. A beating, too. Ain't nothing special."

Duncan looked at the bairn gravely. "It *is* special!" he told her. "Well, not special, but unusual – and wrong. It's wrong to fight, Marigold. The way things were over at the old airport – that's not the way things are supposed to be."

Marigold sighed. "Well," she told Duncan. "I's still learning. But it didn't look so 'orrible to me. Don't we fight at all, on En-Somi?"

"Ha!" Malcolm was amused. "So, answer that one, Duncan!"

★★★

Of course, news of the fight spread all over the island in no time. There were mixed responses on social media. Interestingly, most people who posted comments from our side of En-Somi were supportive of Harris. It sounded as if he had been standing up for the young couple, Quincy and Mo, and we could all clearly hear the assailant call somebody a peasant. Responses from people in and around Storhaven were more mixed. Quite a lot of posts reflected those of the Hus folk, but some people claimed that this was just another sign of the way that life on the island had deteriorated since the refugees had been among us. Some of the posts were really ugly. Someone who called himself – or herself – 'Champion' was keen for some sort of island-wide regulation, banning anyone without 'natural' links to the island from living permanently on En-Somi. Another person calling themselves 'A Friend of En-Somi' wanted to introduce a citizenship test along the lines that the UK had developed way back in 2002, and a third contributor suggested that 'immigrants' to the island should pay a deposit, the way a person might if renting a holiday cottage in the old days, which could only be refunded when the new arrival had lived, trouble free, on En-Somi for three years or more. One person posted that it was time we reintroduced national service, like the Russians, but he only got two 'likes'.

I met Robert and Harry in the shop the next day. I suppose Harry had just walked Mandy's wee one up to the school, and Robert was collecting his post. Elise came in right after me. The conversation, of course, was about the fight.

"*Nei!*" Shona was saying, apparently talking to Robert. "Young Harris was in the same year as our eldest. He wanted to go to art school but he had to settle for economics because he could get a grant for that. He was always a good lad. Just a bit hot-headed."

Elise came in on the conversation. "Aye," she agreed. "I talked to him once or twice when we were over here before. He's got loads of good ideas. But I got the feeling that he finds life on En-Somi a bit frustrating."

"*Aja*, that's as may be," Robert responded. "But I can't find it in my heart to approve of fighting."

Harry was looking from one to the other. "But do we know the full story?" he wondered.

We were all quiet. Of course, we didn't.

"I thought he was standing up for Mo and Quincy," I said. "That's what it sounded like."

"Well, isn't that the right thing to do?" Shona speculated.

"*Aja* – but fighting!" Robert was clearly not happy with the turn of events.

Elise was absent-mindedly staring at the label on a tin of mango slices – probably imported especially for someone's solstice or Christmas feast, and not selling because everyone was so short of money that year.

"Do you think it's all to do with the refugees settling here, then?" she asked.

"*Aja!*" the rest of us all chorused, in accidental unison.

"Then I think I ought to go over to Storhaven," the young reporter suggested. "After all, that's why I came back to En-Somi."

"I can't take you," Robert mourned. "Alf is going to help me to rig up something so that I can harness my ponies, but it'll take us a little while…"

"I'll ask Malcolm," I said. "Our ponies need the exercise."

***

The idea received a very positive response from Malcolm – and also from Duncan.

"Your young man can drive us!" announced Malcolm. "I'm sure you're up to it, Duncan!"

"*Aja!*" Duncan loved the prospect of taking the ponies and trap across the island. "Will you come, Mam? And do you think Sigrid would let Marigold take a day off school?"

"I'd like to see Tom at the ferry," I agreed. "But *nei*, Marigold shouldn't take time out of school. And you, my son, will have to catch up with all the online lessons you miss!"

***

We picked Elise up from the *fi'ilsted* where she was staying, soon after eight-thirty the following morning. It was still dark, although the clouds that were rolling in from the east had thin silver lines on them where the rising sun, still hidden from us, was catching the water vapour. She was wearing a ski suit, and I thought how sensible it was for a journey such as we were about to take. She tossed a sports bag into the back of the trap before climbing on board herself. "Hey! Are you going to drive?" she asked Duncan, sounding impressed.

"*Aja.*" Duncan was playing it cool. He was at an age when he was very aware of a pretty girl only a few years older than him sitting behind him, perhaps watching his every move.

It was, not unusually, a stormy day. The weather was roaring in from the east, from the Norwegian tundra or the Russian steppes. The wind was gusty and icy cold. Malcolm fished a blanket out from under his seat and passed it back to Elise. I was wedged between my son and my partner but I shivered, even so, as we left the village.

Duncan was pretty good with the ponies. Up on top of the *fjell* they became a bit skittish and Malcolm took over until we were east of the pass. We stopped there, just where the track curves round and the slope of the moor provides a brief respite from the gales. Elise took out her camera and filmed the descent. I knew, from the documentary made about the island, that only a tiny amount of all the shots she took would eventually be used.

As the track reached the marshy bottom close to the ruined chapel, Duncan reigned in the ponies and turned to Elise. He pointed to another track, less well-worn, winding off to the north. "Harris lives up there," he told the girl. "With his mam and paps. And that's the way to Lyle's parents' place too. And when we were wee bairns, Alana and me, we were sure that there was a whole *huldufolk* city hidden in the crags you can see over there."

Elise swivelled her camera around to film the rocks Duncan was talking about. "Why?" she wanted to know. "Why did you think the hidden people lived up there?"

"Well." Duncan chuckled, and I suddenly realised how like his father he was becoming. "Alana's paps used to come over every Friday to collect stuff from the ferry, for the shop. And to pick up the post. So, in the holidays he sometimes took us too. Do you remember, Mam? And this one time we saw smoke over there, and it looked just exactly as if it was coming from those crags, and Alana's paps said it was the *huldufolk*, burning their rubbish. And we totally believed him!"

Elise laughed. "How old were you?"

"Oh, I don't know." Duncan turned back to the ponies. "About seven or eight, I suppose," he said over his shoulder. "A bit younger than Marigold is now."

★★★

We didn't have a doctor on the island in those days. It seems surprising when I look back on it. In emergencies they used to send a helicopter over from the Shetlands and we had a nurse with some sort of extra qualifications. The *nasyonii* all had first-aid training, of course, and I think we mostly depended on them. There were some difficult years as the climate got worse, when we could have used emergency medical care but the weather prevented first responders from coming over, and then, finally, we all agreed to employ a medic to live on the island. But that was a few years after the events I'm describing now.

To be honest, I didn't know the nurse at that time. He lived in Storhaven with a wife and two rather unusual children. Over on our side of En-Somi we mostly depended on Sigrid – and Lyle, of course. In Storhaven there was a building we called 'the surgery', which I seem to remember had a waiting room, a consulting room, and two single rooms that we all called *the wards*. We found Harris in one of them.

He was lying in a single bed, a bandage over one eye and

around his head like a television cartoon character, and with scratches all down one side of his face. The nurse with the eccentric children was nowhere to be seen. In fact, there didn't seem to be anyone looking after Harris.

"*Hei!*" he greeted us, cheerfully enough, as we all piled into his small room. "Have you brought me grapes?"

This was a bit of a joke. The availability of exotic fruit had reduced significantly as supply chains deteriorated. Unless we could find ways of growing them ourselves, things like grapes or oranges or bananas were not going to be on our menus. Of course, that was why there had been a tin of mangos in the Gamla Hus shop.

Duncan plonked himself on the side of the bed. "We've brought ourselves!" he remarked cheekily. "Who could ask for more?"

"And the good wishes of everyone in Hus," Malcolm added.

"And a reporter, I see!" Harris sounded approving. "*Hei*, Elise! Have you come to report on the dastardly deeds of the *harkrav*?"

Elise came further into the room. "I have!" she agreed. "I want the whole story. Names. Places. Feelings. Every detail!"

"No problem!" Harris grinned. "I am as putty in your hands! But first, I need some tea. The nurse has gone off and left me, and I'm parched!"

★★★

We chatted for a while. I went out and bought take-away teas in recyclable mugs from Jeanie's café, carrying them back on a wooden tray with the wind blowing directly into my face so that I feared that the mugs would be blown onto the ground. Duncan was in his element. I hadn't realised that he knew Harris, who lived on the other side of Fyrtarn Fjell, but it turned out that Sigrid had asked him to come over and teach the bairns juggling when my son had been in his last year at primary school and Harris was home from his first term at university. There was a lot of laughter from the three younger members of our party.

The nurse came back, popped his head round the door, greeted us all with a friendly *"Morgoni"*, asked Harris if he needed anything, and went away again. After that, Malcolm, Duncan and I left as Elise started to sort out details so that she could film an interview: positioning, adjusting the curtains to achieve the best lighting, and telling Harris that it would be better if he could sit up a bit. We agreed to meet up at the Castle *fi'ilsted* for lunch.

I don't remember now, it's years ago, but I think Malcolm and Duncan went off somewhere. I'm pretty sure that Duncan had friends in Storhaven who went to school with him in Lerwick, so I suppose that he met up with them. I went down to the quay to see Tom. He was something of a favourite with me. When I had first started knitting for the cooperative, it had been Tom who had volunteered to sell my stuff to the ferrymen, and over the years I had made good money that way. Tom refused to take a cut. He said there was something in his contract that forbade him to profit from sales on the side, although Angus thought that was unlikely. "He's just being kind!" Malcolm's son had told me. "He probably thought you needed the money." Anyhow, if I was in Storhaven I liked to catch up with Tom.

He was not in his little office. The ferry wasn't due that day, and he liked to do his paperwork at home. His bothy was right up against the harbour wall – not where the ferry office is now. Sea levels have risen since, but you can still see where it used to be – where the orange buoy is anchored, warning mariners of underwater hazards.

I don't know how old Tom was. He had held that position since before I came to the island, and he had never seemed young. Malcolm thought that there might have been a second employee when he was a bairn on the east of the island and going to school in the little town. There was certainly a second bothy, now empty, across a cobbled area from Tom's home.

Tom, of course, offered me more tea, and I, of course, accepted. He hadn't sold any more of my *gensii* because there had been so few ferries, but he had a bale of untreated wool sent over from Shetland which someone in the cooperative would clean and spin and dye. We talked about the storms and about the bairns coming home early for solstice and Christmas because the authorities were worried that if they didn't do the crossing now, they might not make it at all.

"Half the *harkrav* have left for the holidays already," he told me. "They're worried about the lack of ferries too. This island is becoming more and more isolated."

"*Aja.*" It was undeniable. "But I think we're doing all right, don't you? Apart from the taxes, of course."

"Huh! Those taxes!" Tom sounded disgruntled. "It doesn't affect me. I don't have land, except for my potato plot, which is too small to count – and I do have a wage, for what it's worth. But it's caused a lot of bad feeling. You heard about the fight?"

I explained that we had come over with Elise so that she could interview Harris.

"It wasn't his fault, from what I hear," commented Tom. "It was that lad from that snobby place up on Floirean's Cnoc, you know? 'Sunrise View', it's called, or something equally as English-sounding! Started in on those two youngsters, the couple who sleep in the kirk. Called them names. Told them they were bringing ruin to En-Somi. Harris wasn't having any of it."

We were both quiet for a moment, drinking our tea. Then, to my surprise, Tom added, "I don't like the way things are going, you know. It bothers me. We've always had our differences – *harkrav* and *bondii*, Storhaven and Gamla Hus, but things seemed sort of – balanced. Now we all seem to be at each other's throats. Times are hard and nobody knows who to blame. The *Oyrod*?

(He meant the island council) The refugees? The *harkrav*? Or is it just that the whole world is falling apart? I might lose my job, you know – if the sea's too rough for ferries, what would there be for me to do? And there's so much corruption. I can't get over the idea that people on En-Somi were keeping slaves right on our doorsteps! And I don't understand how we didn't know!"

"*Aja*," I agreed, but added, "it doesn't seem quite like that over in Hus. I think we're all trying to pull together."

"Well, that may be." Tom sounded doubtful. "I've always thought that you were a closer-knit community than us – you're all of a kind, aren't you? All *bondii*. But I think these divisions will come to you, too. I hope they won't, but I think they will…"

I felt a bit depressed when I left Tom's little home a few minutes later. If he was right we had a difficult winter ahead. Or several difficult winters.

CHAPTER 6

It was already dusk again by the time we drove down the track into Gamla Hus. The lights were on in the shop and the school and in one or two bothy windows. A couple of children were kicking a ball up and down the track outside the *fi'ilsted*, calling to each other in a mixture of dialect and English.

"What's happening in the ruins?" Elise asked. Once again she was sitting in the back of Malcolm's cart, and was facing in the opposite direction to the rest of us.

"The ruins?" I asked. There were still a number of disused bothies on En-Somi back then despite the renovations we were making for the refugees.

"Aye – next to Rose's place," Elise said.

There had been two ruined bothies next to the shop until a year ago. Bothan Ross was now fully restored and inhabited but the second tumble-down building was still disused. It consisted of only one main room, like all our dwellings, but it was larger than most, for reasons lost in history. I had only been into it once, for Lyle and Verity's wedding in the summer. It had been ideal for such an occasion, easily accessible, close to the *fi'ilsted* where they had held their party afterwards, but uncluttered, seeming somehow separate from the ordinary life of the village. Lyle and Verity had exchanged the vows they had written themselves, and some of us had spoken briefly, wishing them well, recognising their union. It had been an unconventional ceremony, but moving.

Malcolm had been driving since before we crossed the

pass over Fyrtarn Fjell. He pulled at the reins and looked back to where Elise was pointing. There were beams of torchlight playing over the walls and the broken roof of the building.

"That's interesting!" he said, taking off his hat and scratching his head. "Shall we go and look?"

We all jumped down and left the ponies investigating the grass besides the track. The four of us walked back up to the ruin.

Lyle and Verity were standing in the middle of the bothy, playing their torches against the walls and the roof.

"*Hei!*" we all said as we walked in.

"Thinking of moving?" enquired Malcolm.

"Oh, *hei!*" Verity turned and smiled at us. "We saw you pass just a minute or two ago! How's Storhaven? How's Harris?"

"Harris seems fine," I answered. "What did you think, Elise?"

"Aye, he's good," Elise agreed. "Just a bit shaken up. The other guy hit first – and hardest. Mo was a bit upset by it all, but they were just bystanders, really. It was a good thing Quincy filmed the whole thing. I wanted to talk to the police officer over there but she was up at the other guy's home. I don't suppose she would have told me much, anyhow."

Lyle changed the subject. "Verity's got this idea…" he told us. "Do you want to explain, Verity?"

"*Aja.*" We were all standing in the ruins, the wind gusting around us, two pools of light on the uneven ground from the torches. "I've been wondering about making this into – I don't know what to call it – a place of worship? There's nothing over here, in Gamla Hus. I've never been for as long in my life without taking part in some form of corporate worship as I have since we were married."

Lyle put his arm round his young wife. "It was fine in the summer," he explained. "Verity would just go out onto the moors or down to one of the beaches." He looked at her with a smile. "You like to worship in silence, don't you? But now that winter is here, and these short days and wild weather…"

"A church, then?" I wondered. "Or a chapel?"

"Nothing as formal as that," Verity said. "Nothing as religious. Just a sort of meeting place, or a place where people could come and be quiet. You know, our bothies are small; there's nowhere for people to get away."

"We were thinking of a really simple renovation," Lyle added. "Good insulation, underfloor heating, a wind turbine – like a residential bothy. And then just simple seating. Maybe a little kitchen area, a couple of *cludgii*... We could celebrate special occasions here without having to go over to Storhaven – you know, births, marriages..."

Elise switched on the torch on her phone and shone it on the damaged roof, the gaps where windows ought to be, the uneven floor. "It would take a lot of work," she pointed out.

"*Aja*," Verity agreed. "And permissions for the ground source heating and the wind turbine."

"And nobody has any money," added Lyle. "And these things aren't cheap!"

"But it's a good idea," I said. "If we could make it happen." I turned to Malcolm. "Don't you think so?"

"*Aja*," he agreed. "I really do. I think it's a brilliant idea."

★★★

We applied for a grant. It was the obvious thing to do. To this day it surprises me that there are more refugees in the world than at any time in our history, more hunger, more homelessness, more abuse and addiction and general suffering, but still there are funds available to restore buildings, to create gardens or to erect monuments. We humans can have strange priorities! Malcolm promised to liaise with his son Angus, back on mainland Scotland, and we put in applications to about five funding bodies. Then, with everything else that was happening, we more or less forgot about the idea.

★★★

That afternoon, I remember, we left the ponies and cart outside the *fi'ilsted*. Elise was staying there and we had decided to have a quick drink before heading back down to my place. The conversation on the way home had been mostly about the fight, and about Quincy and Mo.

"Why are they still sleeping in the kirk?" Duncan wanted to know. "Haven't all the other refugees found somewhere to go?"

"Most of them have," agreed Malcolm. "Not Jarvis, of course."

"Oh, Jarvis!" I couldn't tell from his expression what Duncan's exclamation meant. Marigold spoke well of the man, although even she agreed that he was strange, but I think Duncan felt as I did – a little threatened, or anyhow wary.

"So, what do they do all day?" Elise wanted to know.

"Not very much." Malcolm sounded concerned. "I knew bairns like them in Edinburgh. Street people, really. No education, no ambitions – it's not their fault, of course."

"Frankie told me that they wanted to leave the island," I said.

"Lyle asked them that," Malcolm told me. "But they seem to have changed their minds. I don't suppose they know what they want, really."

Robert was sitting at the next table, staring a bit morosely into the fire. He had obviously heard our conversation.

"Perhaps they should be sent back to the mainland," he offered. "En-Somi doesn't have any social services to deal with bairns who haven't been brought up right. Maybe they need to go onto some sort of programme."

Malcolm turned and moved his chair back so that Robert could join our group. "There aren't really any programmes on the mainland for people like Quincy and Mo either. What they need is affection – and security. People are like plants. They need water and good compost. Those programmes are like the flower pots. They don't serve a useful purpose unless there's water and compost – affection and security – inside them."

"Sounds good," remarked Robert, looking unimpressed. "But who's to provide the affection and security you say they need, here on this island? We've got precious little security ourselves!"

"But lots of affection," I pointed out.

"You can't live on affection," answered Robert. He downed the rest of his drink and stood to leave. "I know it sounds mean and selfish," he told us as a parting shot, "but I wish you had never discovered those refugees living out at the old airport. There's been nothing but trouble since then. And it's getting worse!"

When the *fi'ilsted* door had closed behind him, Petter came over and pulled up the chair Robert had been sitting on.

"One of his ponies is sick. He thinks it's nothing serious – the snots – but the other pony is bound to catch it too, and he'll need to rest them until they're well. It could take three months."

"Oh, *nei*!" I was very aware – we all were – that Robert needed those ponies to work. He was pretty well self-sufficient when it came to feeding himself, but he had no other source of actual cash. And, of course, he had already had some of his harnessing taken.

Elise was looking from one to another of us. "I never thought of that," she commented. "It seems so eco-friendly, depending on live animals instead of machines, but machines don't get sick!"

"Well, at least that's not something the refugees can be blamed for!" remarked Duncan. "Malcolm, can I drive the ponies back to your place? Mam, what's for dinner?"

CHAPTER 7

The solstice-*brenni*, or bonfire, that the bairns had built outside my bothy was huge. The amount of driftwood that was accumulating on our beaches at that time was significant. All over the world, as sea levels rose, land was going under water, and whole trees were uprooted and set adrift in the oceans, along with all the detritus of human communities. Huge efforts were being made by concerned organisations and even a few governments to avoid the waters from being polluted by chemicals that never should have been there, but there were islands of rubbish in every ocean. The origins of some of the stuff that washed up on my beach could be identified, but most could not. I know that the year I am telling you about now our bairns found part of a wooden chair bobbing up and down in the sea just as the tide was turning. Marigold waded in as far as my beach used to go before sea levels rose and retrieved it, and it took pride of place, perched on top of the pyramid of wood. We all speculated about where it had come from, but really there was no knowing.

The national news that December included one matter of interest to all of us. The small group of people who had been responsible for enslaving the refugees on En-Somi were to go on trial in Edinburgh. There had been some talk of Lyle going over to the mainland to give evidence, but transport was so uncertain that in the end it was decided he could be questioned over the internet. None of the rest of us who were involved in bringing down the gang had been called to appear in court. Lyle's recordings on his phone were sufficient to prove the alms trading crimes, and several of the refugees would give their accounts of their treatment, also via Lyle's computer. The mainland press, who had been engaged in covering so many other stories in the months since the arrests, started to take an interest in En-Somi again, but nobody actually tried to cross over and meet any of us in person.

Nevertheless, the daily news bulletins seemed to exacerbate bad feeling on the island. Harris was back home by the middle of the month but his paps said that he couldn't go into Storhaven without being the recipient of abuse. A small group of bairns who would normally have been over in Lerwick at school but who were home early because of the storms had formed a gang that called itself, rather grandly, 'The Society for the Protection of the En-Somi Community'. They went around the little town painting the initials SPESC on walls and pavements and warned Jeanie at the Copper Kettle that she wasn't to give Quincy and Mo any free food or drink. Someone claimed to have 'discovered' that the little bakery had supplied bread to the refugees while they were still slaves, and there was a move on the island social media to boycott the shop. It came to nothing, probably because their bread was so good and, anyhow, theirs was the only bakery! It was rather ridiculous, in fact, because the owners of the bakery had sold the bread, perfectly legitimately, to the people who kept the slaves. They had no knowledge of its final destination! Hand-drawn posters appeared on noticeboards blaming the refugees for theft and violence as well as for all sorts of other crimes that, as far as I knew, had not been committed on the island. As quickly as they went up they were taken down, and replaced by other, computer-printed posters with slogans like 'Love Thy Neighbour' and 'Make Love Not War'. Somehow it came about that all those who felt supportive of the refugees started drinking at the Castle *fi'ilsted* in Storhaven, and the 'antis' migrated to the previously less-popular Vikings' Rest.

Things were nothing like as bad in Gamla Hus. I no longer

thought of the newcomers as refugees, although I'm sure there were those who did. We had three little ones in the village school – quite a significant proportion of the total number of pupils – and they had settled well enough. Rose and Si lived right in the village, and Rose helped out in the village shop, so she soon knew pretty much everyone. Baby Thistle was a magnet to some of the older people too. Yanni Sinclair and Harry had fished together in the summer, and had become firm friends. The Kullanders had worked hard to integrate Frankie and her family, who might otherwise have been difficult for our little community to absorb. Even so, we had our problems.

Sigrid mentioned it, a couple of weeks after Harris's fight. We were having a quick catch-up concerning our knitting cooperative. The two of us were sitting in her bothy just down from Lyle's, overlooking the green patch where the bairns took their breaks from lessons. It was later in the afternoon and already dark, with rain or sleet spattering against the window.

"The twins told me something worrying today," she commented, passing me a plate with shortbread biscuits arranged on it. "They said they're fed up with eating porridge. It's all they ever get now. Porridge and neeps and potatoes."

"Ah!" I was not completely surprised. I had heard Marigold talking to Duncan about neeps, wondering what they were and why her classmates didn't like them.

"I've been here before," Sigrid continued. "Way back, in the eighties. You won't remember those days. The government was cutting back on subsidies and benefits. You will have heard of the outcry when free school milk was cut. I was a new young teacher then, full of idealism, not a parent myself but alert enough to see what was happening to the bairns."

"Not hungry but malnourished," I said, thinking of something Malcolm had told me.

"*Aja*, and aware on some level that all is not well. Not worried but ill at ease. They pick up on their parents' concerns."

"It's the taxes, I suppose?" I asked.

"Partly," Sigrid agreed. "And the thefts. But it's more than that. They feel they can't trust the *Oyrod*, and if you can't rely on those you voted for life feels very precarious. And now, every evening on the news, they are reminded of crimes that went on right here, on our own island, committed by people who we had trusted to govern us fairly. It cuts the ground from under people's feet."

We were both quiet, thinking of how hard life was for some of our friends.

Then, "What did you do back then?" I wanted to know. "When you were just starting your career? How did you help the bairns?"

"I didn't do anything," Sigrid answered. "I was a bit out of my depth. Old Buck Stewart, bless his soul, had a cow out behind his bothy where Patrick has built the goat shed now, and he donated all her milk to the school. So we had our own free milk service. He kept it up for years, until the cow died – and then so did Buck." Sigrid was smiling at the memories. "He was a one, that Buck. Do you know, he once propositioned me! I was twenty-one and he was – well, I suppose in his seventies! When I turned him down he took it like a gentleman. 'You can't blame a man for trying!' was all he said." She laughed, almost a giggle. "After that he always winked at me whenever he saw me around the village."

"I'm guessing it's not milk the bairns need now?" I asked.

"*Nei*; one good, appetising meal a day would be ideal," Sigrid agreed. "But I don't think we could stretch to that."

"Porridge and potatoes and *neeps* is not a terrible diet," I suggested. "Boring, but not unhealthy – not like living on chips and pot noodles, the way some of Malcolm's clients did. What our bairns need is variety…"

"*Aja!*" Sigrid suddenly sounded excited. "*Aja!* That's right! So why don't we introduce cooking into the syllabus, and the bairns can make a meal together, once a week? We could ask the parents to contribute what they can…"

"And we could ask Malchi to take the lessons!" I suggested, feeling excited too. "That way every parent will want their bairn to take part!"

We grinned at each other conspiratorially.

"I'll go and talk to Malchi now," I said. Life always feels better if you can see a way of addressing a problem.

CHAPTER 8

Nobody expected our *Oyrod* representative to make an appearance in Gamla Hus. Until a public meeting held over in Storhaven almost a year ago, I would not even have recognised him. His family had owned some land on our side of the island for generations, although like most of the *harkrav* they rented it out to locals. The Munros had long since given up subsistence farming in favour of occupations where a person would wear a tailored suit. I believe Blair Munro was an executive director of an international company based somewhere in Europe, but rumour had it that he spent most of his time in London.

Of course, there are few secrets on En-Somi. If a person wants to keep something to themselves they don't text or message it; they talk, quietly, ideally not in the *fi'ilsted*! But there was nothing secret about our plans to start cookery lessons on Friday afternoons, we wanted to spread the information far and wide, into every bothy west of Fyrtarn Fjell.

The initial response was mixed. The Stewarts, who lived in a bothy that was unique because of the number of rooms it had, had a new son, Hamish, and were really just starting out in life. They were worried about donating some of their limited winter supplies. They had not been the victim of any theft yet but, like all of us, they knew they could be. The Sinclairs over on Hunger Moor also had a youngster, a sweet little baby with sea-green eyes called Rionnag, but they were in full support of the project. The Kullanders, who probably shared with Malcolm and me the honour of being the most financially secure of the Hus households, were also enthusiastic. Malchi, at the *fi'ilsted*, said that he felt honoured to teach cookery. "It's the love of my life," he told us. "After Petter, of course!"

We gathered, as many of us as could make it, in the *fi'ilsted*, about a week before the winter solstice. I remember how dark and cold it was outside, and how warm and welcoming the little tavern felt. It was the first time, too, that I realised how much our community had grown. The newcomers were all there, even Mandy's fifteen-year-old son, who rarely made an appearance in the village. Elise was perched on a stool behind the bar, her camera at the ready to record everything for her next documentary and for posterity. Beside her, also behind the bar, was young Harris, a sketch pad in his hand.

There was quite a bubble of noise. I could distinguish Olaf's gruff voice talking in pure dialect to young Elin, and the three young mothers – Freda Sinclair, Paula Stewart and Rose (also now called Stewart)—who were comparing notes about their little ones, in a mixture of broad island tones combined with something that might have been a London accent, and the odd dialect word. Robert was keeping himself pretty much to himself. He was wary of the newcomers back then, and talked only to other established *En-Som-in-Fedii*. Malcolm was away on the other side of the room talking to Frankie, who had been the leader of the refugees until they were all scattered across the island. I noticed that several of my neighbours had an air of anxiety about them. Even in the soft light of the *fi'ilsted* it looked to me as if the stresses of our lives were telling on people.

I think that Petter was about to open the meeting. He had said something to Elise, and she was fiddling with the lens on her camera. Sigrid had a device ready, presumably to take notes. And it was then that Blair Munro appeared.

Lyle and a group of other men were standing by the door, so when someone tried to come in they all had to shuffle aside, which was not easy in such a crowded space, and that drew everyone's eyes in their direction. It meant that Blair Munro made quite an entrance. I have wondered since, cynically, whether his late arrival was intentional. The man, I realised, was used to taking control of situations.

The last time I had seen our elected representative he had been wearing a tracksuit as if he were planning a trip to the gym, although of course there are no gyms on En-Somi! This time he was dressed more like a typical islander, with a waxed, fur-lined jacket, but his head was bare and I could see that he still wore his hair long, and in a high ponytail. He was a good-looking man if you like that sort of polished, crease-free style, and a smile exhibiting perfect teeth gleaming brightly like a TV advertisement. The word 'inauthentic' popped into my head when I saw him.

There was a lull in the conversations as we all took in who the newcomer was. Blair Munro was smiling benignly at us, for all the world like a politician visiting an infants' school during an election campaign. He held the door open for someone standing behind him, and a young woman with blonde hair squeezed in to stand beside him.

"I hope we're not late?" queried the man in his smart, southern English voice. "It's a wild afternoon for crossing the Fyrtarn pass!"

"Not at all!" responded Petter, seeming to take the situation in his stride. Then he added, making a bit of a dig at our absentee representative, "We don't often see you over here!"

"Well, no!" Blair Munro agreed. "Busy life, you know! Lots to do! But I heard about this venture of yours, and I really had to see for myself! Do you all know Candy Williams? She represents the harbour area of Storhaven."

Candy Williams! I thought. *Candy Williams? What sort of a name is that? How had such a person, with such a foreign name, become a representative on the Oyrod?* She sounded like a YouTube star, or an internet influencer.

"Candy is a Murray by birth," added Blair Munro. "We both want the best for our En-Somi, so we thought we'd come over, and see what's going on. You never know, we might want to replicate it on other parts of the island!"

Malcolm eased his way through the crowd to join me. "Creep!" he muttered into my ear. "*Our* En-Somi, indeed!"

Blair Munro was leading his colleague through the gathered islanders towards the bar. He was obviously a man who liked to be seen at the front of public gatherings, not as one of the crowd. When he reached the bar, he held out his hand to shake Petter's.

"Blair Munro," he announced.

"Petter," responded Petter, using only his first name, so that our representative's introduction seemed overly formal.

"Good turnout!" commented the visitor. "All from my ward?"

"*Aja*," Petter answered, glancing round the room. "Do you not recognise any of us?"

It was another dig at the man who, we had come to realise, had done so little for us in his elected position. Indeed, in the last few months we had come to see him as the enemy. It was this man and his elegant blond colleague who had helped to vote in the taxes that looked set to ruin us. Or, they would if we didn't work together.

Blair Munro turned away from Petter and raised his voice. "Fellow *En-Som-in-Fedii*..." he called out, trying to take over the meeting.

From one corner came the rough voice of Frankie. "'O's 'e, then?" she wanted to know. "Petter, I thought what you was going to lead this meeting."

Petter smiled across at the elderly lady. "You are right!" he agreed. "I am! I'm sure Mr Munro here just wanted to apologise for being late!" Then, turning to Blair Munro, he said, "I think there's space over there," and he indicated a corner by the small window beyond the hearth. "Please take a seat!"

The man had the grace to looked ashamed – or was he,

perhaps, just taken aback? The young woman, Candy, looked indignant, but there was nothing she could do. She followed her companion, and they perched on the window seat, looking uncomfortable.

"So, everyone," Petter started. "I think you all know what we've been thinking. We are facing hard times…" He glanced across at the two *Oyrod* representatives. "Through no fault of our own, I would add! Our bairns are not eating as well as they have done in previous years," and again he looked across at the two representatives. "They are not eating as well as some people on this island!"

There were murmurs of agreement and approval, and angry glances towards the window seat.

"So, this is the idea," Petter continued. "Once a week, on Friday afternoons, Malchi here will take a cookery class with the school children. We will use our kitchen here, because it's suited to catering for more people. For ingredients, we'll accept anything that you think you can spare. Malchi will try to show the bairns how to make a good meal out of whatever is available. And then everyone west of Fyrtarn Fjell is welcome to share the meal the bairns cook – at no further cost to anyone."

There were smiles and murmured comments to neighbours, as everyone thought about the proposal.

"It'll be like over at St Matthew's Bay!" called out Frankie. "We all ate from the same pot there, too!"

"Probably better ingredients this time!" suggested Si, and everyone laughed.

"What if we can't afford to donate any food?" Paula Stewart was probably expressing the concern of quite a lot of people present.

Petter glanced across at Malcolm and me. "We would like to keep this as informal and friendly as possible," he said. "We are a small community. I think we can trust each other. If you can't contribute, that's fine. You'll still be welcome to come and eat."

I butted in. "If you can't contribute," I pointed out, "then you probably *need* to come and eat! Petter and Malchi will collect the contributions here, and nobody else will know who gave what."

"We'll eat over at the school," Sigrid explained, looking up from her device. "It would be impossible to seat everyone in here!"

"And we'll eat early," Petter added. "The bairns will finish cooking when their school day ends, and the food will be served as soon afterwards as we can get organised. So those of you with a long walk home won't be too late."

Blair Munro and his friend had been exchanging glances and whispering to each other. Petter looked across at them, and asked, "Is there anything you'd like to say, Mr Munro?"

The man stood. He looked, I thought, a bit awkward. "It's a noble experiment," he proclaimed. "But aren't you worried that people will take advantage of you? Charity can have a very corrosive effect…"

"A *what*?" called out Frankie.

Petter grinned. "A corrosive effect," he repeated. "Mr Munro means that if we help each other out we'll grow rusty and fall apart. Isn't that right, Mr Munro?"

"I – no!" The man really did look embarrassed this time. "I just meant – I mean – surely, it's better if people help themselves, take a bit of responsibility, rather than depending on other people when the going gets tough!"

"Why?" It was Marigold, sitting on her pap's knee, who had asked the question. She wasn't being cheeky. She really wanted to know.

The question seemed to floor Blair Munro. "Pardon?" he asked, looking bemused.

"Why is it better for people to 'elp themselves than to 'elp others?" Marigold repeated. "It ain't what Sigrid teaches us in school! And it ain't what Verity said when me and Duncan was 'elping Elin and 'er paps with their *brenni*!"

"Duncan and I," corrected Sigrid, ever the schoolteacher, under her breath.

"Yes, well…" The man looked almost sheepish.

"Out of the mouths of babes…" whispered Malcolm to me.

And Shona, who also heard, whispered, "Hear, hear!"

"Of course, it is good to help one another!" Blair Munro was regaining his composure and his sense of control. "That's why Ms Williams and I are here now. We want to help where we can. That's what being an elected representative is all about. But we have to consider the consequences of the help we give. We have to consider whether it's really the best thing for the people we're trying to assist."

Marigold was frowning as she struggled to understand. "But 'ow could it be the best thing *not* to feed a 'ungry person?" she wanted to know. "I 'ates being 'ungry! Don't you?"

"I don't suppose he's ever been hungry in his life!" called out Robert, unexpectedly.

"Well, we all have our own political philosophies," commented Petter. "I can see that Marigold's way of thinking is closer to mine than Mr Munro's here. Still, it's a free country – more or less. So, are we ready to bring the idea to a vote?"

"I is!" announced Marigold.

"Do the children vote?" Blair Munro sounded indignant.

"I don't see why not!" responded Petter, to a chorus of approval.

The vote was not quite unanimous – Blair Munro and Candy Williams abstained. I suppose it was a forgone conclusion. We would have one communal meal before the break for solstice and Christmas, and then start on a regular basis at the beginning of the new school term.

"Why do you think they came?" I asked Malcolm and Duncan as we walked home through the blustery December night.

"Guilty consciences?" suggested Duncan. "They are responsible for all this hardship in the first place!"

"Electoral manoeuvring," was Malcolm's response. "They must know that the next *Oyrod* elections are in two years, and as things stand their prospects can't be looking that good."

CHAPTER 9

The talk of the island next morning was not, after all, our plans for a communal meal, or (in Hus) the unexpected appearance of Blair Munro. It was a bright, cold morning. Before sunrise, when I went out to feed the chickens and Malcolm was trying to wake Duncan ready for his 9.30am online class, the air had felt bitterly cold, and the fading stars were still visible in the sky, looking so close that it felt as if a person could just reach out and touch them. We get these days in December sometimes, days of frost and biting wind when the gulls fly low over the surging sea and their calls seem to echo from the cliffs. On such a day in other years we would have been making our final solstice plans, maybe collecting parcels from the shop to hide away and wrap for Christmas, or doing jobs on the land that such clear mornings make possible.

Instead, when I went up to Hus to talk with Malchi about our first community meal, I found small groups of people standing on the track outside the shop, talking about the latest piece of evidence to be released during the Edinburgh trial.

"They made millions!" Verity was saying, pulling her woollen hat further down over her fears. "How can they ever live with themselves? To make all that money by selling killer drones to such places!"

Si was part of the group. "*Aja!*" he agreed. "And it were all from our work! Us slaves! That million should've been ours! Except, 'o wants to make dosh out of killing other people?"

"One of the London papers calls them traitors," Robert

told us. "They reported it in 'What the Papers Say' at six this morning."

"It makes you want to reintroduce the death penalty!" announced Jamie. "At least, it would if you believed in hanging people! I don't!"

"*Nei!*" Si was quite pink with indignation. "They ought to suffer. Like what we did when we was slaves. Like them poor people what lost loved ones and 'omes and everything, because of them drones!"

Lyle joined the group. "Well," he pointed out, "they're in custody now, and they'll never see freedom again, not if I judge the situation right! So let's let justice take its course!"

"I feels sorry for Jeanie," Si added. "'Er was one of us, you know. 'Er was just trying to make a life for 'erself with that café, and them bosses blackmailed 'er. They made 'er 'elp them! She suffered an' all, and us lot, out at the old airport, we thought what she were our enemy."

"It was that sergeant," Jamie suggested. "Corrupt as they come!"

"*Nei!*" Robert, usually so taciturn, seemed to know all about it. "It was Fox-Drummin and his sidekick, Duncan. And their wives."

"What'll 'appen to all them millions?" Si was wondering.

"I suppose they'll go to the state," Jamie suggested. "Holyrood."

"*Nei!*" Robert seemed certain. "Westminster! We won't see anything of it this side of the border!"

"And definitely not on En-Somi!" Verity was smiling. "But, as Si said, who wants their blood money? Marie, are you here to help Malchi make plans for the meal? I'd like to help, if I can."

★★★

Malchi and Petter had organised one of their outside store rooms as a collection point for any ingredients people might contribute.

Robert had already brought a leg of lamb from his freezer, which was very generous of him considering how much had been stolen from his stores already. Lyle's parents had offered to send over a sack of potatoes. They wouldn't come to the community meal themselves. They were getting old, and the walk from Fremdes Haven over to Hus and back was rather daunting.

"Harris will bring the spuds to us," Malchi told me. "And we'll send him back with two big portions of dinner!"

"Harris seems to be over here a lot," commented Verity.

"*Aja*. Well, we're a whole sight friendlier to him than some of the people in Storhaven," Petter pointed out.

"And I think there's more to attract him here than just our natural warmth!" Malchi added. "Young Elise, for example."

We all grinned. It was true: there did seem to be a natural affinity between them.

"Marigold will be delighted if there's another romance blooming!" I suggested.

"Oh, that bairn!" Verity was smiling broadly. "She doesn't miss anything!"

★★★

The first community meal was scheduled for Friday, 19 December, the last day of term for the bairns in the village school, and a good way to celebrate the beginning of their school holidays. Donations continued to arrive, and were safely locked into the *fi'ilsted* storeroom. Malchi took a critical look at the offered ingredients that Thursday afternoon. "Right," he announced to Sigrid, Verity and me. "There'll be a choice. Lamb stew or chicken and kale hotpot. We'll show the bairns how to cook the potatoes on top of the meat dishes – we use fewer pots that way, and the older potatoes will taste better."

"How many people do you think will come?" I wondered.

Malchi grinned. "Who knows?" he responded. "Quite a few, I think."

Over at the school there was a lot of excitement. Sigrid and Verity had organised the bairns to make decorations – a cheerful mixture of solstice and Christmas images. Hanging from the beams were cut-outs of fir trees (which most of our young ones had never seen in real life) and suns, moons and stars. There were angels and boats and fish and chickens, all to celebrate the bounty of the earth. There was even something that looked suspiciously like an Easter egg. Well, the bairns were small, and some confusion over festivals was to be expected!

Andy, Duncan and Alana had somehow inveigled their way into Sigrid's classroom, ostensibly as helpers, and were busy making paper crowns for all the guests. By the time everyone went home on the Thursday, all that needed to be done was the rearrangement of tables and the erection of the extra trestles that lived in the school broom cupboard.

The little gang of friends were in my bothy, eating cake and drinking dandelion tea with honey in it, to take out the bitterness.

"It's like 'aving a party!" Marigold told me, with her mouth full.

"*Aja*, but with no dancing!" Alana agreed.

Andy giggled. "I can't imagine my mam and paps on a dance floor!"

"Malcolm and Marie can dance!" Marigold sounded proud. "We taught you, didn't we? Down on the beach!"

"Well, they can *sort of* dance," Duncan conceded. "But I don't think they should enter any competitions!"

"Will there be music?" Alana wandered.

"Oh, *aja*! Olaf and Elin have written a new song. They'll sing it to us tomorrow!"

"But we 'as to do lessons in the morning," Marigold told us. "Mafs and reading. Because Sigrid says what we 'ave more than two weeks off, and we mustn't slip back." Then, looking rather complacent, she added, "I won't slip back, 'cos I read with my mam and paps every night. 'Cos they can read now, too! Everyone in my family can read now!" Then she corrected herself. "Well, not Thistle, 'cos she can't talk properly yet. She just calls me 'Gold'. But she'll learn!"

★★★

Since the bairns in the school were doing normal lessons in the morning, we persuaded Duncan to stay at home and do some revision. He was to take exams a week after the beginning of the new term. Alana came down to our place and they worked together, practising their Norwegian and challenging each other over history dates and treaties. Andy was following a different course of study, and wouldn't take exams until May, but his parents also wanted him to keep to term and holiday dates, so I'm sure he was in his room, logged into his computer and studying.

Malcolm had gone over to his place to see to the ponies and to bring back more clothes. Sometimes living in two places can become quite complicated! I was cleaning my windows. It's a never-ending job because, as soon as I have them sparkling clean, another squall comes in from the west and they are caked in sea salt again. Still, I wanted the place to look good on Monday, when I expected crowds for the solstice celebrations.

Until I came to live on En-Somi, I thought that the winter solstice always fell on 21 December. It was only when I arrived on the island that I discovered that sometimes the shortest day of the year is the 22nd. Of course, back in the old days the island men decided on the date, depending on their own observations, and the event was celebrated any time between the 19th and the 23rd. Now we depend on the Royal Observatory way down in Greenwich to give us the correct date, and that year it was definitely the 22nd. So, we had two celebrations very close together – three, if you count Christmas, although Christmas has never been as important as solstice on En-Somi.

I was just washing the cleaning rags when Malcolm came back. He didn't look quite his usual, cheerful self.

"All right?" I asked, squeezing out a piece of cloth that had once been a part of a T-shirt.

"You haven't heard, then?" Malcolm walked over to my south-facing window and stared, frowning, out at the glorious view.

"Heard what?" I could hear the worry in his voice. For a moment the possibility that something had happened to one of his bairns flickered through my mind.

"There's been more theft," Malcolm told me. "At the *fi'ilsted*. Most of the food for today's meal has been taken."

I looked at him, stunned. "But..." I had seen Malchi padlock the storeroom door. It didn't seem possible. And who would do a thing like this?

"Petter phoned me, just now, as I was walking back. He wants us to come over if we can. As soon as possible."

"Right!" I was drying my hands and taking off my slippers. "Duncan and Alana can stay here," I added. "I'll just tell them where we're going – and why."

"Ask them not to tell anyone the news, yet," advised Malcolm. "We'll phone them when we know more."

The bar area of the *fi'ilsted* was empty when we arrived. People would stay at home in the morning working around their bothies and land, if they knew they were going out later in the day. We could hear murmuring coming from the kitchen.

Lyle, Verity, Malchi and Petter were there, standing round the big wooden table where Malchi did so much of his food preparation.

"*Hei!*" It wasn't a cheerful greeting from Lyle, not surprising under the circumstances.

"*Hei!*" Malcolm responded. "So what's the damage?"

"Come and see for yourself."

We all four left the kitchen by the rear door, into the old, paved courtyard. Out there, there were two stone storehouses (there are three now, but that isn't relevant, unless you are trying to follow this story on Google Maps and you can't make sense of my description). The doors of both were open. One had floor-to-ceiling shelving down one side, with cans and packets of all shapes and sizes stacked neatly. Against the other wall was the huge industrial freezer, powered, of course, by electricity from their wind turbine. The other storehouse was also shelved but the shelves were virtually bare. On the floor was a sack of potatoes; there was a row of onions and some bunches of kale and, untouched, a lovely-looking iced cake.

"So is this all we have left?" I asked, remembering the flour and oats, the swedes and dandelion leaves, and two jars of Lyle's home brew that had been there the day before.

"Not quite," Malchi said.

"We brought Robert's leg of lamb into the kitchen last night to finish defrosting, so they didn't get that. The Kullanders didn't bring their contribution down until this morning, so we have one chicken and quite a lot of oats."

"I expect that sack of potatoes was too heavy to carry, on top of everything else," suggested Verity. "Could one person carry everything that's been taken?"

"A strong man, maybe." Lyle was looking thoughtful. "It would be easier with two or three."

"How did they get in?" I had seen the sturdy padlock, and I knew from personal experience that it isn't as easy in real life as it looks on TV dramas to break a lock like that. Lyle, Malcolm and I had spent an uncomfortable time padlocked into somebody's shed, only a year ago.

"Professional job," Lyle told us. "It's been sawn."

Like the lock that held us captive! I thought.

"So, what now?" Verity asked.

Malchi sighed. "I know a few tricks," he told us. "When I first came to the UK, when we were living on tap water and fresh air, we used to bulk out what food we had with oats. It doesn't do much for the taste, but it but it makes it go much further."

"What about your magic ingredient?" Petter asked. Then he explained to us, "His mam taught him how to make this amazing sauce. You'll have experienced it once or twice, when you've eaten here. He won't tell anyone how it's made, or even what it's called. But it's good! I mean, really good!"

Malchi looked thoughtful. "I've never used it with lamb," he considered. "And absolutely never with any recipe that included oats, but I could try... Maybe if we used grated apples? I really need a little exotic fruit, but..."

"There's an unclaimed tin of mangoes in the shop," I remembered.

"*Aja*! That might do it!" Malchi was beginning to look more cheerful. "But I'm not going to teach those bairns how to make my sauce!"

***

I phoned Duncan and asked him to bring a second chicken from our freezer. I had been saving it for Christmas Day but our need was urgent. Petter went up to the shop and claimed the mangoes, and Malchi turned us all out of his kitchen, to create his concoction in private.

We three sat by the fire in the *fi'ilsted* and Petter made Irish coffee to encourage us.

"No leads, then, Lyle?" Malcolm wanted to know, thinking of the thefts.

"None at all." Lyle sighed. "Whoever is doing this seems to be covering their tracks pretty well and, between us, we two *nasyonii* have found a reason to visit just about every bothy on the island. Nobody seems to have extra provisions. Quite the opposite, in fact. It's frightening how basic some people's lives have become in such a short time."

"Well, there are only so many people who could be stealing stuff," Verity reminded us. "The island population isn't that big, and nobody has been coming and going from En-Somi all December. There haven't been any more ferries."

"I'm pretty sure we can rule out everyone in the Hus area," Lyle old us. "For one thing, what would they have to gain? And although Petter told everyone that we wouldn't say who contributed what, I can tell you now that everyone has contributed something! So would they steal from themselves?"

"*Nei*," Malcolm agreed. "So, someone from over Storhaven way? The whole island knows our plans, and there's hardship right cross the island."

"It's possible," agreed Lyle. He sounded reluctant. Who would want to believe that the *bondii* would steal from one another?

"If it isn't *bondii*," suggested Malcolm, who seemed to have read Lyle's thought, "then it must be *harkrav*. Because there isn't anyone else left."

"*Aja*, there is!" I felt mean saying it, but I didn't think we should ignore the obvious.

"If you mean the refugees," Lyle told me, and he sounded very firm, almost as if he were telling me off, "to all intents and purposes we have to think of them as *bondii* now. They live like us, they share with us, their bairns are at school with ours. They have nothing to gain by turning against us."

I felt deeply uncomfortable but I felt I had to say what I was thinking. I trusted these people; they wouldn't think badly of me for expressing my feelings.

"They don't quite *all* live like us," I pointed out. "There's Jarvis, still squatting in the old airport. We don't really know anything about his life."

"And Quincy and Mo, for that matter," Lyle added.

"*Aja*." Malcolm rested a hand on my arm. "It's not a pleasant thought but Marie's right. We can't rule any of these people out."

Just then Malchi called through from the kitchen. "Sauce made!" he told us. "Will somebody go across to the school and tell Sigrid that my lesson will begin at two, and please will she make sure that the children wash their hands before they come, and don't tread mud into my kitchen floor! And dinner will be served at four!"

CHAPTER 10

It was a huge success. Since I wasn't needed in the kitchen of the *fi'ilsted*, I walked up to the Kullanders' place and had a cup of tea with Fiona while the cookery lesson went on in the village below.

The Kullanders' house is unique on En-Somi, built in the Norwegian style, way back when there was oil money on the island. Compared with our bothies, it feels like a large, rambling building, although I dare say it is quite modest by mainland standards. Well, by city standards, anyhow. I know I saw many small, whitewashed single-storey crofts in the Scottish Highlands when I was a bairn.

We walked back down to the school just before four o'clock. I remember standing together – Shona and me in front, Andy and Alf behind, where the path changes direction at Oda's Corner, and looking over the village towards the setting sun. Clouds were rolling in from the north-west and the sky was streaked with orange and red. The sea looked dark, almost deep blue, almost green, almost black. It was stunning.

"It'll be a rough night," warned Alf.

"As long as it's dry on Monday!" Andy said, thinking of the solstice celebrations.

In the village there were lights everywhere. The one thing we were never short of, then as now, was electricity. All our wind turbines were whirling and humming, and a few people had put up brightly coloured little lights outside their homes. They swayed in the strengthening wind, making moving shadows on the rough track. There were two carts outside the shop, the ponies nowhere to be seen, but taken in to shelter, no doubt, in the ruined bothy next to Bothan Ros. Lyle and Verity were walking slowly each side of the old woman whose name I have forgotten, who lived in the bothy by the lower bend in the track as you head down to the summer harbour. Alana came out of the *fi'ilsted* carrying a sort of black cauldron, and called out cheerfully when she saw us. "Hurry up! We're about to serve the food!"

The partition that sometimes divided the infants' class from that of the juniors had been pulled back and the tables were set out in two long rows. The room was crowded already, buzzing with conversation, with activity, with a baby crying, and with the clatter of crockery and cutlery. We had no sooner taken off our jackets and added them to the huge pile by the door when Malchi stood on a chair and announced, "Dinner is served!"

A huge cheer went up and there was much shuffling and waving, beckoning and calling, as people seated themselves beside friends or family. The younger bairns had joined their parents but some of the older ones had been enlisted by Sigrid and Malchi to act as waiters and waitresses. They came round to each person in turn, asking the simple question "Lamb or chicken?" then collecting and delivering the dish of choice, already plated up in the tiny school kitchen.

There were party hats, made to look like crowns, by each place, and in no time at all the scene took on the appearance of something like a medieval banquet. This impression became even stronger when everyone was served, and Olaf and Elin started to sing, accompanied by Olaf's *langspil* and with interludes of the sweet piping of an instrument I had never seen Elin play before.

Malchi, Sigrid, and the child waiters and waitresses were sitting round a low table made of desks from the infants' class, and were balancing their plates rather precariously on their laps. They had been the last to be served, of course, but it wasn't long before Malchi was back on his feet. He came over to where

Malcolm and I were squashed into a corner next to Lyle and Verity. He spoke over my shoulder, between Lyle and me.

"Did we keep the secret?" he wanted to know.

"You mean about the theft? I think so. More or less." Lyle was looking round the assembled crowd. "Actually, quite a few people know – Duncan and Alana, of course, and the Kullanders. We had to tell Elise, and so Harris knows too. Oh, and Sigrid, naturally, and Shona and Patrick. But nobody's talking. You did really well, Malchi."

"*Aja!*" Malcolm leant across to speak to the chef. "This lamb is a masterpiece!"

"Thank Robert for that!" Malchi retorted. "And the bairns. They were wonderful."

"And look at this!" Malchi was holding out his phone, showing us a text. *Hope it goes well this afternoon.*

"Who's that from?" I asked.

"Our representative! Mr Blair Munro, in person!"

"We should have invited him," I said.

"We did!" Malchi answered, and chuckled. "Probably not quite the sort of dining he's used to!"

Apart from the portions saved for outliers like Lyle's parents, we devoured the lot. It amazed me that we had been able to feed so many. "It's like the feeding of the five thousand!" commented Verity, grinning broadly. "Who would have thought we could have pulled this off, given the state of that storehouse this morning!"

★★★

It was, of course, a relief to have managed to feed everyone. If that first meal had failed, I'm sure the project would never have taken off. Even so, we had a big problem, and we all knew it. Malcolm and I talked it over while we ate breakfast the next morning. Duncan was still asleep, the door to his bed space partly open, but he was nearly a teenager by then and nothing seemed to wake him. At that age they need to sleep late sometimes.

"Lyle's right about one thing," Malcolm told me. "We ought to stop thinking of the newcomers as refugees. They really are *bondii* now. Did you see young Shirley sitting on Shona's lap, talking away nineteen to the dozen? And Marigold seemed to know everyone there."

"Oh, I think she does!" I agreed. "When she isn't sure who someone is, she goes up to them and says, ''Ello, I's Marigold Stewart. 'O is you?' People love her!"

Malcolm chuckled. "Of course they do!" Then he looked serious. "We used up more food than we ought to have done yesterday," he pointed out. "We provided an extra chicken, Shona donated the mangoes and several tins of tomatoes, and the extra oats came from Malchi's stores. It won't work as well if the same thing happens again."

"*Nei*," I agreed. "And people will lose heart if they know how precarious it was at one point yesterday."

Just at that moment there was a tap on the door, and Marigold's head peeped round. "Is you awake?" she wanted to know. "Is I too early?"

"*Nei!*" Malcolm smiled at the bairn. "Come on in. Duncan's still in his bed, but Marie and I are up. Do you fancy some breakfast?"

"I's eaten," the bairn announced, taking off her outdoor clothes and boots and leaving them by the door. "It's wild out there!" she told us, perching on the settle. "It's going to be a *voldliggi!*"

"*Aja*, I think you're right," agreed Malcolm, hiding a smile at the old-fashioned dialect word the bairn had used for heavy weather. 'It's going to be *voldliggi*' was one of Olaf's phrases, and the bairn had repeated it with his inflections.

"It were great yesterday, weren't it?" continued Marigold. "I never knew what we put oats in with meat, on En-Somi. I told

Mam what we done, and she said, 'no way!'. She said that oats is for porridge. But then she saw there was oats in the chicken. So now we knows something new!"

"We don't always do that," I felt bound to explain. "That was one of Malchi's special touches."

"'E's a good cook, ain't 'e?" Marigold commented. "But, then, so is my mam!"

"Tea?" offered Malcolm, pouring some for me.

"*Nei*, thanks," answered the child. Her mind was obviously still on the events of the day before. "Frankie were wrong, you know," she told us, looking thoughtful. "It weren't nothing like when we used to eat together before. It weren't just that the food were better. Last night we was 'appy. Over at the old airport, we just ate because we was 'ungry. You 'as to eat. But last night we was eating because it were fun, too."

We heard Duncan grunting and turning over at the other end of the bothy.

"'E's a lazybones!" remarked the bairn. Then she went back to the subject of the community meal. "It were strange not to 'ave all of us there – you know, Charlie and Shawn, and Sheena and 'er boy, and Quincy and Mo. We don't never see them, now."

"Do you miss them?" I asked. The bairn had seen so many changes in the last year. She seemed very resilient, but maybe she needed to talk.

"I – *aja*, I thinks I do, in a way." Marigold looked thoughtful. "When we first came over 'ere, to 'Us and to our bothy, I mostly missed Lavender. It were all right in the daytime, 'cos I were learning so much and it seemed to take up all my head. But at night I would think of 'er, and dream about 'er, and wake up crying."

"But not anymore?" Malcolm spoke lightly, buttering his toast and appearing just to make light conversation, so that the bairn wouldn't feel she was being interrogated.

"*Nei*, not anymore." Marigold got up from the settle and wandered over to the window. "You can see further from your window than we can from ours, in our bothy," she remarked. "Sea, and sea, and sea. Mam says that when she lived down south, before the flooding, she could just see other 'omes when she looked out of 'er window. Flats. 'Omes all built on top of each other. Can you imagine?"

She returned to the settle, and to her earlier conversation. "It were odd," she remarked. "I cried for Lavender when she died, and I 'ad bad dreams. Then I stopped. But when you lot rescued us, and we came over 'ere, I started to cry for 'er again. It were like it all came back to me, because, you know, we was safe, so I could think about 'er. Then I thought what I would miss 'er for ever. And I will, in a way. But that time, you know, when I ran away, and me and Jarvis met at 'er grave, and then afterwards we took a photo and put it up above our washing machine – well, after that I stopped waking up crying."

"And does that feel like a good thing?" I wondered.

"Oh, *aja*! A very good thing!" The bairn seemed certain. "I won't never forget 'er, but Verity says what she's gone to 'eaven. So now I sort of 'ave room to miss the others what used to live with us." She looked down at her toes, warmly clad in green woollen socks. "Do you think Jarvis is all right? He ain't got nobody to look after 'im."

"Perhaps he doesn't want to be looked after?" suggested Malcolm, leaning back in his chair, looking full.

Marigold wrinkled up her nose as she considered this possibility. "I think maybe 'e does," she said. "I think what 'e's a bit odd. 'E used to frighten me to death in the old days, me and Lavender, but now I thinks that's just 'is way. When I ran away and 'e looked after me, I thought what 'e was sad, living all on 'is own over in that ruin."

Just at that moment Duncan emerged, pulling a *gensi* on over his pyjamas, and yawning.

"*Morgoni*, Marigold!" he said, ignoring Malcolm and me. "You're up early!"

"No, I isn't!" she retorted. "You're up late! Your mam and paps 'ave finished their breakfast!"

Malcolm and I exchanged glances. Malcolm wasn't Duncan's father. He and I had only been together for a year or so. I looked at Duncan, to see how he would take this mistake, but he was just yawning again, and stretching.

"I slept so well!" he announced. "And now I'm starving. Have the hens laid? Can I make some scrambled eggs? Marigold, would you like some?"

We left the two bairns making breakfast and talking about the coming solstice celebration, and walked over to Malcolm's bothy. The wind was bitterly cold and the sheep on the moors were all sheltering behind rocks and hillocks. The sea was grey, flecked with white. The whole world seemed green and grey and white – and very beautiful. Malcolm took my hand as we climbed the stile, and didn't let go afterwards, and when we arrived at his place we went back to bed for the rest of the morning. Duncan sleeps like a log, but the privacy of having a bothy to ourselves was wonderful.

CHAPTER 11

Si and Rose were learning our customs quickly. This would be their first solstice celebration, but they had asked lots of questions and had discovered that the *bondii* on our side of the island often met for breakfast before sunrise, and before climbing Fyrtarn Fjell. A little shyly, Rose had asked me about a week earlier if Malcolm, Duncan and I would like to eat with them, and we had agreed to be there by eight. For once Duncan didn't complain about having to get up, and he strode on ahead of us, so that by the time we arrived at Bothan Ros he and Marigold were busy cooking.

"We's frying mashed potatoes!" the bairn told us. "We's calling it 'ash browns!"

"Sounds great!" Malcolm encouraged her, and smiled at Rose, who was watching her daughter proudly.

Those who had been refugees were suffering less from the tax hikes than most people. They farmed no land, and they were still, at that time, receiving resettlement grants from the Climate Emergency Commission. Of course it wasn't much, but they were used to having even less, and they were living among people who were practised in making ends meet. We ate fried potato and bacon, and drank a little too much tea considering that we were about to climb a steep hill, and then we set off together in the dark and the cold.

I am sure that our solstice celebration must have its roots in ancient times. Sigrid once told me that the dialect word for 'sun' is *saulė*, but there is a song that Olaf sings at solstice in which he uses the word *sól*, and that makes sense to me, because of the English word 'solstice'. Anyhow, whatever its origins, it's as big a festival for us as *Huldufolk* Day, and just as hedged about with customs.

Sunrise is a bit after nine on the day of the winter solstice. We scrambled up the *fjell*, occasionally using our torches but generally managing with our night vision. Remember, there are no street lights on En-Somi and we are used to the dark. On the lower slopes where the burn crosses the track, we met the crowd who had eaten at Shona and Patrick's shop, and the Kullanders joined the party not long afterwards from a footpath that looks more like a sheep track, and which joined us from the north. Duncan's little gang were together then, and the bairns went on ahead of us, confident and energetic on a hillside that three of the four of them had known all their lives. By the time we reached the top, the bairns were sitting on a large, tilted rock facing east, dangling their feet over a drop that made me feel slightly queasy, although it is where the young ones always sit, even today.

There is something magical about being on top of a hill in the dark. I remember that it was cold with a strong northerly wind but, even with so many of us crowded into quite a small space, there was a sort of peace. We were small compared with the rocks and the sea and the powerful, invisible wind, no more part of En-Somi than the gulls and the sheep and the burn – and no less.

Very gradually, the sky to the east started to turn from jet black to grey. The *brenni*, or bonfire, that year had been built mostly by the Sinclairs' and Harry's households over on Hunger Moor, and consisted of a lot of off-cuts and left-over pieces of wood from building the new bothy. Petter had dragged up a small tree that had washed up in the summer harbour too, and Shona and Patrick were providing the fireworks, though not as many as we would have seen in more prosperous times. As the sun at last started to creep above the horizon, Mandy's boy, assisted by Yanni, lit the fire, and because of the wind the flames flickered uncertainly for a moment and then caught something highly flammable, and with a *whoosh!* the fire was burning. A sort of subdued cheer, more a murmur of approval, went up from our little crowd, and Patrick set off the first rocket, which exploded with gold and silver stars in the still-grey sky.

After that, we watched the brightness creep down the hill towards the moorland, and eventually Storhaven, as the sun rose. And each time the sun made its first appearance to small groups of *En-Som-in-Fedii* gathered around their *brennii*, we would see a new fire lit, and more fireworks exploding into the dawn. Today would be the shortest day of our year. After this, the warmth of the sun, even in these northerly climes, would slowly return. We drank spiced dandelion tea, made toasts to the rising sun, and when at last daylight had reached the whole island, we slithered back down the *fjell* towards my bothy, where a modest feast was prepared.

It was a good day. Looking back on it, all these years later, it seems as if I had no real worries in the world. I have a clear memory of most of the bairns dancing round the *brenni* outside my bothy, and of refusing to join them despite Marigold's pleading. I know that we went from there to the school, where those who couldn't climb the *fjell* had been eating and drinking and telling stories to each other. We finished our day up at the Kullanders', lighting the last of the fires as the sun set, and watching the final fireworks.

The families dispersed after that, home to their bothies, where parents would have given their bairns gifts, and if there was a courting couple they would have exchanged keepsakes, although I don't think we had any established pairs on our side of the *fjell* that year. We gave Duncan a new phone, and his paps in Norway had sent me the money to install a rather expensive game, which I seem to remember he played until the music that accompanied it drove us nearly to distraction. We knew that in some bothies that winter there would be no solstice presents, nor

Christmas presents either. Most of the *bondii* were economising, stressed by the high taxes, cutting back where they could. We asked Duncan not to tell his friends about his phone, and he agreed, hugging us both and texting his paps his thanks.

★★★

My son had been with his father the previous Christmas, so we wanted to make this one special. Duncan, however, had other ideas. He had brought us back gifts from the Shetlands – a tweed cap for Malcolm that he wore for years, and a little candle holder in the shape of Sumburgh Head Lighthouse for me. Once our presents were opened, though, my son really only wanted to video-call his friends and play on his phone and tablet. I was having to get used to the idea that he was no longer the little boy who liked to spend his time with his mam.

Instead, Malcolm and I went for a long walk, over towards his place and then down to Oden's Inlet. There was a sandy beach there. It used to be wider and longer before the sea levels rose, but it still had quite a generous stretch of sand when Duncan was a boy, and it was one of those beaches where there were always shells. Even today, at low tide, you can see what it was like. The cliffs are high there, and the beach was sheltered. We sat on a rock and watched the tide come in, splashing and foaming around the huge boulders on the southern side of the inlet.

Somehow, we started talking about our previous partners. Malcolm's wife had died of cancer, and he had been bereft. 'Emotionally smashed' was how he described it. "If it hadn't been for the bairns, I don't think I would have survived," he told me. I, on the other hand, had not really been hurt when Bjorn had left. I suppose I had already known that it was over, and he left me with so much – a son, a home, financial security, a place where I belonged. But I, too, had not seriously thought about falling into another relationship. We had both surprised each other.

"It doesn't seem fair, really," I said. "To be so happy when there's so much suffering in this world."

"*Nei*," Malcolm corrected me. "Every ounce of happiness is a good thing. We've got to tip the balance, to make more joy in this world than there is misery."

We sat there for a while, holding hands, watching the waves. Then I suddenly felt Malcolm's fingers twitch. "Look! Up there!" he said, and pointed with his other hand to the top of the cliff opposite.

I followed his outstretched arm with my eyes, and saw what had surprised him. It was a person, a man, standing right on the edge of the cliff looking out to sea. He was wearing a long, dark coat that must have been open. It was blowing in the wind.

"Who is it?" Malcolm wondered. Then, almost in a panic, "Is he going to jump?"

I watched in horror. We were, probably, twenty minutes from whoever it was even if we ran and scrambled back up as quickly as we could. If we called out, would we startle him? Would we cause him to fall, even if he wasn't planning to jump?

Malcolm stood. I suppose it was instinctive. He felt the need to do something. The movement must have attracted the attention of the man and he turned and held his hand to his eyes to shield his vision from the low westerly sun. I felt sure he had seen us. Then he turned, and left, and the cliff was empty.

"It was Jarvis!" I exclaimed. "Right over here, on this side of the island! You know, Jarvis from the old airport!"

Malcolm sat down again. "*Aja*, I think it was," he agreed.

"But why…?" I felt somehow shocked. "What is he doing over here?"

"Well, he can wander where he wants, can't he?" suggested Malcolm. "After all, what are we doing here?"

"*Aja*, but – Jarvis!" It seemed all wrong, that he should be so far from the place where he was squatting. It was like seeing a bluebell at Christmas, or a new-born lamb on solstice.

I suddenly felt cold. "Let's go back, shall we?" I asked. I wanted to be safe in my little bothy with the door and the shutters closed, and with my son and my partner sitting beside the range. And anyhow, it was getting dark.

CHAPTER 12

"What's the problem with Jarvis?" Malcolm wanted to know. "He looked after Marigold well enough, didn't he, when she ran away?"

"*Aja*!" It was true, but I couldn't find it in my heart to like the man. And definitely not to trust him. "But remember," I added, "Verity was there too. He wouldn't harm the bairn with Verity watching!"

"Well..." Malcolm seemed to think I was being a little unreasonable. "He didn't harm Verity when she was alone with him, did he?"

We were walking up the slope from the burn, the wind to our backs, but gusting in a threatening way.

"*Nei*," I had to admit. "But don't you remember, he sided with the slavers, that time up on Floirean's Cnoc? He told Marigold that I was wearing Lavender's cross! He tried to turn the refugees against us!"

"*Aja*, he did that," agreed Malcolm, holding my hand to pull me up the steep bank just before you reach my storehouse. "But he was right, wasn't he? I mean, you *were* wearing Lavender's cross, and you can't blame him for not knowing that your intentions were good!" He paused for a moment. "And maybe he just didn't want anything to change."

I wasn't convinced. Everything Malcolm had said was true, and other than that one incident I didn't know of anything he had ever done actually to hurt anyone. I hadn't liked the way he had looked at me once but, really, I shouldn't be basing my whole judgement of a person's character on one glance, however inappropriate it had felt at the time.

"Ah!" said Malcolm, changing the conversation. "It looks as if Duncan might be cooking us a meal!"

I looked in the direction of Malcolm's gaze, and saw what he meant. The storehouse door was not properly closed.

"That boy!" I started to say, and then stopped. "Hold on, Malcolm!"

I opened the stout wooden door and my stomach gave a sort of lurch. Two whole shelves of food had gone – almost all of the tinned food I had accumulated during the summer to see us through the dark months to come.

To me it seemed obvious. We had seen Jarvis on the clifftop. He clearly knew that we were away from the bothy; he had seen us down on the beach. He was the thief! Then I had a surge of panic. "Duncan!" I cried, and rushed up the slope to the bothy.

He was lying on the settle, one leg hanging over the end, the other knee bent, watching something on his tablet and laughing.

"*Hei*, Mam!" he said as I burst in, then he saw my face. He sat up. "Mam! What's happened!"

Malcolm came in behind me. "*Hei*, Duncan!" he said calmly. "Had a good afternoon?"

"*Aja!*" Duncan was looking from one of us to the other. "Tell me!" he demanded.

"Jarvis has broken into our storehouse!" I exclaimed. "He's taken half our tinned goods!"

"Hold on!" Malcolm was not one to jump to conclusions even when it was so obvious. "We don't actually know it was Jarvis, do we?"

"Malcolm!" I was indignant, partly because I knew he was right, although it was a bit of a coincidence, seeing him like that on the clifftop so far from where he lived, and then discovering the theft.

Duncan was on his feet. "But I've been here all day!" he said.

"I didn't hear anything!" He was putting on his shoes, ready to see for himself.

All three of us went out again, into the blustery dusk. Malcolm clicked on the storehouse light. The two empty shelves seemed to glare at me, wiped clear of all those tins, carefully sorted by produce and use-by dates.

"Well, at least they didn't take the flour or the sugar!" Duncan said, looking at the top shelf on the right.

Malcolm had taken off his tweed cap, and was scratching his head thoughtfully. "*Nei!*" He was agreeing with Duncan. "They've left a lot of things that you'd think a hungry person might want. And look!"

On the top left shelf, we kept treats. This was a recent innovation, brought about by Malcolm, who sometimes liked something sweet to eat in the evenings. Still neatly stacked was a pile of chocolate bars, good, fair-trade stuff brought over by Malcolm's daughter earlier that autumn. Next to the chocolate was a large, old biscuit tin. Duncan lifted it down and opened it.

There were packets and packets of dried fruits: bananas and apricots and raisins, and dried coconut – all things that were harder and harder to get on our isolated little island.

"It doesn't make any sense!" Duncan remarked. "If I were stealing stores, I'd take a bigger variety of stuff! Who wants to live off tinned soup and baked beans when you can make fruit scones?"

I thought I knew the answer to that. "Someone who has lived off tinned food for years?" I suggested. "Someone who cooks over an open fire, who just wants to heat his food up?" Of course, I had Jarvis in mind. It seemed evident to me.

"Maybe." Malcolm was still unwilling to jump to conclusions. "Anyhow, we need to fix a good, sound lock on this door! Marie, can I look in your tool box? Duncan, do you want to help?"

★★★

We didn't text Lyle until a couple of days later. He and Verity had gone over to Fremdes Haven to spend Christmas with Lyle's parents. They were, by all accounts, delighted with their new daughter-in-law, especially now that the young couple had made it clear that they had no plans to leave En-Somi. And anyhow, it was not as if he could do anything except commiserate. Duncan, Malcolm and I had looked carefully all around my bothy, searching for any clues about who had been there, but there was nothing.

Instead, we spent some time comparing Malcolm's winter supplies and mine, and combining the best of both in my storehouse, now sporting a much stronger lock. If we had a really bad storm, we agreed, we would all stay at my place, although Malcolm would need to go back to see to his ponies. "Next summer," he suggested, "we should think about building some stabling over here."

"*Aja.*" It was a sensible enough idea. "But first we'll need to widen the track. Your cart can't make it as far as this yet."

"It'll be heavy work," warned Duncan. "Do you remember, Mam, when they rebuilt the track down to the summer harbour?"

"I do!" It had taken weeks, and most of the men west of Fyrtarn Fjell had helped. "But that was a really big task. I think we could manage it."

"I can see already what I'll be doing all through the next long holidays," Duncan groaned, cheerfully.

We put in an order for more tinned goods, too, but we didn't hold out much hope of them arriving before the spring. They would have to come from the mainland via the Shetlands, and with the weather so unpredictable and supply chains everywhere so precarious, getting anything delivered to En-Somi in the winter months had become almost a miracle. Nor were they cheap. I couldn't afford to keep restocking like this, even with Bjorn's generous allowance.

★★★

The first big storm of that year blew in on 3 January. You probably won't remember it, unless you live way to the north. It skirted Ireland completely, although they were all geared up for it, nor did it do as much damage on mainland Scotland as they had anticipated. We were not so fortunate, and some of the west coast communities in Norway took quite a battering.

I remember waking in the pitch dark with Malcolm lying on his back beside me, and feeling certain that it was morning. Outside I could hear the steady suck and roar of huge breakers beating against rocks. I moved carefully to the ladder down from the sleeping platform (we still used a ladder then. Malcolm and Petter built a proper staircase for my sixtieth birthday). The floor was pleasantly warm under my bare feet, and I padded across to the south-facing windows and opened the shutters.

It was, to use the phrase that Marigold had learnt from Olaf, going to be *voldliggi*, wild. In the dawn light I could see the dark grey sea covered in rolling streaks of foam as waves broke far out, reformed and broke again. Spumes of spray hurtled up into the air and there were tiny droplets on my windows – not rain, but sea-spray carried in the wind. My door was rattling very slightly with the force of the gale. I pulled on my boots and a jacket and went out to battle my way round to check on the chickens. They were still roosting, safe in their warm hen-house, but one had kindly laid an egg.

Back inside, I considered my options. Malcolm and Duncan were both still asleep, although it was late – after nine, and getting light. I didn't want to turn on the radio or start cooking breakfast in case I woke them, but I risked plugging in the kettle, then I borrowed Duncan's tablet, put it on silent and checked the forecast.

The Norwegians had named the storm Haakon, but only declared it a level-two emergency. Ferries and flights, of course, were cancelled, and traffic on the bridge between Sweden and Denmark was restricted to ten miles an hour, with no high-sided vehicles. The Aith lifeboat had been called out for a boat in distress north of the Shetland Islands, and had successfully rescued three fishermen who should have known better than to be out on such a wild night. The London Met Office was warning that the gale would last at least forty-eight hours, and that high winds were expected on the west coast of Scotland, the Orkneys and Shetland. We were not mentioned, which is not unusual.

 I made tea, and settled down to the novel Malcolm had given me for Christmas. He had seen another by the same author in my bookcase, and commissioned his daughter to bring this one over. In a basket at the foot of the settle, my knitting was waiting, and when the others were awake, and if the internet was still working, I would phone Verity about Si and Rose's reading lessons. There was more than enough to keep me occupied until Storm Haakon had blown itself out.

CHAPTER 13

There's something about surviving a storm that seems to put everyone in a good mood. People repair any damage at home, and then check on their neighbours. If the internet is working, devices ping and everyone compares notes. If the phones are down we tend to go visiting. Duncan and Malcolm opted to go by the cliff path round to the Sinclairs' and Harry's households. It would be the first big storm the new bothy had faced, and they were high on the moor, sheltered from the north-east by the slope where their wind turbine had been planted, but facing any weather that might hit them from the south or the west.

I took the old sledge down to my beach to collect driftwood. The pounding waves had eaten away at the grassy bank at the northern end, leaving dark, jagged rocks standing in the churning water and extending the beach another few feet to my right. There was not as much debris as I had expected. It depends a lot on the wind direction and the conflicting currents around the island. I piled up some broken branches, and collected a few pieces of smooth, polished glass that the sea had brought in – green and shiny, the remains of a broken beer bottle, maybe? I would give it to Sigrid when I walked up to meet the others for lunch. The bairns made mosaics with coloured glass salvaged from the sea, glued onto painted boards. Every bothy that had once had bairns at the school had at least one such work of art on a wall, somewhere.

The original agreement was that I would exchange driftwood

for food, but that deal had more or less run its course. I still gave Petter and Malchi the flammable fruits of my scavenging, but since Malcolm came on the scene we bought and paid for all our food at the *fi'ilsted*. On an island with a subsistence economy, we counted ourselves as comparatively wealthy. Petter and Malchi, we felt, ought to save their generosity for those in greater need.

The island – or at least, our part of it – seemed to have weathered the storm well. A chunk of guttering had been torn off the western face of the Kullanders' place, but by the time I reached Hus Andy was already regaling a small group of people with the tale of his father teaching Eric how to use a high ladder safely. It seemed that Eric's baseball cap had blown off when he was at roof level, and Andy had to chase the hat as far as Oda's shrine before he could catch it. "The poor old saint was wearing it!" he finished, referring to the ancient, broken image of Saint Oda.

The pounding seas that had washed away my grassy bank to expose the rock beneath, had, we were told, broken part of the wall that protected the Storhaven harbour and flooded Tom's kitchen area. The burn that ran through the little town had broken its banks, too, and sent water pouring down the main track but, since all the buildings in Storhaven were raised a little above street level, no harm was done.

Duncan was full of his morning, walking the clifftop with Malcolm and visiting Harry's bothy.

"They've made it really bonnie!" he told me. "It's not quite like a normal bothy, because there's a partition, to give Mandy some privacy. Harry and the boy sleep on one side and Mandy and her wee girl sleep on the other, and then they open up the partition in the daytime to make one big room, like a proper bothy. Yanni and Harry made the partition out of driftwood with cloth between the slats. And the bathroom's built right into the hillside, with a tiny window at the top, which is ground floor level from the outside. They're making a sort of seating area outside but Harry doesn't think it'll be finished until the summer."

We were sitting in the *fi'ilsted* as Duncan was telling me all this, waiting for fish stew and dumplings. Malcolm was smiling at my boy's enthusiasm and sipping a whisky.

"It's a good thing Yanni and Harry get on so well," he commented. "They've no other neighbours out there. And I wondered how Freda and Mandy would get on, but they seem all right."

"They survived the storm well enough, then?" I queried.

"Oh, *aja*. Very well, in fact! Harry said it was quieter than any storm out at the old airport, because then there were always parts of the broken roof flapping, whereas everything in and around the bothy is anchored down."

"I think Mandy was a bit scared," Duncan remarked, looking thoughtful. "I suppose she must have memories of whatever happened to make her a climate refugee in the first place."

"*Aja*, of course." Malcolm looked at Duncan approvingly. "Let's hope the fear wears off, now that they are really safe," he added.

We were just tucking into the stew when the *fi'ilsted* door opened, and Elise, Harry and a woman I didn't know came in. They were all carrying bags and looking flushed from being out in the wind.

"*Hei*, Petter! *Hei*, everyone!" Elise was looking cheerful. "We've come bearing gifts!"

Petter came out from behind the bar. "*Morgoni*, Elise and Harry," he said, then, to the stranger, "I'm Petter. Welcome!"

The woman put down her bag and pulled off her woolly hat. She was, I suppose, in her mid-thirties, although it's difficult to tell with the *harkrav* – and *harkrav* she definitely was. They dye their hair and do things to their faces, and of course they spend less time outdoors than we do. This woman had chestnut-coloured hair with golden streaks in it. She was wearing the right sort of clothes for En-Somi but she had wound a pretty scarf, not woollen, but perhaps silk, round her neck. She had pearl studs in her ears, and later I saw that she had a ring with a pearl set into it, on the same finger as her wedding ring.

She pulled off her gloves and, looking a little hesitant, she held out her hand to shake Petter's.

"Hello!" she said, then "*Morgoni*! I'm Freya Munro. My husband, Blair, is your representative on the *Oyrod*?" It sounded like a question, as if she wasn't sure we would recognise his name.

"*Hei*!" Petter greeted the woman again. "It's good to meet you."

We had stopped eating, and were all watching the scene by the bar, which was probably rude of us.

Elise spoke then. "I was interviewing Freya," she explained, "for my project. Ingrid introduced us. And we told her, me and Harry, that the next community dinner is next Friday, because school starts back on Tuesday, and Freya said she'd like to contribute some stuff."

"I wasn't sure what to bring," Freya said. She had a soft, gentle voice. I couldn't place her accent. It was definitely Scottish, but I wasn't sure from which region. "Elise told me that last time you made two large dishes, so I tried to think of things that would mix in well."

She lifted her bag up onto the bar. "I brought cheese," she said, "because we always have a lot, and it goes with most things. And potatoes – Harry's got those. And two onions from my garden. And honey, in case you want to make something sweet."

"Malchi!" Petter called his partner out from the kitchen. "Come and see what Freya Munro's brought for the next communal meal!"

Malchi came out, looking, I thought, a bit stressed. *Perhaps he doesn't sleep well during storms*, I thought. Then he saw what Freya Munro was unloading onto the bar.

Immediately the anxious look vanished. He made some sort of exclamation in his own native language. None of us understood but we all knew he was expressing pleasure.

"This is wonderful!" he said. He picked up the cheese, a huge block of it, opened one corner of the greaseproof paper in which it was wrapped, and lifted it to his face to smell.

"This is *good* cheese!" he exclaimed. He picked up one of the onions and weighed it in his hand, then opened another bulky package. "Sweet potatoes!" he said, almost reverently. "I haven't seen sweet potatoes for years! Where do these treasures come from?"

Freya Munro smiled. "Blair loves them," she said, "so we always bring some back from Edinburgh, if we can get them."

"Won't he miss these?" Malchi was holding one in each hand, as if he were going to start juggling.

"Aye," agreed the woman. "But I'll just tell him we have no more left. Which will be true!"

"So he doesn't know you've come over here?" Petter wondered.

"No. No, he doesn't." She looked, I thought, sad. "He's up on Floirean's Cnoc at the Williams' place, planning something or other. Business, no doubt." She sighed.

A thought crossed my mind: *She isn't happy with Blair.* Then I made a sort of mental correction. Here I was, jumping to conclusions again, judging people with no real evidence.

She glanced at a neat little watch, and said, "Actually, I need to get back. He'll wonder where I am if he comes home and I'm not there!"

"Did you walk over?" Malcolm butted in. "It's a fair distance, and it'll be dark soon!"

"Aye, I did," she replied. "Blair had the ponies, and Elise and Harry were walking over anyway. So I came with them."

"I'll get my cart," Malcolm said, jumping up. "You can't walk back that way on your own, and in the dark!" Then, to Duncan and me, "Do either of you want to come?"

★★★

It was eight at night by the time he returned. Duncan and I had decided not to go, but Malchi had hitched a lift because he wanted to pick up some stores that had been awaiting collection at the Old Castle *fi'ilsted* for at least a month.

"That was an interesting development," Malcolm remarked as he took off his coat and shoes, checked the kettle to see if there was any water in it, and switched it on. "I'm making tea. Would either of you like any?"

"She seemed sweet," I said. "Not a bit like her husband. No tea for me, thanks."

"*Nei*, not a bit," agreed Malcolm. He turned the range up a notch and made his tea. "But I'm not sure how sweet she is. Some of her comments as we drove to Storhaven… I wondered if she had just donated that food to spite her husband! But perhaps I wouldn't blame her if that was the case. Anyhow, Malchi and I ate at the Castle," he told us, changing the subject. "The food was good, but honestly, it's not a scratch on Malchi's! And they've put their prices up. It was mostly *harkrav* eating in there, and not many of them. These high taxes'll hit everyone in the end."

"How far did you have to go," Duncan wanted to know, "to reach the Munro place?"

"Oh, not far." Malcolm was holding his mug of tea with both hands wrapped round it, trying to get warm. "The Munros live just out of Storhaven, in that bothy you can see from Aeloff's Hill if you look back towards the town." He settled in his rocking chair. "There were no lights on," he added. "So I suppose Blair was still with his friends."

"Poor Mrs Munro," Duncan commented. "Mam, Malcolm, do you mind if I go to bed to watch 'The Death of the Last Spy' on my tablet?"

★★★

A couple of hours later, as we lay cosily together on the sleeping platform, Malcolm said, "If you believed in prayer, Freya Munro would be the answer to one."

I shifted a little to make myself more comfortable. "She would?" I queried, sleepily.

"*Aja*." Malcolm had one arm round me, and was absent-mindedly stroking my bare shoulder. "Malchi was really worried about this community dinner. Hardly anyone has contributed anything. Sigrid gave him a big bunch of kale, and Si and Rose bought two large tins of chicken soup from the shop with their allowance, and there were a few other bits and pieces, but not enough to make a whole meal. And then Freya Munro turns up with all that food!"

"Olaf would thank the *huldufolk*," I suggested.

"*Aja*!" Malcolm gave a little grunt of amusement. "And Verity would thank her god!"

"Well…" I was more asleep than awake. "Someone deserves some thanks!"

"*Aja*, so they do," agreed Malcolm. And then I was asleep.

CHAPTER 14

Shona was of the opinion that his parents were too hard on Harris. They had only the one bairn, born late to them, and raised strictly. Their bothy was isolated between Fremdes Haven and Caldbrae, so Harris had to walk quite a distance to reach the Storhaven school, and he didn't do well there, by all accounts. None of us knew him until he went off to school in Lerwick, when two of Shona's older bairns became friendly with him.

"He used to come over here," Shona told me. "For a while I thought he was keen on our eldest, but nothing came of it. He wanted to go to art school, I think. He had his eye on a couple of good places on the mainland, but his parents were having none of it. So he got some sort of enterprise grant to study economics, but it wasn't his thing."

Shona was stacking shelves. Actually, she wasn't – she was rearranging them. There had been no ferry for five weeks and, even with people trying to spend as little as possible, stocks were running low.

"He doesn't look like my idea of an economist!" I commented. "Too much untamed hair!"

"*Aja!*" Shona chuckled. "I've always had a soft spot for the laddie. He was full of ideas when he used to come here – plans to start a drama group on En-Somi, or open an art gallery, or start some sort of singing group. He was a bit of an odd man out."

She inspected the sell-by date on a jar of pickles and placed it in a prominent place at the front of a shelf. "He's always been a bit of a one-off, on an island like ours."

"Well," I said, "he seems to have found a kindred spirit with Elise."

Shona looked down at me from the top step of her ladder. "*Aja*," she agreed. "I wonder what his parents think of that?"

★★★

The younger bairns had gone back to school. It was a cold, comparatively calm day. For a while I had heard the distant noise of some sort of team game going on outside the building, but all was quiet now. Sigrid must have taken them inside for their lessons. The background roar of the waves was more subdued that morning than it had been for weeks. The air felt crisp and the breeze cutting. There was a soft sun, filtered by low, grey clouds that seemed to give it a halo. I felt like going for a walk.

I headed up to the village and then down the track that leads to the summer harbour, past the bothies of Lyle and Verity, Sigrid, Robert, and a couple of other families, to the corner where an old lady lived – I think she was another of the Stewarts. Once the track wound round to the east I could see the ocean, sparkling in the soft light, the steep dark rocks that marked the entrance to Loch Innsjen, and the battered cove that is our summer harbour. The track is steep just there and, despite the good work of our community a few years earlier, it had been eroded by the weather. I had to keep an eye on where I was treading. The roar of the sea was greater by then. Even on a calm day, there are certain stages of an incoming tide when the waves break against the dark, tumbled rocks that do a rather inadequate job of sheltering our harbour, and the noise of the crashing and foaming of the water filled the air. I remember how happy I was feeling, grateful for Malcolm and Duncan, for the little community of Gamla Hus, for the wind and the sea and the gulls. I turned, and looked back towards the village, which is hidden from sight just there, so that all I could see was Norse Hill and beyond it, stark in the bright air, Fyrtarn Fjell. I felt my heart lift towards – towards what? I didn't know, but at that moment I was convinced there was something – something or someone good and true.

There were sheep on the moor moving lazily around, intent on their own simple business. Their wool looked heavy, white from a distance but grey and tangled closer up. I seemed to be the only human being on earth, and it was glorious.

Except – as I looked up towards Hunger Moor, something caught my eye. I looked more carefully. A darker cloud drifted across the grey-white sky, and for a few moments shadows moved across the marshy ground. Perhaps it was just sheep, or a trick of the light? But I seemed to have seen a figure on the hillside, moving up towards the Sinclair's bothy. I blinked, and looked again. There was nothing. I thought I must have imagined it. Then it occurred to me that it was probably Yanni or Harry, checking their sheep or tending to a broken drystone wall. There are always things that need to be done, if you are a crofter.

I walked on down to the summer harbour. The rising sea levels and the pounding of the waves had done an enormous amount of harm. The old stone wall that used to be the quay was broken, and water was rippling over it, even then when the tide was not yet at its highest. The small rowing boats that we use for fishing in the summer were upside down on a sort of rocky shelf on the western side of the cove. They had been wintered there all the time I had lived on En-Somi, but I saw for the first time how close they were now to the sea. On a really rough day it would not just be the spray that would reach them but the rolling, crashing breakers. We would need to find a safer place to rest our little boats when it was too rough to go out to sea. And, with the old quay under water, where would we tie them up in the summer?

Then, again, I saw movement, and this time I could see who

it was. Yanni, Harry and Mandy's lad were standing on a flat rock below the place where the boats are wintered, and further out in the cove. They were fishing, using rods.

They seemed to have seen me at about the same time that I saw them. "*Hei*, Marie!" called Yanni. "Coming to join us?"

"*Nei!*" I didn't even know how I would get out to the rock they were standing on, even if I had wanted to. "Is the fishing good?" I shouted.

In response, Harry reached into a sort of hessian sack he had looped over his shoulder, and held up a fish by the tail.

"Better than nothing!" called back Yanni.

Mandy's lad was struggling with something. I watched as Yanni helped him to reel in another fish, and then hold it up to me. "Dinner tonight!" he shouted. "Sea trout!"

I did an exaggerated thumbs-up sign, to show that I had heard. I watched for a few minutes longer but I didn't see them catch anything else.

I considered what I had seen, as I walked back up to the village. January is the wrong time of the year to fish for sea trout. They had obviously caught some, but the fish would not be good eating. Yanni was *En-Som-in-Fedi*, an islander born and bred, and he would know as well as anyone when to fish and when not to. So why were they there in January, rods in hand? It seemed obvious to me – and worrying. No islander would be out angling if their barrels of fish at home were full. The Sinclairs' and Harry's households must be short of food.

Then another thought occurred to me. If the men were down at the summer harbour, who had I glimpsed climbing the moor?

★★★

When I got home that morning, I had an email that rather distracted me. The school in Lerwick had contacted all the En-Somi parents, about half a dozen of us. They were proposing that we should give up trying to send our bairns to the Shetlands in the winter. There was too great a chance that they would be stuck there, unable to return to En-Somi for months. Then, too, there was the question of the cost. Travel and boarding expenses were all covered by the Education Department, but retaining domestic staff and heating a building that wasn't used for more than half the year was a dubious use of limited funds. We were presented with a proposal that the money be spent, instead, on employing staff with expertise in distance learning, and of replacing all-year-round boarding with an intensive summer school immediately after Easter, leading up to the examination season.

Duncan and I had a discussion with Bjorn via our computers that evening. Duncan himself was initially uncertain about what he felt. "I like school, Mam," he pointed out. "And I'm doing well…"

"*Aja*. But you have missed a lot this year, because of the weather…"

"You could always come here, and live with Gudrun and me," Bjorn suggested. "The schools are good, and the girls would love to have you."

I felt my heart lurch. It was one thing for Duncan to go and visit his paps. I was happy for him to do so. In fact, I thought it was a really good thing. But for Duncan to go and live in Norway, to come to En-Somi only now and again… I knew I needed to think about what was best for my son, and I knew that Gudrun and Bjorn would be good to Duncan. The girls were his half-sisters, too, and they might all benefit from living together for a while. But even so…

"*Nei…*" Duncan was hesitant, thinking things through. "Thanks, Paps," he replied at last. "But, you know, I'm an *En-Som-in-Fedi*, I belong here. And all my friends are here…"

"*Aja*." Bjorn was understanding, even if he looked a little disappointed. "Well, there's always university, when you get that far!"

Duncan grinned. "Oh, that would be great!" he responded. "But I'll have to work hard at my Norwegian!"

Shona and Patrick were quite pleased with the suggestion of the Shetland school. They had seen one after another of their bairns heading off for the Lerwick, and later to Aberdeen and Edinburgh. Alana was their youngest and they liked the thought of her staying around for longer. Andy Kullander was already taking distance lessons, for health reasons, although it was a long while since the lad had suffered any episodes. Over on the other side of the island, a couple of families chose, like us, to keep their bairns at home, but the people who lived next to the stables in Frigg Alley decided to sell up and move to the mainland. Apparently, they felt that life was becoming just too difficult on En-Somi.

With all that on my mind, I didn't think much more about my morning walk down to the summer harbour. Not, that is, until I next saw Freda Sinclair.

CHAPTER 15

There was a certain amount of sheepishness from some of the adults that week. Everyone wanted to know whether the community meal was still on, but I suppose most of them knew that they hadn't contributed, and suspected that others hadn't too. Those of us who were aware that, thanks mostly to Freya Munro, we were in for a really good feast made a point of talking enthusiastically about it, and Sigrid reminded all the bairns that their parents were welcome.

Even so, there was not quite the same excitement in the air that Friday, as there had been before Christmas. Then the bairns had been preparing for the winter break, and there had been a feeling of festivity, even though one of the reasons for us gathering together was the very real struggle on the part of some of the *bondii* to feed their families a nutritious and varied diet. The weather didn't help, either. That Friday was one of those bleak, grey days when it doesn't seem to get light at all, and it's hard to feel motivated to do anything other than sit by the range and dream of summer.

Apparently, Marigold had summed it up, when the bairns went up to the *fi'ilsted* for their afternoon cookery lesson.

Malchi had gathered the class in the main seating area, and given them his talk about safety with food and in the kitchen, about hand washing and sharp knives and hot surfaces. He explained how dumplings are made, and then set the younger ones to mixing the ingredients in huge, round mixing bowls. Meanwhile, he suggested, the older bairns should come into the kitchen to prepare the main dish.

He told me later that Marigold had sighed at that point, and exclaimed in a weary voice, "But, Malchi, can't we just eat soup out of tins? All this cooking is 'ard work, and we been doing maths *all* morning!"

Things looked up a bit when the wee chefs were shown the sweet potatoes. "Not *more* red food!" Marigold had commented, and indeed the two large specimens did look red in the bright kitchen light. "Is they just potatoes what are sweeter than usual?" she wanted to know. "And where does they come from?"

Of course, I had no part in the preparations. I spent the morning reading through the materials; pages and pages of them, that the school in Lerwick had already forwarded to us. A new tutor was about to be appointed, a young woman who had taught bairns in the Australian outback. There was the suggestion that, if possible, pupils should form study groups, and I wondered whether young Andy Kullander would join Alana and Duncan.

At lunch time, as we ate bacon sandwiches, Duncan asked, "Can I go up to the village now, to help with the preparations?"

The lad had been studying all morning, wearing his headphones so that I couldn't hear the teacher's side of the conversation but only his answers. The last hour or so had been Norwegian, and I found myself thinking that his accent was already quite good, although I expected that he would always have that En-Somi sing-song lilt when he spoke.

"I'll see you up there," I agreed.

It was an ordinary sort of day. I think I might have put a load of laundry into the machine and done a few routine checks on the heat pump and the turbine. Malcolm was over at his place, tending his ponies and catching up on emails. I followed my son up to Hus in time to give any last-minute help, if it were needed.

The school room was set out as before. Duncan was carrying all the cutlery from the *fi'ilsted* across, and Alana and Andy seemed to be collecting forks and spoons from all the village bothies. It had not occurred to me, at our last meal, how there could be enough place settings for so many people!

Marigold rushed up to meet me as I took off my jacket. "Malcolm's already 'ere," she told me. "'E's over there, talking to Yanni. And we made cheese and sweet potato pie, and you mustn't muddle up sweet potatoes with yams, what are different from what we cooked. And they come from South America – not *these* sweet potatoes, but the first ones. And it's a mystery 'ow we come to 'ave sweet potatoes on En-Somi because it ain't – isn't – a usual part of our diet! But it's a secret, 'o gives what, so we won't never know!"

I was relieved to see that so many people had turned up. A group of men including Malcolm were gathered in the corner where there are pegs at different heights, for the bairns to hang their coats. They looked as if they were having a serious conversation and I didn't want to interrupt. Freda Sinclair and Rose were sitting together, their little ones on their knees, and Rose saw me and waved, so I went over and joined them.

Baby Thistle seemed to be changing by the day. I remember thinking, *she looks like a little girl now, not a baby!* Although both women greeted me with smiles, they too looked serious.

"'Ave you 'eard?" Rose asked me. "About Freda and Yanni 'aving their store'ouse raided?"

Suddenly I was remembering that person on the moor a couple of days earlier when I had walked down to the summer harbour.

"When did that happen?" I asked. "Have you lost much?"

"It could have been worse," Freda told me. "I was just telling Rose. We heard about the theft at Jamie's place, on *Huldufolk* Day, and we were still making the final touches to Harry's bothy, so we built his storehouse into the hillside, next to their bathroom, and you access it from inside the bothy. Quite a lot of our stuff was in there too. We only finished putting the shelves in after Christmas. Petter came over to help. If they'd come a week earlier, we'd have lost much more."

"So they broke into your storeroom?" I checked.

"*Aja*, and all they found were potatoes and neeps, and not so many of them, because Yanni has built a clamp to keep them fresh." She chuckled, then. "And there's an old bike that Yanni's brother brought over at solstice. His bairns have grown out of it, and of course Rionnag won't want it for a while yet!" She patted her baby fondly.

"When did this happen?" I asked.

"Tuesday," Freda told me. "That's right, isn't it, Rose? Because it was Monday when Paula and I met up at your place."

"*Aja*. Monday," Rose agreed. "Marigold 'adn't gone back to school. She and Andy Kullander were just getting ready to call on your Duncan. And it 'adn't 'appened then."

"It didn't happen at night, either," Freda added. "I went in there on Tuesday morning, to fetch some parsley and everything was all right. And then Yanni went to fetch some potatoes to fry up with the fish they caught down in the summer harbour, and half the potatoes had gone!"

"*Aja*," I told them. "I saw the men fishing. And I thought I saw someone up on the moor below your bothy, too. But I wasn't sure."

"Well." Freda sounded resigned. "I suppose that was him. The thief. We've told Lyle, but what can he do?"

"It's 'orrible, 'aving your stuff stolen," sympathised Rose. "It used to 'appen to us all the time, when we was in them camps. If there's anything me and Si can do…"

"Dinner is served!" called Malchi. The group of men in the corner broke up, and various husbands joined their wives around the table. Malcolm beckoned me over to a place he was saving for me.

"I'll see you later," I promised, and left the two friends commiserating with each other.

★★★

The food was delicious. It was only part way through that I realised it was a vegetarian meal – nobody had donated any meat or fish. When I pointed this out to Malcolm, he nodded, his mouth full. When he could speak again, he said, "I saw you talking to Freda. Did she tell you that they've had a theft, too?"

"*Aja.*" It seemed that by then most of us had heard. "It's making life really difficult for everyone," I commented. "As if things weren't tough enough. Did I tell you that I saw Yanni and Harry fishing down in the summer harbour? In January?"

"Then all they'll be eating is skin and bones," was Malcolm's response. We both knew that the sea trout are never plump in the winter.

I looked across the room, to where Duncan and Alana were beginning to take round second helpings. "They seem to be eating well tonight," I commented, watching Duncan spoon more food onto Yanni's plate.

"Well, it is good!" Malcolm grinned. "I don't know how Petter manages to live with Malchi and not put on weight!"

CHAPTER 16

Marigold and Alana called for Duncan as it was just getting light the next morning. The dull grey weather of earlier that week had been replaced with a brisk northern wind, carrying in squalls of sleet. Both lassies had pink cheeks from being out in the fresh air, and they were giggling together about something that had happened the day before.

"Is Duncan ready?" Alana asked, peering round the bothy door.

Marigold, on the other hand, just came straight in, taking off her shoes at the door. "'E's never ready!" she announced. "'E just sleeps and sleeps! Come on, Duncan! Wakey, wakey!"

From inside his sleeping closet, Duncan groaned. "It *can't* be morning already!" he complained.

"It's nearly afternoon!" Marigold declared, untruthfully. "It'll soon be dinner time!"

Alana was giggling again. "My mam says that Paps would sleep all day if she let him!" she said. "But she never lets him!"

"Doing anything interesting today?" Malcolm asked the lassies. We could hear Duncan closing the bathroom door, and the shower running.

"We's going over to Fremdes 'Aven," Marigold told us. "We's taking two portions of yesterday's food, for Lyle's mam and paps. Because they don't like to walk over 'ere in the winter. And we's going to bring back a contribution from them, for the next meal."

"That's quite a trek," Malcolm pointed out.

"*Aja*, that's what Lyle said too. But 'e's phoned 'is mam, and she's going to make us something to eat. It's funny, really, we's taking over two servings, eating four, and bringing food back 'ere. They'd be better off if we stayed at 'ome!"

"Ah, but they wouldn't have the benefit of our wonderful company!" butted in Duncan. He was dressed, and trying to towel-dry his hair.

"Give them my love," I told the bairns. "I haven't seen them for ages!"

Duncan's phone pinged and he checked it. "Andy says he's waiting at the shop," he told his friends. "Hurry up, you two, we don't want to keep him hanging around!"

"Huh!" Marigold was unimpressed. "Weren't us what was still in bed!"

"Take an apple," I called as the trio left, Duncan still zipping up his jacket. "You haven't had any breakfast!"

★★★

Verity and Lyle came to lunch that day. It was Lyle's day off, but if they stayed at home in the *nasyonihuss* there was nothing to stop people from calling in to report this or that, or to ask for help with filling in forms. "I've got my phone with me," he told us. "Someone'll reach me if it's an emergency."

We sat round the range, eating savoury pancakes with forks, and talking about Lyle's parents.

"Mam has these stiff knees," he told us. "I want her to see a specialist, over in Lerwick or on the mainland, but she says it runs in the family. Her mam had stiff knees, and her mam before her... She won't accept that treatments might have moved on a bit since those days!"

"And your paps doesn't see so well, does he?" added Verity.

"*Nei*," agreed Lyle. "Mind you, he never did! He's great at seeing into the distance, but it's years since he's been able to read anything without peering at it and squinting. He's got glasses but he never wears them!"

"I wish they lived a bit closer," Verity told us. "Then we could just pop round. It's pretty lonely out there, where they live."

"*Aja.*" Lyle was looking thoughtful. Then he grinned. "There's another reason we'd like them closer too!" He looked at Verity. "Shall I tell them?"

"They've probably guessed," Verity answered, and blushed. "I'm pregnant!" she said.

There was much hugging and back-slapping, and Malcolm said, "I suppose it would be rather inappropriate to make a toast!" So we drank some more tea, and talked about summer babies.

"Sigrid will be delighted," I pointed out. "So many wee ones in Gamla Hus! The future of our school must be guaranteed!"

"*Aja!*" Lyle was still grinning. "Although that wasn't our main thought, when this little one was conceived!"

"Well, *nei*, I would hope not!" I laughed.

They stayed all afternoon. It was relaxing and comfortable, spending time with them. We knew each other well, we'd had adventures together, and sat round tables and campfires, talking about the issues closest to our hearts. The wind whistled round my chimneys and the waves foamed against the rocks on my beach, and the world seemed good.

★★★

They were still there when the bairns crashed in, excited and happy, and bringing the cold in with them on their jackets and in their hair. From inside the bothy, with the lights on, it already looked as if it was dark outside, but in fact it was still the long, slow, winter dusk.

Duncan dumped two large cake tins on the kitchen work surface. "Your mam's been baking!" he announced, looking at Lyle. "There's cake and scones here, for next Friday. Only she told us to tell you not to store them in any outside storehouse. She doesn't want them stolen!"

"What did you 'ave for lunch?" Marigold wanted to know.

"We 'ad *pylsa*, which Duncan says they calls "'ot dogs' in English. And your Duncan 'ad three!"

"Well, I hadn't had any breakfast!" my son pointed out. "And it was a long walk!"

"*Aja*, it were!" Marigold was kneeling by the range, her hands spread out to the warm glow. "And you'll never guess 'o we met, on the way back?"

I cast my mind over the people who lived over on the remote north of En-Somi. "Harris?" I suggested.

"*Nei!*" Marigold was dismissive. "'Arris is always where Elise is, and Elise don't go over there! Try again!"

"Olaf?" suggested Malcolm. "There's nowhere on the island that he doesn't go."

"*Nei*, not Olaf! You'll never guess!" She looked at her three friends, and put a finger to her lips. "Don't tell!" she instructed.

The three older bairns were smiling. They were more than tolerant of Marigold's liveliness, they enjoyed it.

"Can I put the kettle on?" Duncan was waiting for one of us to guess again.

"Of course," I answered, then, to Marigold, "A small group of *huldufolk*, gathering dandelion leaves for a winter salad?"

"Don't be silly!" Marigold giggled. "Anyway, Sigrid says what you can't see *huldufolk*, they's invisible to the 'uman eye!"

"*Nei!*" Andy liked people to be accurate. "You can see them," he insisted, "if they decide to let you see them." Then he added, "But we didn't. See any *huldufolk*, I mean."

"Then I give up," sighed Malcolm. "What do you say, Lyle? You're the *nasyoni* round here. You ought to know who's out and about!"

"It's no use asking me," Lyle responded. "I'm off duty!"

"I give up, too," Verity said. "I don't know the people who

live on that coast – or over by the old lighthouse either. I've still got a lot to learn!"

Marigold stood up. "Well," she announced proudly. "We saw Jarvis, and 'e didn't even know 'o we was!"

★★★

Then the story tumbled out, told mainly by Marigold but with the other three butting in. Duncan had made them all tea, and the four bairns were sitting on the floor by the range, excited and happy.

"We was walking down the track from Lyle's mam and paps's place, just where there's that little bridge thing, like a plank, over the burn. You know?"

"I know," agreed Lyle. "I used to walk that way to school!"

"*Aja*. Well, so you knows. We 'ad to walk single file, and Alana was at the front, and you know that big rock? Well, there was this huge white bird perched on top of it, and we all stopped to look, and then suddenly there 'e was!"

"I nearly jumped out of my skin!" Alana giggled.

"You screamed!" Andy told her, sounding disgusted.

"*Aja*! Well, it was a shock!" Alana told him, sounding indignant.

"'E must 'ave been coming down from that other moor…" Marigold was ignoring the interruptions.

"Caldbrae," Duncan explained, and to Marigold. "It's where Holti lives."

"'O's 'Olti?" she wanted to know, momentarily distracted. "Any'ow, there 'e was, just standing there!"

"I'd heard of him, from Marigold," Andy butted in. "He looked after you when you ran away, didn't he? When you hid out at the old airport?"

"*Aja*, 'e did," agreed the bairn. "When we was slaves I were frightened of 'im, because 'e always seemed weird and unfriendly, and I never knew what 'e'd do next, but when 'e found me up by Lavender's grave 'e were kind. Only, 'e wanted me to live with 'im, and not come back to 'Us. 'E thought what someone would take me away from Mam and Paps, and put me in a 'ome."

"And that's the strange thing," Duncan said. "He must have known Marigold…"

"'E knew me all my life!" the bairn exclaimed. "I were born 'ere!"

"*Aja*. Exactly!" agreed Duncan. "But his first words were, 'Who are you, what are you doing here?' He sounded really angry."

"So I says, 'It's me, Marigold!' And 'e looks at me really strangely. Like 'e doesn't know whether to believe me."

"*Aja*, that's right," Andy agreed. "It was as if Marigold was someone he's met once, from the other side of En-Somi, or maybe in Lerwick, and he was trying to recall who she was!"

"And 'e says again, 'Marigold?' 'E sounded sort of uncertain. I doesn't know the right word. Puzzled?"

"Puzzled is good," Duncan agreed.

"I was frightened of him," Alana told us. "He is rather strange-looking, isn't he?"

"Well, I doesn't know." Marigold seemed to think that Jarvis's appearance was the least unusual thing about their encounter.

"He was wearing a long, dark coat," Andy explained. "Black, or maybe very dark green, and he was carrying this big thing, like a sack, over one shoulder. And he had bare feet! Bare feet, in January, on the moors!"

"Oh, 'e never wears shoes!" Marigold told us. "It's 'is thing."

I thought back to the times that I had met Jarvis, and of course she was right. I might perhaps have seen him with something on his feet once, but generally he went around without footwear.

"So, we was all standing there," Marigold continued. "Alana, then me, then Duncan, then Andy, in a line on the track, and Jarvis was just standing on a rock, and we was all looking at each other."

"I thought he might hurt us," Alana said.

"Oh, 'e wouldn't 'urt nobody," Marigold reassured her friend. "At least, I don't think so!"

"It was a stand-off!" Andy announced, dramatically.

"What's a stand-off?" Marigold wondered, but then continued her story without waiting for an answer. "So I says, ''Ow is you doing nowadays, Jarvis. Is you all right?' And 'e says, 'Yeah, I'm fine. Getting by.' So, I says, 'What is you doing out 'ere on the moors?' and 'e says, 'This and that,' like 'e didn't want to tell me. But I thought what 'e 'ad remembered 'o I was, because 'e said, 'Is this your friends, what you told me about?' So, I says, '*Aja*,' and I told 'im 'o everyone was."

"And he sort of smiled," Duncan said. "And looked much more normal!"

"*Aja*," Marigold agreed. "'E says, 'So you really 'as got friends!' Like I would 'ave been making it up, when I told 'im I 'ad! And 'e says, ''Ow is your mam and paps?'."

"Only he said, 'mum and dad', like the English do," corrected Andy.

"*Aja*. 'E did say that. We was all English, when we was slaves," the bairn agreed, comfortably.

"And then 'e says something really odd," Marigold continued. "'E says, 'Is you 'ungry?' I mean, doesn't you think that's odd? Is that what you would say, if you was meeting someone again for the first time in months? 'Is you 'ungry?' I mean, if you met Sigrid, coming over Fyrtarn Fjell, there's all sorts of things you might say. ''As you been to Stor'aven?' or ''Ow's your granddaughter?' or 'I likes your new coat!' But not, 'Is you 'ungry?'."

"Perhaps he was hungry," suggested Malcolm, who, like all of us, had been riveted to the tale.

Alana giggled. "Duncan told him everything we'd eaten at your mam's, Lyle. And told him that we were bringing scones and cake back for the community meal. I don't think he needed to know all that!"

"*Aja*, but 'e were pleased, you could tell," Marigold insisted.

"Well, he seemed to have got it into his head that we were starving!" Duncan was indignant at Alana's criticism. "I wanted to convince him that we were all right."

"I think you done right," Marigold reassured my son. "I don't think what 'e were 'ungry, Malcolm. I think what 'e were worried about us."

"'Was'," Andy corrected Marigold. "He was worried about us."

"I was worried about *him*!" Alana told us. "I didn't know what he'd do next!"

"*Aja*. But all 'e did was turn around, and walk back up the slope!" Marigold told us. "'E didn't say, 'bye' or 'see you later'! 'E just turned round and went back the way 'e 'ad come!"

"And then we were on our own again," Andy said. "As if it hadn't happened!"

"You were really frightened, weren't you, Alana?" Duncan looked at his friend sympathetically.

"She wanted to run 'ome!" Marigold told us. "But we wouldn't. Duncan said that we'd only 'urt ourselves if we ran, and Andy said what Jarvis 'ad gone now any'ow, and I remembered that Sigrid told us we must always watch where we's going if we's out on the moors, so we walked here."

"But quite quickly," Alana agreed. "We didn't hang around."

CHAPTER 17

"Those bairns have so much energy!" Malcolm sounded quite envious. They had only stayed long enough to devour some bread and honey and phone their parents, before they were off again, all set to have a sleepover at Andy's home, the only place on our side of the island large enough comfortably to accommodate three extra young people without warning.

"It's so good to see them all together," Verity said. "I hope our wee one has such a good group of friends when he or she is that age!"

"*Aja*," I agreed. "Their friendship has been the making of Marigold. It seems to have given her confidence. Sigrid says she plays much more happily with bairns her own age now. Especially young Christian."

Lyle and Verity had come for lunch initially, but it was dark by then, after four in the afternoon, and Malcolm was thinking of cooking. "Stay for dinner!" he insisted, and the young couple didn't need any persuading.

"What did you make of their encounter with Jarvis?" Lyle wondered, watching Malcolm peeling potatoes.

"Quite strange," Malcolm answered. "If he'd been one of my clients, I'd have wanted him assessed. There're all sorts of conditions that might explain his peculiar behaviour."

"Perhaps we should just accept him as he is?" I wondered. I was thinking about my resolution to be less judgemental.

"Well, *aja*, of course we should!" Verity agreed. "Will we eat on our laps, or shall I move this stuff off the table?"

"Better move it," Malcolm said. "The thing is, if we knew what his problem is, we might be able to help."

"He's obviously been hurt," Lyle remarked. "He doesn't trust authority at all."

"That could be considered a sign of sanity," Malcolm grumbled. "Some of the decisions politicians made when I was working...! You wondered what planet they were on!"

"I don't think it's just that he's been hurt," Verity told us. "I think it's something else."

"It's all this business of not recognising people," I suggested. "Do you think he blocks things out? Do you think it's a defence mechanism?"

"Well, it could be." Verity was staring into the flickering light in the glass window of my range. "Do you remember that I went over to his squat when I was trying to decide whether to marry Lyle?"

"Oh, I remember that!" Lyle groaned. "How could I forget? I thought I'd lost you!"

"*Aja!*" Verity held out her hand instinctively and touched Lyle's arm comfortingly. "I didn't mean to hurt you, you know that! I was just confused."

"So was I!" Lyle grinned. "I wouldn't want to go through that again!"

"Well," Verity continued, "we seemed to get on quite well, Jarvis and me. When we left, I suggested I might go back and visit sometime. He didn't seem too keen, but he said a strange thing. He said I should wear my blue jacket. It was that pretty waterproof summer jacket, you know?"

"You do look very good wearing it." Lyle sounded approving.

"Thank you!" She smiled warmly at her husband, but then went on explaining her thoughts. "I heard a programme once, a podcast. It was about this woman who had a car accident, and afterwards she couldn't recognise anyone's faces. Not just the first time she met them again after the crash. Every time. Even her own family! She just couldn't tell faces apart anymore."

"So do you think Jarvis has experienced some sort of physical trauma?" Lyle wondered. "How could we find out? The records of those refugees have been lost long since."

"Well, maybe. But the podcast didn't stop with the woman in the accident. It seems it's a real thing, face blindness. Some people have it from birth – like colour blindness, or an inability to hold a tune. There's a name for it."

I took out my phone and typed in 'face blindness'. Up it came, at once. *Prosopagnosia.* There was a lot about it.

I started reading bits out. "Listen to this," I said, "'The effects of it can be depression, social anxiety, social withdrawal, a lack of confidence, difficulty in maintaining relationships'. That could be Jarvis, couldn't it?"

"It would make sense," Verity said. "If he was worried that he wouldn't recognise me, then me wearing the blue coat would help him to know who I was."

"It would explain why he didn't recognise Marigold today," Malcolm added.

"It would explain a lot of things." Lyle was looking thoughtful. "It could be the reason he hasn't moved into town. Can you imagine how hard it would be to manage, if you kept meeting people and you didn't know if you'd met them before?"

"So he lives on his own, out on the moors," I said. "Wandering around, like some sort of wild man."

"It must be a hard life," Malcolm said, putting a casserole dish into the oven. "I wouldn't fancy it."

"We ought to try to help him," Verity suggested.

"My love!" Lyle sounded indulgent. "She wants to help everyone!" he told us, smiling fondly at her.

★★★

Much later, when Lyle and Verity had left, arm-in-arm despite the narrow track, and after Malcolm and I had cleared up from the meal, we went down to the beach.

It was, of course, pitch dark, although there were bright little lights sparkling in the water – one of nature's special touches, some bioluminescence that we only seem to see in the winter. We stood on the pebbly ground and watched the waves heaving and breaking against the newly exposed rocks.

"Of course," Malcolm said, thoughtfully, "we don't really know that face blindness is his problem. That's just us, speculating."

"*Aja.*" The same thought had occurred to me. "But it would make sense. He notices other things about people, as if he's always looking for clues. He saw that I was wearing Lavender's cross, back before the refugees were freed. Nobody else had noticed."

We were both quiet. Somewhere a sea bird squawked loudly, and was silent again. The foam from a bigger wave rushed up the beach towards us, and instinctively Malcolm pulled me back.

"But we do know that he wanders all over the island." He was still thinking about Jarvis. "We saw him on the cliffs, and the bairns saw him coming over from Caldbrae. And they said he was carrying some sort of bag over his shoulder."

"*Aja.*" I could see where this was going.

"He could be our thief, you know." Malcolm sounded almost sad. "It feels a bit mean to say so. I know you were thinking the same thing a while back, and I think you might be right."

For a while we were both silent. There's something peaceful about the heave and crash of waves on rock. Malcolm's arm was round me, and I felt warm in my thick winter jacket. A few weeks earlier I had been convinced that Jarvis was a villain, but the events of the day, his concern in case the bairns were hungry, and the reminder that Jarvis had once looked after Marigold when she was finding life hard – all these things made me feel more kindly towards the man. The truth is, I was beginning to feel reluctant, almost guilty, in believing that Jarvis was stealing from the *bondii*.

As if he had guessed what I was thinking, Malcolm gave my shoulder a little squeeze, and said, "We need to keep an open mind, you know."

"*Aja*, of course," I agreed. "But if Jarvis isn't the person stealing all that food, who is? And what did he have in the bag he was carrying?"

A gust of wind blew in from the sea, and I shivered.

"Bedtime?" Malcolm asked, and we turned to climb the slope to my welcoming bothy.

CHAPTER 18

"The thing is, it's making Malchi stressed," Petter was telling us.

We were standing in front of the *fi'ilsted*, and Malchi was further down the track by the school, talking to Sigrid.

"I suppose we both thought that people would contribute to these meals. Not a lot, of course, because times are hard, but we thought most people would donate something. But it's Tuesday already, and all we have is the cake and scones Lyle's mam baked, and the shortbread you made, Marie, so that there'd be enough sweet things for everybody to have a taste."

"Well, you know." I was thinking aloud. "People didn't donate last time, but there was plenty of food to go around. Nobody knows how few people contributed, or that it was thanks to Freya Munro that we had such a good dinner. So maybe each household thinks that everyone else is helping, and that they don't need to?"

Petter looked worried. "*Aja*, maybe you're right," he agreed. "But we can't go on like this. Malchi was awake in the middle of last night, surfing the internet for recipes using wild food…"

"Let's give it one more week," Malcolm suggested. "Lyle could visit a few bothies and remind people that we need ingredients for the bairns to cook with, and Sigrid could mention it to the young ones. If need be, I can give you half a barrel of fish for this week, and then, if we still don't have a range of donations, we'll have to tell everyone the problem we're having. You do still have potatoes, don't you?"

Petter sighed. "We do. But that seems to be what's being

eaten in most bothies – potatoes and neeps. Malchi was hoping to introduce a bit more variety."

"Is Lyle around?" Malcolm wondered. "I'm taking the pony and trap over to Charlie's bothy. Their storage battery was installed months ago, and their wind turbine was turned on last week, at last, so they'll have electricity in abundance! Would you like to come, Marie? Sheena promised me that if they ever managed to get everything working she'd cook me a hot meal to celebrate. Mind you, I think they'd almost despaired of it ever happening! Fancy going right through last autumn depending on an open fire!"

"He's gone over to see Jamie," Petter told us, talking about Lyle. "He won't be back 'til later. Jamie's querying the amount of land he's being taxed on. The maps the *Oyrod* used to calculate what we all owe were drawn up years ago. That low meadow by Michaelmas Bay is more or less under water now, what with sea levels rising. He doesn't think he ought to be taxed on it. Lyle's going to help him fill in the claim forms."

"Bother!" Malcolm muttered. "I'd better send him a text, then, about telling everyone we need donations for Friday."

"It's no problem," I told him. "I'll go down and see Verity. She'll pass on the message. But will you give my apologies to Shona?"

★★★

Verity was reading a book on some sort of device. The bothy was neat and cosy, and there was gentle music – a harp, I think – playing on the radio in the background. She smiled as I came in.

"Marie! I was just going to make coffee!" she exclaimed. "You must have read my mind!" Then, while she put the kettle on, she added, "I'm trying to do lots of reading while I still can. Everyone tells me that I won't have a moment to myself once the baby comes!"

"That's what they say!" I agreed, leaving my boots by the door. "But you won't find it a hardship. I loved every minute of Duncan's baby years – except the nappies, of course!"

"I wanted to talk to you, actually," Verity told me, spooning ground coffee into her cafetière. "We've had two replies about grants to create a meeting house. Well, four, actually, but two were straight-out rejections." She laughed. "Look!" she said. "The Rocks and Plowman Heritage Fund wrote back that they only offer grants within the UK. They think we're not British!"

"They've probably never heard of En-Somi," I pointed out. "But you'd think they would know, since we have a postcode!"

"*Aja!*" Verity laughed again, pouring in the hot water. "One postcode for the whole island, which nobody ever uses!"

We sat at the little round table, looking out at the track that is the main street of the village. There wasn't anyone around, but gulls were swooping and diving close to the green area where the bairns play during their breaks from lessons.

"Those birds are not daft!" Verity remarked. "They sit on the roof of our bothy and wait for Sigrid to call the young ones back in, and then they swoop down, looking for crumbs. Sigrid gives the bairns oat biscuits when they go out to play!"

I laughed. "They've been doing that for years!" I told her. "I remember the same thing when Duncan was at the school!"

"So, can I show you these grant responses?" Verity asked. "There's one that I don't think will work for us, but the other one is quite interesting."

"*Aja*," I agreed, sipping my coffee.

She stood up and went through to Lyle's office, the only other room in their bothy, and came back with a pile of papers.

"Lyle printed them off so that we could take them up to Petter to look at. And we hoped to show them to you and Malcolm."

One of the two positive responses was from a construction company in Glasgow. Their main business was building eco-friendly homes, but as a way of 'giving back' (that's what their documentation said) they also built community hubs.

"But looking closely," Verity pointed out, "their offer isn't without strings. Look at the small print on page five. Although they say that grants are not 'contingent' on being given planning permission to build homes nearby, it's clear that's what they really want."

I scanned through until I found the passage she was referring to. "*Aja*," I agreed. "You're right. And there's no way we could have houses like those on En-Somi. We wouldn't want them!"

"*Nei*, and the *Oyrod* wouldn't give planning permission. And for once they'd be right! And, when they saw the sort of terrain we're dealing with, these builders wouldn't want to build here!"

"What about the other organisation?" I asked.

"Well, it's interesting." Verity stacked the papers concerning the first offer, and slipped them back into a cardboard folder that said 'Police Scotland. Highlands and Islands Division'. Then she spread out a rather thinner stack of papers. "More coffee?" she offered, as she showed me the documents.

This grant offer came from an obscure little charity based on the Isle of Man. Their particular interest was in rejuvenating rural communities, and helping ordinary people to navigate the enormous amount of red tape that can accompany even the simplest of projects. They had certain stipulations. They wouldn't give money to any new build that wasn't in character with the existing architecture of the area, or that wasn't eco-friendly. They required grid references, and photographs of the village. If they were satisfied that our plans were good, they would pay for materials, but not for the labour, with the exception of electrical and insulation work, which had to be done by qualified specialists. They didn't usually deal with religious organisations, but they recognised that many small communities didn't have churches, or mosques, or temples, and they were happy for the buildings they sponsored to be used as places of worship, as long as they were not exclusive to one religion. Where the need arose, they were willing to do the hard graft of putting in planning applications. They had, they said, experienced volunteers with proven records of getting things done.

"It looks promising," I agreed. "Is there a catch?"

"I really don't know! Lyle looked through all the stuff when it arrived yesterday, and he's used to official papers. He couldn't see any hitches. Except one."

"What's that?" I already felt disappointed at the very thought of a problem.

"Well, they only fund, on average, two projects a year," Verity pointed out. "So we think the competition might be quite tough."

We surfed round on the internet and found a couple of other projects that the Manx charity had funded. Both were built specifically for community needs. One was attached to a pub in a hamlet in Yorkshire, and was to serve as a post office, shop, food bank and meeting place for Brownies and Cubs. The other was in East Anglia, and was intended to host a surgery once a week from a visiting doctor – made necessary by the closure of the only remaining bus service in the area.

"They look like our sort of people," commented Verity. "What do you think?"

Just them Lyle came in. As usual when he was working on our side of the island, he wasn't in any sort of uniform. He ducked as he came in – he is, I dare say, an inch or so taller than the bothy door when he's wearing his boots.

He went over to Verity and kissed her, then greeted me. "*Hei*, Marie! How are you? I thought I saw Malcolm with his cart, crossing over Fyrtarn Fjell. You can see for miles from Jamie's place."

"*Aja*. He's gone to see Charlie's bothy, now that it's finally finished."

Verity was pouring coffee for her husband. "They've got electricity, at last!" she told him.

"*Aja*, Jamie was telling me. They'll feel the difference!"

"Actually," I remembered, "I nearly forgot. I've got a message for you, from Petter." I explained about the lack of contributions for our community dinners, and the idea that Lyle might prompt people to be a little more generous when he was on his rounds.

"No problem," he agreed. "But I don't know if it'll work. Everyone I talk to nowadays is worried. The *En-Som-in-Fedii* used to look forward to the spring, but everyone's dreading April now, because that's when we get the next tax bills. Jamie MacLoughlan has wondered about selling up and leaving the island. Blair Munro has made an offer for the tilling rights to his land – not as much as it's worth, of course, but beggars can't be choosers. The only thing that's stopping him is the fact that his brother Mac lives over on Frigg Moor. He doesn't want to move away from family."

I felt quite shocked. "They'd be the second family to leave the island," I pointed out. "Didn't those people in Storhaven go, when it was decided that the older bairns would be distance-educated?"

"They did," Lyle looked serious. "Or, rather, they will. There hasn't been a ferry for weeks, but Tom says we're expecting one this Friday, and they plan to go then. And there's another family leaving, too – those relatives of Holti who live along from Fremdes Haven. Mam was telling me on the phone last night."

It was a bit depressing. "We do seem to be fighting an uphill battle," I said. "It all seems so difficult. I don't know what else we can do to encourage everyone!"

"I do," said Verity, speaking quietly, and looking at her husband. "We can pray!"

CHAPTER 19

I very rarely feel low. Way back, when my grandmother died, I remember that I cried quite a lot, but that was grief, not depression. The two are quite different. Nor would I say that I was depressed, exactly, after talking to Petter and then to Lyle and Verity. I felt, I suppose, rather flat, as if the fun had gone out of life for the moment.

Malcolm had returned home late from Charlie's place, and weary. He told me that they were doing well over there – Charlie, his son Shawn, Sheena and her boy.

"I can't work out the relationships there," he told me. "Both boys call Charlie 'dad', but only the younger one calls Sheena 'mum'. And it looks to me as if Charlie and Sheena are a proper couple now, but they weren't, were they, when they were still slaves?"

I thought about that. "How would we know?" I wondered. "It was a strange set-up. Do they seem happy?"

Malcolm scratched his head thoughtfully. "Well – *aja*, I would say that they do. Sheena is so quiet, it's hard to tell, and I think Charlie bosses her around a bit, but the boys seem cheerful. Oh! And Sheena was teaching her boy reading, so that he can start at the Storhaven school after the Easter break. That'll give them a few more contacts in their area. At the moment, it sounds to me, the only *En-Som-in-Fedii* they see regularly is Holti, they're so isolated over there. And maybe the new *nasyoni*."

Duncan had been watching something on his tablet, wearing earphones, but he had taken them off and paused his viewing when Malcolm came in.

"Did you ask Shawn if he'd like to come over?" he wanted to know. The two lads had hit it off during the summer solstice picnic the previous year.

"*Aja*, and I think he will," Malcolm said. "But they're still working hard on that bothy when the weather allows. They had all those drainage problems, and it's been heavy work, sorting it out. He seems like a good lad, although I have to listen hard to understand what he's saying. That accent!"

"You ought to watch soap operas based in England!" Duncan suggested. "That way your ears would get attuned to their way of speaking. I understood him all right last summer – well, most of the time!"

Malcolm was slumped in his usual rocking chair. It had been a long day because he had first walked over to his bothy in the morning to pick up his ponies and trap, driven over to Charlie's place beyond Storhaven, and then reversed the whole journey, in the dark, at the end of the day. "And now I ought to go and look out that half barrel of fish!" he groaned, "Ready to take it up to Malchi tomorrow morning."

"Don't worry, Malcolm!" Duncan stood up and stretched. "I'll do it in the morning. I'm going up to Alana's for a maths lesson at nine-thirty. Why do classes have to start so early?"

★★★

It was the sound of my phone bleeping that woke me up. I had been deeply asleep, dreaming that I was knitting a really complicated pattern and couldn't get it right. Each time I finished a row, I would look back and find a mistake. And all the while, someone was waiting for me to finish the garment. In my sleep I felt flustered, and when my phone started to bleep I thought it was my grandmother's doorbell ringing, and that my buyer had come for her finished garment.

Malcolm was still sleeping deeply and there were no sounds

coming from Duncan's direction. I crawled out of bed and down the ladder and went over to the charging socket, where most of our devices were lined up for the night.

Of course, the phone had stopped ringing by the time I got to it. I would have recognised the number even if Malchi's name hadn't come up. I felt a pang of anxiety. Why would Malchi be phoning us – it was actually Malcolm's phone that had been bleeping – so early in the morning? It was barely seven o'clock.

I put the kettle on, and spooned instant coffee into the mug that Duncan had given me years earlier ('The best mum in the world' was its motto) and put my jacket and boots on. I took my phone and the coffee outside. The night air would help me to wake up, and I didn't want to disturb the others.

It was a cold morning. There was frost on the ground and the wind was bitter on my face. It was still pitch dark, the sky was brilliant with sparkling stars and the sea was swishing and sucking, almost gently, on my beach. I shivered.

"Malchi?" I asked, when he answered on the second ring. "Is everything all right?"

He sounded strange at the other end. I couldn't tell if he was laughing or crying. "*Aja!*" he answered. "Everything's fine – good. Can you and Malcolm come up here, please? As soon as possible?"

"Malchi – of course we can!" I responded, feeling slightly panicky. "Can you tell me what's happened? Do we need to bring anything? What—"

"Just come!" Malchi demanded in that strange, strangled voice, and the phone went dead.

I rushed inside. "Malcolm, wake up!" I called. "Duncan, it's morning!"

Malcolm peered over the edge of the sleeping platform. He looked dishevelled and sleepy. "Marie?" he asked. "What's the matter?"

"Malchi phoned. He wants us to go up there as soon as possible."

"Why? What?" Malcolm was understandably confused.

"I don't know!" I told him, guessing the meaning of his questions. "He sounded odd."

Duncan was standing in his sleep shorts, looking at me. "Mam?" he asked.

"I think something must have happened at the *fi'ilsted*," I said. "We need to there, Malcolm and I. Do you want to come too, or will you have your breakfast here and go up to Alana's, as planned?"

"Oh, I'm coming with you!" Duncan responded. "What if Petter's ill? Or if the *fi'ilsted* was broken into again last night?"

None of us had showers, and I was the only one to have drunk any coffee. We were out on my narrow track, up the slope by the wind turbine, and heading for the village within ten minutes.

Of course it was still dark, and the freezing air hurt our lungs as we clambered and strode towards Hus.

"If Petter's ill," Duncan was gasping, "at least it's still enough for a helicopter to come over from the Shetlands!"

"*Aja*," Malcolm answered, also breathing heavily. "Malchi will have rung them before he phoned us."

"But if it's another theft," I suggested, "then there's not much we can do."

"Perhaps it's Sigrid," Duncan wondered. "Or someone else – one of the bairns, maybe?"

There's a place where the track up from my bothy reaches a few feet of flat land, and from there a person can see the bothies at the higher end of the village track. There was a light on in the shop, and all three of the *fi'ilsted* windows glowed, but the rest of Hus was still in darkness.

Malcolm stopped, breathing deeply. "It doesn't look like a general emergency," he commented.

"*Nei*," Duncan agreed.

"Well, I hope it's not!" I added, but I felt pessimistic. I couldn't recall Malchi ever phoning us so early in the morning, or sounding so strange.

★★★

We went straight to the *fi'ilsted*. The door was unlocked (actually, I'm not sure it's ever had a lock!). I was the first one in.

"Malchi?" I called.

At once Petter came through from the kitchen area. He was grinning; even in the low light his eyes seemed to be shining.

"Wow!" he exclaimed. "You got here quickly. Come through; we're all at the back!"

I could smell coffee, and a teapot was standing on the kitchen table with a couple of mugs. It didn't look like the scene of a disaster.

"We're out here!" Petter said, leading us out into the tiny, cobbled courtyard and across to one of the stone buildings where they kept foods that weren't too perishable.

Shona and Patrick from the shop were there, and Sigrid, and of course Malchi, all gathered round the open door, looking into the lit storehouse.

"Let Marie see!" demanded Petter, and the little crowd stood back, so that we could see what the others had been staring at.

"We've had another break-in," Malchi said, and now that I could see his face I realised that he sounded strange because he was smiling so much, trying not to laugh.

We three peered in.

It was amazing. The shelves were neatly stacked, as they always were, but on the floor were heaps and piles of food. There were tins of sweetcorn and lentils, soup and Scottish broth. There was a catering bag of flour and a box of demerara sugar. Two small bags turned out to contain apples, and another had fish wrapped in brown paper, thawing by then but obviously recently frozen. There were two slabs of imported butter, the sort that you sometimes see at the Castle in Storhaven.

Everyone was quiet as we took it all in. Then, "Some break-in!" Duncan exclaimed, and suddenly we were all talking and laughing, hugging each other, checking the labels on the tins.

At that moment, Lyle arrived, and a moment later Verity. We stood back to let them see, just as everyone had cleared the way for us. The little courtyard was crowded by then, as Lyle knelt on the ground to look more closely at the treasure trove.

"And you locked the door, of course?" he checked with Malchi and Petter.

"*Aja!*" the two men said in unison, and Malchi held out a broken padlock. The hook part had been neatly sawn apart.

"And you didn't have any of these supplies in here last night?"

"*Nei!* All our stores were on the shelves, as they always are."

"Except those potatoes," added Malchi, pointing to a hessian sack in the far corner. "Those were the only contributions we'd had for Friday's meal when we went to bed, last night."

"*Nei*, we've got some baked food inside," Petter reminded him.

Lyle stood up and took a step backwards. "Well," he said, "it looks like breaking and entering, all right, but I hardly think we want to prosecute the person who did this!"

"I was so worried," Malchi told us. "I couldn't think how we could feed everyone the day after tomorrow, unless the *bondii* started bringing us food, and now this! It's like a miracle!"

"It's an answer to prayer!" suggested Verity, quietly.

"Even so," Petter said, taking the damaged padlock from his partner, "my first job of the day is to rig up another lock!"

"And my first job is to feed all you people!" Malchi added. "I can't give you a full Scottish breakfast, but there's porridge and toast, and as much tea or coffee as you want!"

CHAPTER 20

The bairns were given Friday morning off. Sigrid had to go over to Storhaven to see the nurse about something, she wasn't saying what, and the message went round on WhatsApp groups and emails that parents were not to send the young ones in until after lunch. The cookery lesson at the *fi'ilsted* and the meal to follow was to happen as usual, and everybody was welcome, whether they had felt able to contribute or not. We had one or two requests from the east of the island, mostly people who had family on the west and had heard all about the previous two meals. We weren't quite sure what to do about them. It was a big enough task just feeding the folk in and around Hus.

I wasn't expecting to go up to the village early. Duncan and Alana were studying at my place, and Malcolm was digging a few potatoes out of his clamp and doing some basic maintenance around his bothy. Until Duncan had come home semi-permanently, we had spread our time about equally between the two bothies but it wasn't as easy now, and Malcolm had only slept a couple of nights over there since before solstice.

Then Malchi phoned, wondering if I would be on call to help with the wee ones in case Sigrid wasn't back in time, so I strolled up to Hus right after an early lunch.

As I approached the village, I could hear the excited voices of bairns. Marigold's voice, of course, I recognised at once. At first, I thought that they were playing outside Bothan Ros, Marigold's home, but as I got closer I realised that several children were in the old ruin next door.

"*Nei!*" I heard the piping voice of wee Shirley, the bairn who lived next to the Kullanders up on the hill. "We're the slaves, and you are the baddies!"

In a broad island accent, Christian responded, "But I was a baddie last time! I want to be one of the slaves now!"

"You can be a slave next time!" Marigold was placating the bairn. "And me and Shirley will be the goodies what set you free. But first you 'as to bring us food, and make us work!"

I could see that Marigold and Shirley were sitting on the ground in the ruin. They had built a pyramid of plant stalks to resemble a fire, and they were both huddled close to it, as if they were cold.

"All right!" the other village boy agreed. To Christian he added, "If we're bad, we'd better be really bad!" He picked up a piece of broken wood that must have fallen from the roof, and waved it about in the air. "Work! Work!" he demanded shrilly. "Or I'll put you in chains!"

"We wasn't that sort of slaves!" Marigold reprimanded the lad. "They never 'ad no chains, the bosses. They just said what if we didn't work, they'd send us back where we came from!"

"Well," Christian objected. "It doesn't sound so threatening if you say that. Can't we just pretend there were chains?"

"*Aja!*" Wee Shirley was more than happy with the idea. "And a whipping block, like Sigrid told us, in Barbados."

"Good!" The lad was happy with that. The game started up again. "Work! Work!" the second lad shouted.

"I doesn't want to!" Marigold was pretending to be cowed. "I's 'ungry!"

"Work, or we'll put you in chains!" Christian threatened.

Shirley pretended to cry. "All right," she agreed. "I'll work!"

She stated picking up stones from the uneven floor, and piling them up in one corner.

"That's enough!" declared Marigold. Then, to the boys, "Does you want to be slaves now?"

I chuckled to myself as I went on down to the *fi'ilsted*. It was, in a way, a pity that the bairns had to know about such things, but it seemed to me that what I had just seen was healthy. I thought they might play it out of their systems.

★★★

As it happened, Sigrid was back in time, arriving on Robert's cart, pulled by his two ponies wearing a very effective makeshift harnesses. A trickle of bairns arrived from the outlying bothies, and the village children gave up their games and joined the wee crowd as they started their cookery lesson. Verity, Lyle and I organised the tables in the school, and Verity wrote a beautiful 'Welcome!' sign on the whiteboard. As dusk fell, not long after three that afternoon, delicious smells started to waft around the village, and by four the usual crowd had gathered.

Although this was only our third community meal, a sort of routine was developing. I noticed that some people already went to the same seats as last time. The wee bairns, the ones not yet in school, knew what to expect, and were less clingy. The older children were taking it in turns to carry round the plates of food, and they, too, were more confident. Olaf our bard, and wee Elin, already his apprentice, sat together in the corner, where Sigrid had organised a small library, and accompanied us with songs and instrumentals.

I don't know the name of the dish Malchi and the children had created that day, if indeed it had a name. They had used the apples in the savoury course, and I would say there was some ginger in it. Whatever it was, it was served on beds of mashed potato, and it was delicious. I was surprised anyone had room for cake, shortbread or scones afterwards, but they did!

It was probably close to five in the afternoon by the time the meal was finished. People were leaning back in their chairs or sitting sideways on benches to talk to people behind them.

Olaf and Elin were taking a break as they ate their meal, and Elin's paps was sitting with them, talking to Olaf and laughing about something. Possibly Olaf had been telling him one of his interminable tales.

Then there was a sort of scuffle at the doorway as two elderly men moved their chairs to let a newcomer pass, and to the astonishment of most of us, Blair Munro came in. And behind him, just as when he had dropped into our meeting before solstice, was Candy Williams.

At first, of course, not everyone noticed that he had arrived. Petter went over and shook hands with him, and the people at that end of the room were aware of the new arrivals. Over where Malcolm and I were sitting it took a little longer. I noticed Duncan nudge Andy and Marigold, and the bairns all looked in that direction.

Oddly, the whole room went quiet. Everyone was looking at the two *harkrav* interlopers, wondering what they were doing there. Blair Munro looked a little uncomfortable. It was not a welcoming silence that had greeted them.

He gave a sort of cough. "Goodness!" he exclaimed, looking at the empty plates littering the tables. "Have you finished already?"

"*Aja!*" Petter was calm and polite. "We've had a real feast this afternoon!"

"I'd forgotten how early you *bondii* eat!" tittered Ms Williams into the still room, and somehow it felt like a criticism.

"Oh, *aja!*" Petter still sounded jovial, although the last comment carried such a weight of scorn for our unsophisticated habits. "Early, but well! I'm sorry you missed it."

"I'm surprised," the man said, looking around. "I had heard – well, that is… the rumour is, that you're quite short of food over here. Thefts, and so on?"

"A few wee problems," agreed Petter. "Nothing we can't handle."

"Well." Blair Munro seemed almost lost for words. "I'm glad to hear it."

"Oh *nei*, he isn't!" Malcolm whispered to me. "Why do I think he came over here? To help us, or to gloat?"

Robert, who was sitting on the other side of Malcolm, leant forward and muttered to us both, "I don't trust yon *harkrav* gentleman as far as I can see him. He's what my paps would call a rum 'un."

"*Aja!*" We were both in total agreement.

They didn't stay long. Blair Munro shook a few hands, and made a fuss of little Hamish Stewart, for all the world like a Westminster politician on a walk-about. Candy Williams spoke to Malchi about something, and he looked rather taken aback, then they both left.

"She asked me where I came from!" Malchi told us afterwards. "I've lived on En-Somi for twenty years! What does it matter where I was born?"

"Aye," Elise was there while we were discussing the unexpected visitors. "When I interviewed them, over on the other side of the island, Blair Munro asked me the same thing. And I was born here! In Scotland, I mean, obviously not on this island! His wife, Freya, looked really uncomfortable."

"It's because you're not white." Harris was pointing out the obvious.

"*Aja!*" Petter put an arm round his partner. "That'll be it. He's just stunned by your exotic beauty!"

Malchi laughed, and looked more relaxed. "I forget that there are still people like that," he told us. "It's ages – years – since anyone on En-Somi commented on my race. It took me by surprise."

★★★

We were, of course, all intrigued by where the unexpected bounty in the *fi'ilsted* storehouse had come from.

"It must have been Freya Munro!" Petter insisted. "After all, she brought over food for the second meal, didn't she?"

"*Aja*." Malcolm wasn't convinced. "But she didn't bring it secretly. She arrived in the middle of the day, and showed us her contributions. Whoever gave us the food this time did it in secret, in the night."

"Perhaps she thought it better to keep it from her husband?" As we all had, I had noticed that we only ever seemed to see Blair Munro with Candy Williams. I felt quite sorry for his wife.

"Maybe." Lyle looked unconvinced. "I can't see how she would have managed it, though. I mean, how would she carry all that food over from her home, over the Fyrtarn pass, break the padlock, stack the food and get home again, without that arrogant husband of hers knowing anything about it?"

He was right, of course. It was difficult to imagine how Freya Munro could have achieved such a thing.

"There's something else, too." Malchi was looking thoughtful. "It was a strange mixture of food that we were given. I noticed while we were cooking – the bairns and I. Some of the tins had those little price labels that Shona and Patrick use, so you'd think they had been bought in our village shop, but the demerara sugar came from Fortnum and Mason. Isn't that some sort of luxury store in London?"

"I should have noticed that!" Lyle looked ashamed. "Some *nasyoni* I am!"

"So, who on this island shops at Shona and Patrick's but also has goods shipped in from London?" Petter wondered.

We looked at each other, confused. Everyone knew the answer – nobody.

CHAPTER 21

The *nasyoni* from Storhaven wanted to come over and visit Lyle. She was still new to the island and faced a tough job. The previous officer, Sergeant Stenson, had been arrested and taken off the island for his part in keeping the refugees as slaves out at the old airport, and for arms dealing. He had been moderately popular, and the *harkrav* islanders who had been arrested with him were also deemed by many to have achieved good things for En-Somi in the past. It meant that her arrival as the representative of a new administration was not greeted with universal approval.

This new officer, Mirren, knew about island life, but she came from a larger, more connected community. I think she had been a little taken aback by the mixed reception she received. Lye had gone over to Storhaven to greet her from the ferry when she arrived, and had attempted to brief her on the situation and to settle her into her new home. That had been a bit tricky, too. Sergeant Stenson's wife, Annie, hadn't known about her husband's criminal activities, and so she hadn't been arrested. She continued to live in the Storhaven *nasyonihuss*, the bothy provided for the resident law-enforcer, and had refused point blank to move out. Of course, she had no right to continue to live there, but the *Oyrod*, the island council, were embarrassed at the thought of evicting her, and so she had stayed. Instead, Mirren had been given a wee bothy at the top of the hill out of Storhaven. It had only one room and no office, but at least it had a good view.

Of course, Malcolm and I didn't meet her on that first occasion when she came to Hus, but Verity told us all about it.

"I like her!" Verity told us. "She's not young – her bairns have grown up, and she's a widow. Her husband volunteered for the lifeboat crew and was drowned in one of those big storms. Her son still serves on the same lifeboat – can you imagine how stressful that must be? She says she never wanted promotion. She wouldn't have applied to be transferred to En-Somi if it had been a sergeant's post, although she's passed all her exams. Her big thing is community."

"I like the sound of her," Malcolm said. He was just getting ready to go over to his bothy, and Duncan was up at the Kullanders' with Alana. Verity had come over to keep me company.

It was one of those calm February mornings when spring seems to be in the air, even though we could still suffer some serious storms yet. We were sitting outside on the southern corner of the patio where the morning sun just creeps over the hill where my turbine is planted. We were wearing our winter jackets and boots, but enjoying the feel of the distant sun on our faces. The sea was remarkably calm. Such days occur only very occasionally in the winter, and seem all the more lovely for that reason. There were a few white caps way out on the ocean and we could hear the gentle swoosh and gurgle of the waves on my beach. Nearby, sheep were grazing placidly, 'baaing' now and again in a contented fashion, as if they were having a desultory conversation about something.

"She mostly wanted to know about how the island community works," Verity told me. "She called it our caste system, and actually that's a pretty good description, isn't it?"

"*Aja.*" I thought so too. "Although, really, isn't the whole of the UK like us – privileged and wealthy people at the top, ordinary folk making up the rest of the population? Isn't the whole world like that?"

Verity stretched her legs out, enjoying the low sun and the

gentle breeze. "But it's so stark, here on En-Somi. I mean, do other societies have names for the different groups, the way we do: *harkrav* and *bondii*?"

"*Nei*, perhaps not." I thought about it, staring out over the sea. "Unless you want to talk about classes – you know, working class and middle class?"

"Well... Anyhow, Mirren has had a few problems with some of the *harkrav*. She told us that they seemed to think that she was some sort of agent for them. They invited her to a meeting of the *Oyrod*, and spent the whole evening giving her instructions – or that's what it felt like to her!"

"Oh, poor Mirren!" I could just imagine how it might have been. "What were they instructing her to do?"

"It was rather unpleasant, actually," Verity told me. "For one thing, they wanted her to collect island taxes. They told her that Sergeant Stenson had always gone to the outlying bothies to save the *bondii* from coming into town, and they wanted Mirren to do the same."

"I'm not sure that's right," I told my friend. "Lyle's never collected the taxes over here. The bills come over from Storhaven, and either people go over to the town offices in person or the return envelopes are collected up at the shop and all taken over together."

"*Aja*. Mirren didn't think it was right either, and she told them so. Apparently, they weren't best pleased! But that wasn't all."

I shivered as the breeze strengthened a little. "What else?" I asked.

"They were talking to her about our newcomers," Verity explained. "Blair Munro told her that the refugees were here, on En-Somi, because nobody else would take them. He said that they were known thieves and that some of them are violent criminals. He said that the *bondii* have been taken in by sob stories, and that it is the job of the *Oyrod* and the law-enforcement agencies to protect the community. They warned her to stand no nonsense, to arrest anyone who puts a foot out of line."

"That's rather harsh!" I commented. "And has anyone put a foot out of line?"

"Well, that's the interesting thing," Verity told me. "The newcomers rarely go into town. There aren't that many of them east of Fyrtarn Fjell and, of those who are over there, Charlie and his crowd rarely leave the moors where they live. So there's just that young couple, Quincy and Mo. Mirren said that there have been a few rather vocal arguments in the street, especially after people have been to the *fi'ilstedi*, but they are between different groups of *bondii* – those who want the newcomers to go and those who are happy for them to stay. And, of course, she's checked the island social media, and she's seen that some of it's pretty toxic, but by and large the newcomers don't post anything. So again, it's mostly just *bondii* throwing brickbats at each other!"

"Is there anyone left on our side of En-Somi," I wondered, "who wants the refugees to go?"

Verity thought about it. The sun had moved south, and was behind the patch of moorland that separates my bothy from Malcolm's. "Shall we go back inside?" she asked. "It's got colder!"

Once in my snug bothy, with jackets and boots off and fresh coffee in our mugs, the conversation continued.

"I think Robert was suspicious of the newcomers," she told me. "And, of course, he was one of the first to have stuff stolen, so you can understand it. But I saw him going into Rose Stewart's bothy with Si the other day. The two men were laughing at something Marigold was telling them, and they looked as thick as thieves."

"*Aja!*" I chuckled. "Marigold loves Robert's ponies. Well, she loves all ponies! She goes down there and talks to them, so Petter told me. It's a sure way to Robert's heart!"

"To be honest, I think having Rose and Si right in the village has done a lot to help all our newcomers. People know them, and so they don't see them as refugees anymore, just as Si and Rose." Verity was looking thoughtful. "Whose idea was it, anyhow, to house them over here?"

"Your Lyle's," I told her, smiling. "He invited them to live in his office! And then Shona and Patrick. The idea of renovating that bothy was theirs. And, as you know, all the other renovations came from that."

"Maybe it's a shame that nobody housed any newcomers right in Storhaven," Verity suggested. "Then, perhaps, Mirren wouldn't have such a difficult job. I should have thought of that when I was still living over there."

"You had enough on your hands, if I remember rightly!" I suggested. "More coffee?"

★★★

The knitting cooperative was growing. Rose had been the first to become a new member, although she was making macramé hammocks, not knitting. Lots of people had seen them in use in the school and the *fi'ilsted*, and Rose was happy to give them away to *bondii*, which was much appreciated in such straightened times. Of course, she brought baby Thistle with her to our meetings, which slowed us all down because the baby was happy to be passed from person to person for cuddles and games. That persuaded Freda Sinclair to come over with her little girl. Freda was already a fine knitter, although socks were her speciality, knitted properly on four needles. Freda had been at school with Paula Stewart, so when they met in the shop she encouraged Paula, who was by nature a bit shy, to bring little Hamish, already a toddler, and to join our circle. We used to meet in Sigrid's bothy at one time, but with additional members, and wee ones needing floor space to crawl or explore, we moved to the *fi'ilsted*. It was not ideal. Young Hamish was forever bumping his head on chairs and tables, and had a fascination for the round stools, which he wanted to climb.

Petter pretty much stayed away while the knitters were there, but Malchi was always around, serving us tea and shortcake and playing with the bairns. He told us once that he had started a degree to become a teacher back in the country of his birth, but another student 'outed' him and he had to leave in a hurry. Once in the UK, life was for several years just a matter of survival. Like any asylum seeker he was eligible for a tiny level of support – it amounted to less than £7.00 a day to cover everything including accommodation, and he wasn't allowed to work. He had lived in one room in a crowded house, and had barely coped for the three years that it had taken for the Home Office to approve his application. Then he had met Petter on a gay pride march in Southampton. "And the rest is history!" he finished, happily.

"We always thought what asylum seekers took all the 'omes from us Brits!" Rose told him. "The guards in the camps, that's what they told us!"

"*Aja.*" Malchi frowned. "That's what people thought, but it was never that way. I moved up here with Petter, but I stayed in touch with other asylum seekers for a bit. They ended up in some pretty dismal places." He picked up Thistle, who showed every sign of wanting to suck Malchi's trouser leg. Then he gave a broad grin. "I've been so lucky! I couldn't have wished for a better life!"

Thistle reached out and clasped a handful of Malchi's hair. "And that's despite being terrorised by this wee bairn!" he added.

Malchi was much more relaxed by then. For three weeks the same amazing provision of food had occurred, though not always in the same way. Two days before the next Friday meal, when the lock on the door of the *fi'ilsted* storehouse had been replaced, a neat pile of tins and packets had been left in the cobbled yard. The following week it was put on the bar in the *fi'ilsted*, and after that they stopped locking the storehouse. Bit by bit all the *bondii* west of Fyrtarn Fjell learnt about these surprising gifts, and although there was much speculation among the adults about who might be helping so much, the bairns had no doubts.

"It's the *huldufolk*, obviously!" Marigold told me. "We made them lovely wee *huss* and burnt them down at the summer 'arbour, and they knows we respect 'em. That's why you 'as to stay on the right side of 'em!"

Duncan smiled across at me, behind Marigold's back.

★★★

It was, though, something of a mystery. If the *huldufolk* were helping us out in our time of need, some other, malign, force was still working against us. Shona and Patrick had a break-in at the shop and a whole shelf of tinned fruit was taken, along with precious cash from the till. Fruit had become a bit of an issue that winter because we were seeing so few ferries bringing us fresh perishables from further south. Over on the east of the island, too, *bondii* were suffering losses. Tom, at the ferry port, had three tins of fresh-baked bread taken from his kitchen in broad daylight, when he had been standing less than twenty feet away talking to Mirren. Holti had been very badly hit too. His storehouse had been raided three times despite the fact that his bothy was so remote.

"It's as if someone has a particular grudge against him!" Ingrid told me on the phone.

The Storhaven people were less united than us. Some folk from that side of the island had started to travel over to Hus to share in our Friday meals. Now that we seemed to have a regular supply of ingredients, we saw no reason not to include them, especially as they were good at contributing small items to the feasts. We enjoyed their company. Most of them, after all, were related to some of us. But the school was becoming very crowded on Friday afternoons, and there was no getting away from the fact that they seemed to bring the tensions of their side of the island with them.

I remember talking to a couple from over on Frigg Moor just up from the old oat field, who told me that their cousins in Storhaven had stopped talking to them altogether. The issue, it seemed, was the refugees. "They say we never should have let them stay!" the husband told me. "En-Somi was a peaceful place before they came!"

"Peaceful for us," his wife corrected. "Not so good for those poor folk over at the old airport!"

"*Aja*, well…" The husband had sounded less than convinced. "But they caused us no trouble while they were out there! And now look at our crime rate! It's as bad as inner-city Glasgow!"

"Hardly!" his wife corrected wearily, and I had the distinct impression this conversation had been rehearsed by these people over and over. I feared that the same things were being repeated around the hearths of many bothies across the island.

CHAPTER 22

It must have been the end of February or the beginning of March, and a wild, windy morning at that. For no obvious reason both Malcolm and I had woken early, well before seven. We lay in bed talking quietly, listening to the creaks and groans of the wind turbine, the slight hum of batteries charging, and the crash of waves against rocks. Malcolm went down to make some tea, and opened the shutters in the kitchen area. He came back with two steaming mugs and the news that it was going to be a fine morning.

"We could climb Fyrtarn Fjell," he suggested. "If we set off at once we might catch the sunrise."

"Oh, *aja*! Let's!" I agreed. "But quietly! We don't want to waken Duncan!"

We scrabbled about, donning jeans and *gensii*, and then warm winter jackets and sturdy boots. Malcolm grabbed half a loaf of bread and a slab of cheese, I took water, and we were off.

It was still night, but with that grey darkness that comes before sunrise. Fyrtarn Fjell loomed black and a little forbidding in front of us. We climbed the steep path up to the village, not talking much but giggling a little.

"This is the sort of thing I would have done when I was a wee bairn!" Malcolm told me.

"Without your mam and paps knowing?" I wondered.

"Definitely without them knowing!" He laughed. "They would have thought it far too frivolous, climbing the fjell without any particular reason!"

In the village there were already lights in some of the windows. Sigrid was obviously up, and Robert, but the shop and the *fi'ilsted* were still in darkness, and there was a dim light creeping between the shutters of Bothan Ros, suggesting that most of that household was still asleep. Perhaps Rose had needed to feed Thistle. Shona's goats were a little restless, bleating in that sad way they have, and a sheep was surprised by our arrival and lurched to its feet from the track ahead, scampering onto the grass by the broken stone wall.

We took the track out of the village and then veered north, to join the footpath that links Hunger Moor and the Kullanders' place with the summit of the fjell. We had last climbed this in the company of others on solstice day. It was easier with just the two of us, and we made good progress. I remember that the sky to the east, beyond the mountain, was grey rather than black by the time we reached the top.

We stood there looking east, our backpacks at our feet, Malcolm's arm around me. Down in the valley, where the land is marshy, criss-crossed with drystone walls, everything was still dark and mysterious, but over towards Storhaven there were little pinpricks of light from the town and a streak of brightness low in the sky. We dusted off the sheep droppings from the flat rock and sat down. Malcolm tore a lump of bread from the loaf for each of us, and passed me some cheese. We shared my water. The strange, squawking dawn chorus of En-Somi had begun. Then there was a bright flash of gold as the sun rose above the horizon, and long streaks of light streamed across the higher moors.

It was beautiful. We turned to look at each other but neither of us said anything. There were no words for such a view.

Then, at the same time, we both heard something. Over to the north, where a path no larger than a sheep track comes up from the direction of the summer harbour, came the distinct sounds of someone else climbing the fjell.

"We weren't the only ones with this idea!" commented Malcolm, in a hushed voice.

We were both looking in the direction of the scuffling and slight panting, and so we both saw him at the same time. It was Jarvis.

He stopped dead when he saw us. He had still not quite reached the top of the mountain; we could only see him from the waist up. He stared at us, and we stared at him, and for a fraction of time nobody said anything.

Then Malcolm stood and held out his hand to pull Jarvis up the last, steep patch and onto the rock where we were sitting.

"*Hei*!" he greeted the man as if it were the most natural thing to encounter another human being on top of the fjell at sunrise.

I remembered the conversation we had had with Verity and Lyle. What if Jarvis didn't recognise us?

"*Hei*!" I said. "It's Malcolm and Marie – you know, we met you at the old airport?"

"Oh… hi!" Jarvis was standing on our rock now, taller than Malcolm even in his bare feet. "There ain't usually nobody 'ere when the sun comes up."

"I don't suppose there is," agreed Malcolm. "We woke early and decided to come up here on the spur of the moment."

"Would you like some bread and cheese?" I offered. "We've got water too."

Malcolm and Jarvis both sat down again. "I always 'as water," Jarvis told us. "I carries it wiv me. I doesn't know if it's good to drink out of them streams. You know, 'cos the sheep poo in them. But I likes bread and cheese, if you 'as enough."

"They do," agreed Malcolm, talking about the domestic habits of the sheep. "And we've got plenty of bread and cheese. Marie was baking yesterday."

We sat in companionable silence for a few minutes, eating our breakfast. Then Jarvis said, as if checking his facts, "It were you and your friends what freed us from the bosses? And you knows Marigold, 'ose sister got drownded."

"*Aja*," we both agreed in unison. Then I added, "You looked after Marigold when she went looking for her sister's grave."

Jarvis turned to me and smiled. It may have been the first time I had ever seen him smiling. "Yeah, I did!" he agreed. "You remembered!"

"It was a good thing you did," Malcolm told the man. "And it was good of you to mark where Lavender had been buried too. Si and Rose have a photo of the grave on the wall of their bothy – their house."

"Si and Rose," repeated Jarvis. "And they 'ave a baby. Thistle. Is she still alive?"

"Oh, *aja*," I told him, smiling at the thought of that wee bairn. "She's crawling now, and into everything. And Marigold goes to the village school, and has learnt to read and write."

Jarvis gave a little sigh, and stuffed the last of his bread into his mouth. "That's good," he told us. "So they didn't take 'er away and give 'er to no foster parents?"

"No, they didn't do that," I agreed.

Again, we sat in silence. Then, to my surprise, Jarvis said, "It's beau'iful, ain't it? 'Ills and streams and rocks and sea, and sheep and birds, and day and night…"

"*Aja*." Malcolm sounded as moved as I felt by the man's outburst. "Beautiful."

"I 'ad't never seen nothing like this, before I came 'ere," he continued. "And then, when we was working for them bosses, I never thought about it. I just thought about – you know – surviving I suppose. Just not getting into no trouble. And then 'aving a drink at the end of the day, and food to get you through. And keeping warm. It feels like I weren't properly awake. Just living. Now I's awake."

"But are you all right?" I wasn't sure if it was best to ask, but it troubled me that this strange man was so alone. "There's nobody with you over there at the old airport, is there? Aren't you lonely?"

For a few moments he was silent, frowning into the distance.

"I don't know if I's lonely," he finally confessed. "I feels like I bin alone all my life. I's used to it. And I watches, you know. I sees what uver people does when they fink nobody's watching. I knows what goes on."

"You've explored a lot of the island, haven't you?" Malcolm asked. "We saw you once, standing on top of the cliff by our places, looking out to sea."

"Yeah!" Then he turned and grinned at us again. "You scared me!" he told us. "I thought what I must 'ave been on private land, and you'd call the cops, and 'ave me taken away! So I skedaddled!" Then he looked serious again. "I doesn't know what's private and what ain't, on this island. Them bosses, they didn't like us to go nowhere, but Quincy and Mo, they used to go a-roaming, and nobody arrested them. So I tries to stay out of sight. But I knows what's going on. I sees it all."

"And what is going on?" Malcolm wondered.

"Ah, well, there you 'as it!" Jarvis said obliquely. "More'n ought to be going on, that's for sure! You's good people, but ain't everyone on this lump of rock good. Oh no!"

"So who are the bad ones?" I asked. I wondered if he was thinking about the thefts. "It would really help to know."

"The same ones 'as 'ave always been bad!" Jarvis told us.

Then he stood, brushing bread crumbs off his filthy clothes. "I's off now," he announced. "Say 'ello to Si and Rose, and young Marigold. And the vicar lady, if you sees 'er." Then he was gone, back the way he had come, walking as confidently over the rocks and marsh as if he were wearing good walking boots instead of going barefoot.

"What an interesting morning!" remarked Malcolm, as we gathered up the remains of our breakfast.

"Very," I agreed.

CHAPTER 23

Tom, at the ferry port, asked if he could come to one of our Friday meals. It was Yanni Sinclair who asked on his behalf – Yanni's brother worked on the ferries and knew Tom well. "He just wants to see how we manage," Yanni told us.

Of course we agreed. Normally the ferry came in on Fridays, but that sturdy little boat was being repaired following another rough crossing, and wouldn't be calling on En-Somi that week. I suppose it was the fourth week of our almost-miraculous supplies, and a ripple of excitement had replaced any anxiety about having enough food to go around. What would we be presented with this week? I am fairly sure that on the occasion I'm remembering it was four large catering tins of duck breasts and the ingredients to make a plum sauce. As Malchi pointed out, we were eating better than the *harkrav*, at least once a week!

"It's the sort of dish you'd expect to have served up at a formal dinner," he said. "I just don't believe any *bondi* would have anything like this in their storehouse. There's no getting away from it: someone from the *harkrav* is helping us!"

"*Aja*, but..." I just couldn't imagine anyone we had come across from that community who would see the need to help *bondii* – except just possibly Freya Munro, and I wasn't even sure about her. And how would she manage to bring such largess over to us, over and over again, in the middle of the night, without her husband finding out?

To add to the mystery, some of the goods that arrived anonymously were recognised by people from Hus. I was actually one of the first to notice it. I had learnt from Bjorn, when I first arrived on the island, the importance of storing tinned food with the earliest sell-by dates at the front. "If it's a good winter," he had told me, "we might not eat it all, so some of the cans could be more than a year old. It never seems to go off, but we ought to be careful…"

It was wise advice. Sometimes, though, the sell-by or use-by dates were hard to read, and so when I stacked the food in the storehouse I made my own records of when I had purchased the food, on sticky tabs on the tins. And then one of my cans of sweetcorn turned up in one of the donations – not the week of the duck breasts but before that.

"That's crazy," I pointed out. I was holding the tin, looking at my own writing, feeling confused. "Why would anyone steal from us and then return our food? It doesn't make any sense!"

I was standing in the *fi'ilsted* kitchen, having just brought a batch of bread up for the feast. Malchi hadn't realised that the tin had once been mine; he was just pointing out that it had a note on it.

"That's not all," he told me. "Last week we had two jars of Sigrid's preserves in our food parcel!"

We looked at each other, mystified. "I wish these cans and jars could talk!" remarked Malchi. "Something very odd is going on here!"

★★★

Some of the bairns had taken to the cooking as if they were born to it, but a few of them were less enthusiastic. Marigold had become Malchi's sous chef, and she, in turn, bossed Christian around unmercifully. Elin was not interested in the creation of meals, and spent Friday afternoons with Olaf practising for the evening. The older bairns, those who were now being educated online, generally helped with the setting up and organisation when school ended. Tom, when he arrived, was amazed at how slick the operation had become after just a few Fridays.

"So, who gives you the food?" he wanted to know.

"Oh, various people," I told him, vaguely. I wasn't sure if the news of our donations, now much discussed west of Fyrtarn Fjell but not mentioned on social media, was known beyond our community.

"And you feed people who haven't contributed?" he asked.

"That's the whole point," Petter explained. "Some people over here are really struggling."

"*Aja*, over in Storhaven too," Tom agreed. "And even more out on the moors. *Bondii* with no cash incomes have almost stopped coming into the town, except the bairns, of course, to go to school. Jeanie was telling me that the people from Caldbrae, who used to travel in together most Fridays to meet the ferry and then to have lunch at her place, have just stopped coming. They don't have any spare cash, you see. Every last penny is needed for the taxes."

"It makes me angry," I told him. "The *Oyrod* must have known what would happen when they changed the tax rules. It seems so vindictive!"

"*Aja*, that's the word for it," agreed Tom. "Vindictive. Mind you, there are *bondii* who support what they've done. They tried to rope me in, the crowd who drink at the Vikings' Rest. The ones who are paid salaries. The ones with money in the bank."

"You're paid a salary!" I pointed out.

"Oh, *aja*," Tom agreed. "And I'm glad of it, but that doesn't help my friends. That's why I wanted to see what you were doing. Gamla Hus has always been a kindly community."

★★★

It was early dusk by the time we all gathered in the school. Tom looked around, apparently impressed by all that he saw. He went over to talk to the Sinclairs but sat with Malcolm and me for the meal, with Rose and Si on the other side. Inevitably, he was captivated by baby Thistle and quickly got into conversation with Si and Rose. I noticed that Rose told him, "We's Si and Rose Stewart," in her softening English accent, and that Tom managed not to show a flicker of surprise.

The older bairns with Malchi and Petter were just bringing in the steaming caldron of duck and the side dishes, when Freya Munro appeared with Verity and Lyle. They had invited her over as a thank you for her earlier kindness, and had been really pleased when she had texted, earlier that day, to say that her husband had another engagement, but that she would love to come. Even though I guessed she had dressed down for the occasion, there was something about her that made her stand out from the rest of us. Somehow, even in her trousers and *gensi*, she had a sort of air about her, a sense of style that we didn't have. Nevertheless, her smile was genuine and her appreciation of the food was evident. She seemed quite at ease with Verity and Lyle, and said something to young Christian, when he offered her potatoes, that made him laugh. I decided that I liked her – but with reservations!

It seemed to me that we were particularly noisy that evening. There was a rousing chorus of 'Happy Birthday', sung to Freda Sinclair, and then Olaf played the introduction to 'Flower of Scotland' and everyone started singing. As you probably know, it's a song of rebellion; it expressed how we were all feeling, and so did 'Scotland the Brave', which followed. Then Alf Kullander raised an arm into the air to quieten us all, and started to sing 'No Peace in the Glen', which I am told comes from the terrible days of the enclosures. Others stood, and then we were all standing, arms round each other's shoulders, swaying to the heartbreaking song of loss and destruction. I glanced across at Rose, just as we sang the line 'to see thee no more', and she had tears pouring down her face. She and Si had not been uprooted by enclosures but they had lost everything, just as had our mainland ancestors. Across the room, Frankie, also a refugee, looked grim-faced and stoical. These people had been through so much.

Then, "My God!" The exclamation came from Tom, who was staring at the door, as in came Blair Munro and Candy Williams.

Of course, not everyone noticed. A good number of people had their backs to the door or were just not looking in that direction, and there are always some folk who sing those enclosure songs with their eyes closed, almost as if they are praying, but even so there was a sort of hesitation in the singing, and at that moment I think it might have stopped altogether, had it not been for Olaf. We were on the last verse but he started at once at the beginning again, and Alf, who had a deep and powerful voice, followed his lead.

It saved the day, at least for the Munros. Freya had seen her husband come in – the husband who had been unable to accompany her to the meal because of another engagement, and who had now arrived with another woman. I don't know how long it might have taken Blair to realise that his wife was there but Candy Williams noticed at once and nudged the man, pointing. Freya went very red and stopped swaying to the music, Blair looked like a small child caught stealing a biscuit. Candy Williams, however, held her head high and waved across at Freya, as if they were old friends meeting at a cocktail party.

Marigold, who had been sitting with the other bairns, had come across to join her parents when the singing began. She took in the situation at once. "Them's bosses," she told me. "'E's seeing that blonde one behind 'er back. 'E's a lying cheat!"

"*Aja!*" It was Si responding. "And when you's grown up I never, ever want to 'ear that you done such a thing! I wants you to be the sort of girl what can be trusted, like your mum!"

The song ended, and chairs scraped on the floor as some

people sat down again, and others began to mingle. Olaf started to play an instrumental version of one of our dialect songs, and the room was full of conversation again.

I looked across the room. Verity had turned to Freya and put one hand on her shoulder. She said something and the two women stood. Verity led the way to the door. Freya had to walk right past her husband to get out. She didn't look at him, and he pretended not to see her.

"She didn't know!" exclaimed Tom, almost under his breath. "Everyone in Storhaven knew, but she didn't! That poor lass!"

Blair Munro and Candy Williams obviously intended to brazen it out. Blair started to approach people – people who might vote for him at the next *Oyrod* elections. He smiled his white-toothed smile and held out his hand to shake those to whom he was hoping to speak. He reached the place where Petter and Malchi were standing. Petter looked away as if he hadn't seen the man approaching. Munro pretended he hadn't noticed the slight, and extended his right hand to Malchi.

Malchi paused and calmly looked the man up and down, as if he were inspecting the guard. Then he turned away, a look of utter scorn on his face.

"Well done, Malchi!" Malcolm said, beside me.

CHAPTER 24

When the ferry next came in it brought a small mountain of goods that had been held up by the weather or the general logistical difficulties that an unpredictable climate was causing everywhere. Malcolm had ordered all that he needed to build a small rowing boat, which he planned to keep close to my beach. The currents run fast there, it's why it's such a good source of driftwood, but Malcolm hoped that the same movement of water would bring lots of fish across the mouth of the little bay.

Verity was showing me the gifts that her family had sent over: little hand-knitted matinee jackets, a musical mobile to hang above a cot, toys for a baby to play with in the bath and a baby book, to fill in all the landmarks of the wee one's development.

"They're so excited!" she told me, referring to her mother and stepfather. "I hope they'll make it over here this summer. Their first grandchild!"

I remember how thrilled Bjorn's father had been when we had told him that Duncan was on the way. "*Aja*," I agreed. "It's a very special time."

"I used to think I wouldn't want bairns," Verity went on. "The world seems like such an uncertain place to bring a wee one into. But here on En-Somi…"

"I know," I agreed, guessing what my friend was thinking. "It feels safe here. As if the world might destroy itself, and here we'd still be, planting our kale and singing our songs…"

Then Verity chuckled. "But let's have some coffee, while we can still get it!" she suggested.

Lyle came in just then, ducking under the lintel, leaving his boots in the entrance, kissing his wife and hugging me.

"So, Tom's taking the bit between his teeth!" he announced, checking a tin for biscuits. "He's trying to get the Storhaven people to have communal meals, like ours."

"Good for him!" I said.

"*Aja*, but will it work?" Verity was frowning as she poured in the milk. "There's a much bigger mix of people over at Storhaven. You know how some folk objected to us feeding the refugees in the kirk, and then there's the crowd that drink at the Vikings' Rest... And the *harkrav*..."

"I know," Lyle agreed. "I wondered about that. They've got a problem about where to meet, too. The *Oyrod* has pronounced that the school is not an appropriate venue for such an event, and the people at the Castle are worried about offending customers if they allow Tom to hire their back room. Ingrid and Dougie are all in favour of the idea, but Ingrid thinks it would be tactless to ask to use the kirk – and she's sure the answer would be 'no' anyhow!"

"I would think they'd have a problem of distance, too," Verity commented. "It's one thing to come down from Hunger Moor or over from Michaelmas Fjell for a meal in Hus, but would the people from beyond Caldbrae really go down to Storhaven? Even for a good meal? And it's easier to come to us than to go to Storhaven for the *bondii* who live over towards Fremdes Haven or Frigg Moor."

"Well... Tom's asked to use the room in the town hall where they do weddings," Lyle explained. "I don't think they can say no. And it's worth a try. He's started putting out the word around the town and on social media. Jeanie says she'll help..."

"Good luck to him!" I said warmly but, I have to admit, I didn't think it would work.

★★★

I was right, though it's a sad reflection on our island that Tom's innocent attempt to help brought about such trouble.

It began, predictably enough, with a few posts on social media. The anonymous contributor Champion was upset because not only had taxes gone up but now those who were 'self-sufficient' were being asked to feed the scroungers and layabouts who 'abounded' on our island. Champion was backed up by others, with remarks about the loss of backbone among *En-Som-in-Fedii*, about our 'once proud tradition' of standing on our own two feet being eroded by an influx of newcomers, and about 'spineless' *bondii* who had lost the simple skills that enabled our ancestors to survive real privations with a smile. Some of it became very personal. One of Champion's supporters blamed 'a small group of activists in the kirk' for introducing 'foreign' ideas to well-meaning worshippers and then abandoning them when her efforts were 'discovered'. We recognised Verity from those comments, but she maintained she was not bothered. Another post complained about the influence of those 'with connections to communist regimes', who had never understood the simple biblical injunction that 'those who don't work don't eat'. Several islanders had connections with Norway, of course, but Malcolm was convinced that was a reference to me, although to think of Norway as communist was pretty outlandish – Norway, with its royal family and thriving competitive industries around sustainable energy!

Tom took a photo of graffiti drawn on the side of his bothy, the words 'blood and soil' and a swastika, but he commented wryly that the 'artist' had used chalk, and he had been able to wash his wall clean in a matter of minutes.

"They don't know what this stuff means," suggested Lyle.

"Oh, I think they do!" Malcolm was looking grim. "I'm glad Malchi is over here with us, away from the trouble."

Mirren, the *nasyoni* from Storhaven, came over to talk to Lyle and to get away from the unpleasant atmosphere for a few hours. Lyle and Verity brought her to the *fi'ilsted* for lunch, and they joined Malcolm and me.

"Is it the *harkrav* youth?" I wondered. "My Duncan never mentioned any right-wing influences at the school in Lerwick."

"*Nei*, not as far as I can tell." Mirren might have been new but she already had a good grasp of the social landscape of the island. "There aren't many of their bairns on the island. They're all in school on the mainland. The lad who beat up Harris is in Edinburgh now. And anyhow I'm not sure it's bairns doing all this."

"But adults…" Verity was finding it hard to believe that any civilised human could be responsible for the sorts of things that were happening on the east of our island.

"Who is 'Champion'? Do you know?" Malcolm asked.

"*Nei*. Lyle and I were just discussing that. There's no way for us to tell who's posting stuff. The people in Aberdeen might be up to finding out, but from their point of view this is small fry. Hardly worth glancing at."

I was perplexed. "But I don't really see why anyone would object so strongly to Tom trying to help the *bondii* on his side of the island. I mean, all he wants to do is to get them together, encourage them a bit, feed their bairns…"

"Politics!" was Malcolm's one-word explanation.

"*Aja*." Lyle was in complete agreement. "Look at it from the point of view of the *harkrav*. Tom's introducing a whole new approach to the difficulties facing ordinary people. It's an approach that says 'we're all in this together'. It says, 'we're a community'. It implies that if I have food on the table and you don't, I ought to share it."

"'Love thy neighbour as thyself'," quoted Verity.

"Exactly!" Malcolm smiled at Verity almost conspiratorially. "Now, there's a revolutionary slogan if ever I heard one!"

"I suppose it eats away at people's core beliefs…" Lyle was thinking aloud. "You can't be comfortable sitting down at a laden table while knowing that someone up on the moors is only eating neeps and potatoes, unless you think that their poverty is somehow their fault. Otherwise, how would you look at yourself in the mirror?"

"So, then, if someone challenges the idea that they're responsible for their own hunger, you feel threatened…" Verity was thinking it through.

"*Aja!*" Mirren smiled across at Verity. "But the trouble is that, from all I hear over in Storhaven, life on the island really has deteriorated. There's a lot of theft. Far more than I encountered in my last posting. It's affecting everyone, especially those living out on the moors. The owners of the big bothies on Floirean's Cnoc have been complaining that they don't dare leave home even just to spend an evening with neighbours half a mile away. The risk of coming home to find their storehouses raided is just too great! And nobody seems to be exempt. It doesn't seem to make any difference whether you are a company director using En-Somi as a convenient tax haven or a simple crofter just trying to keep body and soul together! I can't imagine where all this food is going!"

Lyle, Verity, Malcolm and I exchanged surreptitious glances. We knew where the food was going; we just didn't know who was responsible for the redistributions – or why. There seemed to be, though, a tacit agreement that at this point we wouldn't tell Mirren too much. She was, after all, a newcomer.

★★★

Malchi was worried about Elise – or, rather, he was worried for her. "That wee lassie shouldn't be over in Storhaven," he told me. "I know she's keen to film everything that's happening, but it's not a happy town just now, and she's an obvious target. We've invited her to stay here, at the *fi'ilsted*."

"That's a good plan," I agreed. We were sitting at Malchi's hearth, and I was braiding Marigold's hair in a high plait at the back of her head, in a style that was briefly fashionable among the bairns because of a Norwegian rapper.

"Won't work!" volunteered Marigold.

Malchi laughed. "Why's that, young Marigold?" he asked.

Marigold sighed. She obviously found us adults very slow on the uptake. "'Cos 'Arris goes over there to work!" she explained.

"Ah – *aja* – I see your point!" Malchi was still grinning. We had all noticed how close those two had become.

"Perhaps Harris ought to come over here too?" I suggested. "He certainly isn't high on the popularity stakes among the people who drink at the Vikings' Rest!"

"His parents wouldn't have it!" Malchi was very up to date with island concerns. "He has that job in Storhaven. It's not much but it brings in a little cash – I mean actual money – and his parents will need it when the next quarter's taxes come due."

Then I had a bright idea. Malcolm was over at his place. He had been sighing and grumbling over breakfast about the need to walk over to his bothy so frequently. I had just seen a way of killing two birds with one stone. I went outside, leaving poor Marigold holding an unfinished plait so that it didn't unravel, and phoned my partner out of earshot of the others. When I came back in, I'm sure I was smiling.

I sat down again and resumed my hairdressing. "We might have a solution," I volunteered. "Of course, it's up to Harris. But, if he wants it, Malcolm can offer him a job house-sitting and looking after his ponies. It can be a real nuisance, when he's living at mine, to keep having to go over to his bothy. And Malcolm's pension is in real money, so he can pay Harris in cash, and Harris can go on helping his parents…"

"Not 'ouse-sitting!" Marigold corrected me. "Bothy-sitting! Honestly, Marie, anyone would think what you was English!"

CHAPTER 25

Things were getting worse. A couple of days after Harris moved into Malcolm's bothy, Mirren phoned Lyle. This time it was not just theft. Holti had surprised someone in the act of trying to raid his storehouse again, and the thief had hit him over the head with the handle of his yard brush. Holti had only been unconscious for a short while, which was just as well because it was a bitterly cold night and if he had lain there for very long he would certainly have suffered from hypothermia. As soon as he came round, he had phoned his nearest neighbour – another of the Stewart cousins, I think – and got help. As it happened, nothing had been taken, but the use of violence was frightening.

"I'm worried about Holti," Lyle told me over the phone. "He lives alone up there on Caldbrae, and he's not as young as he was."

I had the four bairns in my bothy at the time. Malcolm had offered to teach Duncan some of his whittling techniques, and they had decided they all wanted to learn. They had salvaged wood from my beach before lunch, and now the four of them were sitting round my range with Malcolm, making clothes pegs and littering my floor with wood shavings.

Of course, they had heard about Holti.

"'O would 'it a' old man on the 'ead like that?" Marigold was indignant. "Just for some neeps and spuds!"

"My mam says he ought not to be living on his own, at his age," Alana offered. "She wouldn't mind him coming over to us in a few years, when I'm out of her hair. He's Pap's second cousin, or something."

"I bet he wouldn't come!" Andy remarked. "How many old people do you know who move in with family on En-Somi?"

"Is this all right, Malcolm?" Marigold was holding out a rather neat peg for my partner to inspect. "I wouldn't want to move in with no second cousin," she added sagely, "if I'd been living all on me own for years!"

"*Nei*," Duncan agreed. "When you're used to your own ways."

"It would be better if someone moved in with 'im," Marigold suggested. "Then 'e'd still be boss of 'is own 'ome!"

"*Aja.*" The bairn was right, of course. "But it's not that easy. Holti's bairns left the island years ago. One's in Australia, the other's in – I'm not sure – over near Stranraer? Somewhere on the west coast, anyhow."

"Quincy and Mo," said Marigold.

"Who are Quincy and Mo?" asked Andy.

"Those two *un-fedii* who Harris was standing up for in that fight," Alana explained.

"What about Quincy and Mo?" Duncan had stopped whittling and was looking at Marigold with one eyebrow raised.

"Quincy and Mo 'as nowhere to live," the bairn explained. "'Olti needs some young'uns around 'im. Didn't you tell me, Marie, what 'Olti said in that meeting – the meeting we never went to, that 'e could do with some young ones around? And I seen Quincy fight Charlie once, when we was slaves, and 'e would've won too, but Frankie stopped 'em. And 'e weren't as big then as 'e is now."

Duncan was impressed. "You're a genius!" he told Marigold. "Do you think they would? Move in with Holti, I mean?"

"Do you think Holti would have them?" I queried, but I must admit, I was impressed too.

★★★

The *Oyrod*, the island council, had asked Lyle and Mirren to meet with them in closed session. They were worried about the escalating crime rate. Well, we all were. Lyle had fitted a lock onto the door of his parents' bothy when he and Verity went over for Sunday lunch. "There's been a bothy there since before anyone can remember," he told us. "And this is the first time there's ever been a lock on the door. The storehouse, maybe, but not the bothy…"

It was quite a crowd that went over to Storhaven with Lyle. Elise wanted to film an interview with Holti and Harris was there, ostensibly to protect her. My four, Duncan, Marigold, Alana and Andy, all wanted to persuade Quincy and Mo to move out to Holti's place, and to talk Holti into having them. Harry was hoping to have a word with Charlie. They took Malcolm's ponies and trap. The ponies needed the exercise, and several of the group were experienced enough to drive them.

Malcolm and I enjoyed a quiet day at home. It was almost April by then. Malcolm was sitting in front of my bothy making the finishing touches to the boat. He had a tin of quick-drying eco-friendly yacht varnish at his elbow, and was deciphering instructions written in Norwegian as he went along. I had cleaned out the chickens and had a long Zoom call with one of Duncan's teachers. It would be several years yet before he would take his Nationals but the online teaching staff were keen that their students should have regular experience of exam-taking. I gave them Sigrid's contact details. It would be best, I thought, if the Hus bairns took their end-of-term tests in the school, even if it meant giving the younger ones a day or two off.

It was pleasant, being alone with Malcolm. There had been a time, only a year or two earlier, when I might have spent days without any human company and not minded at all. I had never felt lonely, but I had to admit to myself as I made Duncan's bed (he was supposed to make it himself, of course!) that having him home was better than speaking to my son once a week over the internet, and the thought of not seeing Malcolm every day was awful. I folded Duncan's pyjamas and put them under his pillow, and was just thinking about lunch, when I heard voices outside.

"Marie!" Malcolm had put his head round the door. "Is there any coffee brewing?"

I slid the door across Duncan's sleeping place and went to see who our visitor was.

It was Jarvis. For a moment I almost couldn't believe it. Then Malcolm said, "Here's Marie, Jarvis!"

"And you's Malcolm!" Jarvis sounded pleased with himself. "You was wearing them same things when I saw you on top of the 'ill."

"I probably was," agreed my partner. "It's nice of you to call. Would you like some coffee? Or tea, maybe? Anyhow, do sit down."

Jarvis didn't join Malcolm on the bench but sat on the edge of the slated area, his bare feet in the grass. "I bin watching you!" he announced, "To be sure 'o lives 'ere. You got a boy, and them uver kids comes over a lot, and Marigold. But only you is 'ere today."

He seemed completely unashamed of his spying activities, as if it hadn't occurred to him that watching one's neighbours like that might not be quite acceptable behaviour.

"*Aja*," I agreed. "Tea or coffee?"

"I 'ad coffee once," he answered. "In one of them camps. It were bitter. We never drank no coffee when I were a kid. Just Coke and beer. But you don't drink no Coke on this island. Ain't never seen a can of the stuff anywhere!"

"You might prefer tea, then," suggested Malcolm. "Me too, I think." Then he called through to me, "Tea for both us, please – with lots of sugar!"

I sat next to Malcolm and the three of us wrapped our hands round our warm mugs. Every time the sun went behind a cloud it felt really cold. A sheep, with purple marking identifying it as one of Jamie's, wandered up to look at us but scuttled away when Jarvis changed his position. For a few minutes nobody spoke.

Jarvis slurped his tea. "This is good!" he offered. "Real tea!"

"It's what attracted me to Marie," Malcolm lied. "The fact that she knows how to brew a pot of tea!"

"Is you going fishing?" Jarvis asked, nodding towards the newly varnished boat. "That sea's dangerous, you know."

"*Aja*," Malcolm agreed. "It can be dangerous. You have to know what you're doing."

There was a brief silence while we all sipped – or gulped – our drinks.

"I'm glad you decided to visit," Malcolm said. "Is there anything in particular that brought you here?"

"I walked!" answered Jarvis, misunderstanding. "Ain't no other way to get around except feet and 'orses, and I ain't got no 'orse."

"I see that." Malcolm sounded mildly interested. "So, did you come for any particular reason? I mean, we're really pleased to see you, but did you want some help with anything?"

"Yeah – well, no!" Jarvis hesitated. "I just fought, well – you know! If there's trouble – cops and all that 'assle… I just 'oped that if I asked, you'd keep an eye out for that little Marigold. You know, keep 'er safe. If there's trouble."

I felt really touched. My first impressions of Jarvis had clearly been quite wrong – or, anyhow, over simplified.

"Of course we will!" I exclaimed.

"More tea?" offered Malcolm, getting up to refill the pot. Then, as he poured our second cups and ladled more sugar into Jarvis's mug, he asked, "Do you think there will be trouble?"

"Oh, yeah!" There was not a shadow of a doubt in Jarvis's mind. "There's already trouble, and there'll be more. Them bosses… And don't let 'em 'urt that vicar lady, nor that fella what says 'e's the fuzz but ain't really. Them's good people!"

"But who would want to hurt them?" I asked.

"It's always the same people what 'urt uvers!" Jarvis told us. "You knows that!"

Then he rose to his feet, and left, heading off down towards my beach.

"The same people?" ruminated Malcolm. "It's always the same people who hurt others? Who do you think he means?"

"Well, it was the *harkrav* who hurt the refugees," I commented.

"*Aja*! But not *all* the *harkrav*!" Malcolm pointed out. "Just five or six of them, and they've all been arrested. They're not on the island anymore!"

"But he sounded as if he knew what he was talking about," I said. "He was warning us, wasn't he? And asking for our help to protect the people he's fond of."

"I wish," said Malcolm as he tested the varnish to see if it was dry, "that I had some idea about what is going on! Honestly, life was more straightforward in Edinburgh!"

★★★

"Mission accomplished!" shouted Duncan as he burst into the bothy not long after sunset. "And, Mam, did you know that Marigold can count to a hundred in dialect? She couldn't even count to a hundred in English when I first met her!"

"Wow! That is impressive!" I exclaimed. "So, what do you mean, about mission accomplished?"

My son threw his jacket towards the coat pegs, then sighed when it fell on the floor. He padded over in his stockinged feet to retrieve it. "Quincy and Mo are going to stay at Holti's. He really liked the idea, and so did Mo, but Quincy was worried that Holti would tell them what to do all the time. Holti says he won't, but in the end they agreed to have a trial period."

"That's great!" I was really pleased. The two refugees were still young, and I hated to think of them dossing in the kirk when almost everyone else in their group had found somewhere permanent to live.

"*Aja,*" my son said, leaning against the breakfast bar and watching me peeling potatoes. "Only just in time, really. Storhaven's horrible now, Mam. There's writing on walls saying things like 'refugees go home' and 'island for the islanders'. And someone realised that Harry was *un-fed* and yelled across the track that he had no right to be here, and one of the nurse's bairns told him to leave off, and they spat at her! Oh, and where's Malcolm?"

"Down on the beach," I told Duncan. "He's finished the boat."

"Oh, brilliant! I think I'll go down and see for myself!"

"Tell him dinner'll be ready in twenty minutes," I called, as Duncan slammed the door behind him.

★★★

Malcolm and I were lying in bed, talking. Once again, we had woken early, but we didn't feel like jumping up and climbing Fyrtarn Fjell again. Rain was beating against the shutters and the noise from the wind turbine told me it was a north-wester.

"I read once," Malcolm told me, stretching comfortably and putting one hand behind his head, "there's research that shows that the bigger the income gap between the wealthiest in a society and the poorest, the higher the crime rate. There's a direct correlation."

"It makes sense," I commented.

"I think it's true of health outcomes too – the greater the disparities in income, the greater the differences in longevity."

"What, even in countries like ours, where everyone has access to health care?"

"I think so. *Aja.* So this author claimed. Backed her argument up with some very convincing statistics, too."

"Well…" I was considering our situation on En-Somi. "I don't suppose the rich have got any richer. Not on the island. But I'm sure the poor have got poorer – quite a lot poorer."

"*Aja!*" Malcolm gave a contented yawn. "So why haven't we seen increased crime on our side of the island?"

"We have!" I pointed out. "Not violence, thank goodness. But a lot of theft!" Then I added, "I don't think it's Jarvis, doing the stealing."

"I hope it isn't," Malcolm replied. "I'm getting to quite like that man. To be honest, I'm struggling to make any sense of the situation. I thought at first it was just hungry people getting desperate, and I was rather shocked that people would take food from neighbours who they had known all their lives. I wondered if it was our newcomers, but we were all in and out of their homes working on renovations, and none of us saw any sign of anything purloined. But since we've started receiving these food gifts, and we know it's stolen food… Well, it just doesn't add up."

I grunted my agreement. "Then there's the theft of the harnessing for Robert's ponies," I added. "That doesn't fit any sort of pattern!"

"Tea, you two?" It was Duncan, standing at the foot of the steps up to our sleeping platform. "I slept so well last night. I hadn't got a clue this storm had even arrived until I woke up just now!"

CHAPTER 26

There was a lot to talk about in the *fi'ilsted* the following Friday. There had been another successful meal – some sort of bean casserole and baked potatoes, I think, and chocolate biscuits (a rare treat), sent over by Verity's family along with all the baby stuff. The fun of the event, though, had been dampened a bit because when Lyle came back from his meeting with the *Oyrod* he had brought those ominous brown envelopes with the next quarter's tax bills. A lot of the *bondii* had found out how to log into the new website by then and they were forewarned, but not everyone.

Most people drifted over to the *fi'ilsted* when we had finished eating. Petter had a whole system of bartering going on to avoid asking people to use their precious cash, so most households could manage one round of drinks before they headed off home. It was lighter by then, of course. The sun wouldn't set until after seven, and even then there'd be a long, slow dusk.

Sigrid's daughter Kenna had come over with her baby, and was planning to stay in Hus all weekend. Mackerel fishing was about to start and a lot of the men on the east of En-Somi were relaunching their boats after the winter. The mackerel wouldn't be at their best yet, but on the other hand the sea was still too rough for rowing out very far, and the boats hardly had to go out any distance before they started casting for mackerel, so it was relatively safe.

It was good to have Kenna there. We had appointed her to keep the accounts of the fund we had set up to help people with their tax bills. Of course, she could have joined us via her computer, but people liked to go across and have quiet words with her. Most *bondii* were deeply unhappy about the thought of getting into debt, even if our bankers were family and friends.

It was a pretty wild night, although the storm of earlier in the week had calmed a bit. Or, rather, it had passed us and headed towards the Continent, where it would cause absolute havoc. A lot of the bairns were playing outside on the track or in and out of the ruined bothy next to Bothan Ros. A few of the younger ones were seated on laps or on the narrow window seat, and Olaf was telling one of his unlikely tales to a group of older men, who must have heard all his stories dozens of times before.

I wouldn't say there was an air of gloom. It wasn't the way it had been the first time we received those huge tax demands, but the atmosphere was definitely subdued. People were talking in small groups seated around tables, or leaning up against the bar. Then Petter rang the bell they kept (and still keep) on the bar, and called us all to order.

"Well, *En-Som-in-Fedii*," he began, "we've made it through the first quarter and here we are again!" He waved his own brown envelope in the air.

"*Aja*, by the skin of our teeth!" grumbled someone.

"No thanks to the thief!" added someone else.

"No thanks to the *Oyrod*, either!"

"But thanks to the *huldufolk*!" murmured someone at the table next to ours.

Perhaps Petter heard that last remark. "Whoever else we feel we need to thank," he told us, "we definitely have a debt of gratitude to Kenna. She spent the whole morning on the new *Oyrod* website, and she's done her maths, and here she is, to give us an update on our funds!"

Kenna passed her wee one to Sigrid and stood. I wouldn't say that she was normally blessed with a happy face but when she smiled Kenna looked so like her mother I couldn't help liking her. She was smiling now.

"Well," she told the listening crowd, "I'll tell you the good news first, so that nobody needs to be worrying. Our fund is fine. It's true that we have less in reserve than we started with, but there's enough money to cover everyone's bills."

"How can that be?" someone wondered, sounding doubtful.

Kenna looked down at her tablet. "Several different things have worked together in our favour," she told us. "A number of you have relatives on the mainland or in Norway, and they have helped a lot. The Alba film crew have donated all the profits from the sale of their documentary abroad to our fund – we're lucky the BBC don't own that film or we wouldn't have seen a penny of it!"

There was a gentle ripple of laughter at that. Everyone knew that the BBC was strapped for cash.

"Well done, Elise!" called out someone from the back, and the people nearest our young reporter patted her on the back, or nodded their thanks.

"*Aja*, that film has really been useful," Kenna smiled across the room. "We've had two very generous donations that have helped a lot, and several much smaller gifts, which all add up…"

"And on the downside?" asked Robert.

"On the downside," Kenna explained, "there hasn't been any fundraising on Lerwick because the bairns aren't at school there anymore, and the folk on Shetland have problems enough of their own with all these storms. And then there's the question of our newcomers."

"*Nei!*" It was Robert again. "We'll not be blaming them for anything!"

Lyle stepped in at that point. "Quite right!" he agreed, rising to his feet. "But the new *nasyoni* and I had a meeting with the *Oyrod* earlier this week. The relocation funds stop on 1 May. Up until now we've used those funds to help with the costs of renovations, and they are more or less complete now, and to provide basic groceries. So, from 1 May our new neighbours will have to feed themselves, and we all know that, despite their best efforts, they're not going to find that easy!"

Verity stayed seated but her voice rang out clearly enough. "So we'll need to look out for each other even more than we have been doing!" she said.

Then Olaf was on his feet. His eyes twinkled as he smiled at us, and I wondered, for a moment, what he found so amusing in our situation. Things weren't going to get any easier.

"So let battle commence!" he exclaimed. "The battle for our better natures! The battle to see generosity defeat selfishness! The battle not just to survive but to survive with grace!"

"The battle to defeat the *harkrav*!" called out young Harris, and everyone cheered.

★★★

"But did they call you over to Storhaven just to tell you that?" Duncan was indignant. "They could have emailed or phoned to let you know that the allowances of the newcomers were about to end! It's not as if you can just pop in and be back with Verity ten minutes later!"

There were six of us in my bothy but it didn't feel crowded. Duncan and Marigold were sitting on the edge of the sleeping platform, their tablets to hand, their legs dangling over the edge. Verity was lying on the settle, Lyle and I were in the rocking chairs and Malcolm was on the floor by the range. The bairns and Verity were drinking dandelion tea. I must admit that the rest of us had opened the last of the Edinburgh gins brought over by Malcolm's daughter.

"*Nei*," Lyle answered. "That was just a side issue, although I thought Blair Munro seemed unnecessarily pleased that our new friends would soon have to fend for themselves. *Nei*, what they really wanted to talk about was the crime."

"Well, it's a big issue," Malcolm commented. "And, for once, the *Oyrod* did the right thing, asking to talk the situation over with you and Mirren."

"Humph!" Lyle was unimpressed. "If they had wanted to 'talk it over' with us they would indeed have been doing the right thing, but that isn't what happened!"

"Now, why am I surprised?" Malcolm queried, and sipped his drink.

"First of all, they expressed their displeasure with Mirren. Fin Murray said he was speaking for all of them when he told her that they had hoped she might be able to get on top of the situation. He said that he understood that the *bondii* can be difficult to police, and that having some of the dregs of the English refugee crisis foisted onto the island was bound to make for difficulties, but things had actually got worse since her arrival, not better!"

"What's *foisted*?" Marigold wanted to know. "Jarvis was afraid I would be foisted, that time I ran away."

Duncan swung his long, dangling leg sideways to give the lassie a gentle kick. "*Nei!*" he told her. "He thought you would be fostered. Taken away from your mam and paps and made to live in some other family!"

"So what's *foisted*?" the bairn persisted.

Duncan looked helplessly at Malcolm.

"*Foisted* means – well, handed to someone who doesn't want it."

"Sounds like the same thing to me!" announced Marigold, and finished her tea.

Lyle continued his story. "So once they had put Mirren firmly in her place – or, at least, tried to – they rounded on me and said that by all accounts things are no better over here in Hus. In fact, that Candy Williams woman said that she had heard that we are harbouring troublemakers, and that such action could only result in more trouble!"

"Is we harbouring troublemakers?" Marigold sounded as if that possibility was quite attractive.

"*Nei!*" Lyle was laughing. "It turned out that they were referring to Harris, and to his house-sitting!"

"Bothy-sitting," Marigold corrected, with a sigh.

"So, then what?" Duncan wanted to know.

"Well, so then they said that, as we had proven so ineffective, they had come to the conclusion that there needed to be a public meeting – or, actually, a series of public meetings. That Fin Murray said that, if the police couldn't control the situation, it was time that the people took responsibility for themselves."

"What are they hoping for?" Malcolm sounded scornful. "Are they planning to raise a militia?"

"They're planning something, that's for sure!" Lyle told us. "Verity, my love, you look exhausted! Do you want to go home?"

★★★

Sure enough, the message came round on social media, the *Oyrod* was planning a series of public meetings to discuss the crime surge. The first gathering was to be the coming Saturday in the kirk. Everyone with voting rights was welcome.

"Does I 'ave voting rights?" Marigold wanted to know.

"*Nei!* You're not thirteen yet!" Duncan was teasing her.

I looked at Malcolm, who had his tablet open on the website. "They say that only genuine islanders will be allowed to vote, and that outsiders are not welcome to these sessions, which will deal with issues peculiar to En-Somi. In other words, our newcomers aren't welcome!"

"I don't think they have the power to keep them away," I reminded my partner. "Anyone can watch the proceedings."

"They could make people feel pretty unwelcome," was Malcolm's grumbled response.

CHAPTER 27

We had a quiet week leading up to that first public meeting. The Easter break was due to begin that Thursday, but by general agreement we had our community meal on Friday, even though Good Friday is not supposed to be a feast day. We were not a very religious bunch, as I've mentioned before. At Malchi's suggestion we had fish, and there was some fresh-caught mackerel to add to the pot, although the plumpest fish arrive on our plates later in the year.

With Marigold still in school and the older three bairns studying online, most of that week was comfortably routine. Andy and Duncan were working together on an extra project for their Norwegian teacher, who was showing an interest in our dialect, but Alana was less concerned about language. Her fascination was ecology, I seem to remember, although she worked through several areas of interest before she eventually decided she wanted to be a human rights lawyer. But that was years later, and not part of the story I'm telling you now.

The general response of the *bondii* west of Fyrtarn Fjell to the holding of open meetings in Storhaven to discuss crime was of total disinterest.

"What, go all the way over there to hear them spouting off about falling standards?" Yanni more or less summed up the general feeling.

"I won't be told how to behave by an adulterer!" Robert was scornful. Most people had seen the look on poor Freya Munro's face when Blair had walked in on our Friday feast with Candy

Williams, and those who hadn't witnessed the occasion had certainly been told about it. Given that we all knew that Freya had donated food on at least one occasion, there was no doubting where our sympathies lay.

"Lyle and that Mirren woman is doing their best!" Rose felt the same as the rest of us. "Does they think the *nasyonii* just sits around doing nothing? If it 'adn't been for Lyle and 'is lot, we'd still be slaves! Weren't no posh *Oyrod* 'elping us!"

We were in the *fi'ilsted*, of course. It was Saturday morning, and the ferry had come in the day before, so people were collecting mail and packages from the village shop and dropping in on Malchi and Petter before they went home. People from the outlying bothies probably wouldn't see any but their nearest neighbours again until the new term started at the school, so they were willing to linger for an hour or so, despite all the work that needs to be done on the land at that time of year.

I was about to pay Petter for my coffee – I was one of the few *bondii* who still had actual currency – when Marigold put her head round the door.

"'As anyone seen Lyle or Verity?" she wanted to know. "There's a lady 'ere what wants to talk to 'em!"

"They've gone over to Fremdes Haven," Petter answered. "Show the 'lady' in, Marigold!"

Marigold turned and said something to the visitor, then said, "'Ere she is!" And behind Marigold, looking, I thought, rather shy, came Freya Munro.

At once there were warm smiles on several faces. "*Goddi morgoni!*" Petter greeted the woman almost formally. "Would you like some coffee? Have you come over on your own?"

Freya Munro had walked just a few steps into the *fi'ilsted* and was standing looking, I thought, quite distressed.

"I wanted to see... I hoped... Is Verity around?" she asked. "Or her husband?"

"*Nei*, they're over at Lyle's parents' place," Robert told the woman. "They won't be back 'til sunset. They borrowed my ponies and cart."

"O – Oh!" It was obvious that Freya Munro was unhappy, and none of us really knew her. I stepped forward.

"Are you in a hurry?" I asked. "We could go down to my place for coffee, if you'd like – and you can phone Lyle from there and talk to him. Or Verity, if you prefer."

"*Aja!*" Petter liked the idea. A *fi'ilsted* full of curious people is not a good place for someone in distress.

"Oh, thank you! I'm Freya Munro."

"*Aja*, we met briefly," I reminded her, as I put on my jacket. "That time when you brought over food for our meal. I'm Marie."

We made desultory conversation on the way down to my bothy. I could tell that she had something on her mind. To be honest, I thought she had probably left Blair Munro, and I didn't blame her at all. But where can a fleeing wife go on an island as small and remote as En-Somi? I guessed she had come to Hus hoping to find refuge with two of the few people she knew who weren't part of the close *harkrav* circle.

It turned out, though, that I was wrong. When we arrived at my bothy Malcolm and Duncan were getting ready to go down to the beach to try out the new boat. They were already dressed in their warm clothes and boots, and were performing routine checks on their life jackets.

"*Morgoni!*" Malcolm greeted her, and I read the surprise on his face. He held out his hand. "Malcolm McDough," he introduced himself.

"Good morning," responded Freya Munro, shaking hands. "I'm sorry to intrude. Your wife invited me… I was really looking for Verity or your police officer. Lyle?"

"It's their day off," Duncan told her. He didn't go in for formality. "They often leave Hus when Lyle isn't on duty. They'll be visiting friends, I should think. I'm Duncan." He smiled at the bemused woman in a friendly way.

"Hello, Duncan…" Freya Munro still had that lost look about her.

Malcolm was always quick to sum up situations. "Well, we're off now. I want to catch the tide. Come on, Duncan, bring the rods, will you?" He kissed me on the cheek and they were gone.

I ushered the woman inside. She saw me remove my footwear and took hers off too. She was wearing stout walking boots, and I guessed she had come over on foot. It's a long way for somebody who isn't used to the exercise.

"Tea or coffee?" I asked.

"If it's no bother…" She was standing in the middle of the room, looking around. "What a charming little cottage – bothy!" she said. She walked over to the bookcase against the east wall, and looked at my photo of Duncan. "Is he your only one?" she asked.

"*Aja*," I answered. "But he's kept me on my toes!"

"And have you always lived here?" she wondered. "These bothies always look so small from the outside, but really…"

"I came here with my husband," I told her. "I didn't even know of the existence of this island until I met him at university!"

"I guessed he was an educated man," Freya told me, wondering over to look out of my west-facing window. I realised she was talking about Malcolm but it didn't seem like quite the moment to clarify the situation.

I poured the tea and handed Freya Munro her mug. "Sugar? Do sit down!"

She perched on the edge of her rocking chair, still looking ill at ease. "Thank you!" She was quiet for a moment. Then, "You've got a wonderful view," she commented. "I always thought we had the best location on En-Somi – over on Floirean's Cnoc, I mean, but this is stunning."

"You get the morning sun," I told her. "But we get wonderful sunsets." I thought it was time to get to the point. "Mrs Munro," I said, "would you like some privacy while you phone Lyle? I can go outside. I want to check on my chickens anyhow!"

"No! No!" She suddenly looked animated. "And please call me Freya. No… The thing is… Can I talk to you? I mean, aren't you friends with Verity and the police officer? Then you can tell me whether I need to intrude on their day off."

"*Aja!* Of course! If that's what you want!"

Finally, she sat back in the rocking chair and took a sip of her tea. "Well… you obviously know that I'm married to Blair…"

Here we go! I thought. "*Aja.*"

"Mm, well, he's not a good husband, but that's neither here nor there! I dare say you know about his current affair with Candy Williams? I'm guessing the whole island knows. He doesn't really try to keep it a secret…" She stared out through the window for a moment or two. "I'll leave him one of these days," she said in a matter-of-fact tone. "When I'm ready. But that isn't what I've come to talk to Verity about."

That was a surprise to me, and intriguing, but I didn't say anything. I just nodded for her to go on.

"Well, of course, living with a man like Blair, and seeing other people who live on Floirean's Cnoc, I hear a few things…"

"I suppose so," I encouraged her.

"They really hate having these refugees here," she told me. "It was fine when they were all over at the old airport. We all knew they were there, of course. Did you realise that? Half the people on the Cnoc had shares of sorts in that drone company. It was a very lucrative business, and not just because of the free labour… But now that the workers are living in the community, and the drone business has closed for the moment, well – you can see how it changes everything! Instead of being people with no rights, they're suddenly entitled to everything everyone else on En-Somi has. You know, homes and education and health care… And those things cost money. And we're the ones who have got the money…"

"Well…" How was I going to explain to her that because of the changes to the tax laws it was us, the *bondii*, who were going to foot the bill for the newcomers?

I suppose she got there before me. "No!" she said. "I imagine you're thinking that when the *Oyrod* started to tax you on the land you farm they were shifting all the expense to you, but, to be honest, your increased payments won't cover the costs. We'll end up subsidising the refugees too. They just wanted to punish you, because you prevented them from getting rid of those people as soon as their existence was discovered. They like to punish people, my husband and his friends!"

"But…" I was taking it all in. So, many of the *harkrav* had known about the refugees all along? "You *knew*!" I exclaimed. "All that time… for ten years those people lived out there at the old airport, and you all knew it?"

"It does sound pretty despicable," Freya Munro admitted, and looked a little ashamed. "I suppose we thought… well, I thought… you know, they had to live somewhere, and work somewhere, and people like that… you know, not everyone can live as we do! Not everyone would want to. I always thought, well, there are lots of people worse off than them! Blair assured me that they were well fed. Poppy Fox-Drummin started her nurse's training before she met Dom, and she provided their health care. I just thought… Well, we didn't talk about it much but I assumed they were happy enough!"

I felt a surge of anger. How could anyone be so blind, or so callous?

"They're still determined to get rid of them," Freya continued. "The refugees, I mean. They won't stand for you *bondii* getting in the way. That's what I came over to tell Verity. They've got a scheme… But I've seen what you've achieved over here, and I think they're making a mistake. So, I thought I'd warn you… and I wouldn't mind doing a little punishing myself!"

"I think you need to talk to Lyle and Verity," I told her. I was thinking, *Verity definitely won't go along with the idea of punishing anyone. That's really not her style!*

"Yes, maybe…" She was hesitating again. "But I'd rather

talk to someone face to face. I've been thinking about telling someone, planning what to say, all the time I was walking over here. And if Lyle won't be back until this evening... and I can't always get away. In fact, I really must be back by mid-afternoon. Blair's... well, he's got a busy evening coming up. Would you mind if I told you about their plans? Then at least there'll be someone over here who knows. The thing is, they're starting tonight..."

"That's fine," I said. "I can speak to Lyle and Verity this evening."

"You're not going to this meeting then? I mean the one the *Oyrod* has called? Isn't anyone from over here going?"

"Not as far as I know," I told her.

"You're playing into their hands!" Freya said, looking dejected again.

"Are we?" I asked. "Honestly, Mrs Munro – I mean Freya – what more can they do to us?"

"Oh, quite a lot!" Once again she stared out of my window towards the clouds and the churning sea. "This is their plan: they're stirring up trouble all over the island—"

"Not here!" I interrupted.

"No, not here," she agreed. "Or, anyhow, not yet. But everywhere else. They've managed to persuade half the population that all these thefts and the violence are the result of the refugees coming into town. I talked to our police officer – you know, the new one? She told me that there's no evidence that it's them who are responsible, but do you realise that they're the only ones who haven't had break-ins? I mean, that tells you something, doesn't it?" She looked at me, waiting for my response.

"Well," I said, "it could tell you that there's nothing to steal in their bothies?"

"Yes. Yes, I know. That's what the police officer said... Anyhow, my lot – I mean Blair and his cronies – they're getting everyone stirred up, blaming the refugees. Their plan is to hold these public meetings, and to try to get the majority of islanders so worried and angry about the dangers the refugees pose, that in the end they'll vote to have them removed. It's the only way, you see, that the vote to keep them can be overturned."

"Ah! *Aja*, I see!" I suppose until then I had underestimated how devious some people can be, as well as how desperate the *harkrav* might be to get rid of the newcomers. It had been at a public meeting of the *Oyrod* more than a year earlier that the decision had been made to allow the refugees to stay. It hadn't occurred to me that it could be overturned. "Perhaps we should have decided to go to their meeting!"

Freya Munro gave a sort of mirthless laugh. "Oh, they're banking on you not turning up! You western *bondii* have been the main source of their problems all along!" She frowned. "I don't really think you can do anything about it," she told me. "They're used to getting their own way, you know. I've seen it over and over again. And things have already gone quite a long way on my side of the island. I just thought you ought to know…"

"Thank you!" I said. She was right, we needed to know. But what could any of us do about it?

CHAPTER 28

I walked back up to the main track with Mrs Munro. She told me about her bairns, one in school in Hampshire, the other at Exeter University. "I'm not close to them," she told me. "We sent them away to school as soon as each one turned eight. It wasn't my idea, of course, but Blair didn't want them to pick up En-Somi accents, and to be honest I don't think he much liked having them around. They're turning out like their father. Well, I suppose that was always the plan, but I was young when I met Blair, and I thought he knew what was best. And I've had a good life, I suppose, all things considered."

It sounded pretty grim to me. "What do you do all day?" I wondered, and only when I'd spoken did it occur to me that it was rather a rude question.

"Oh, this and that!" she replied. "There are dinner parties. We have barbecues down on the beach in the summer, and Blair keeps a little sailing dingy in Storhaven harbour, although we hardly ever go out in it now, the weather's become too unpredictable. I play the piano – not professionally, nothing like that! But it keeps me occupied. And we try to get away three or four times a year. We were hoping to drop in on the Edinburgh Fringe last summer, but then there was all that flooding..."

We had reached the track up to the fjell by then. "Do you know your way from here?" I checked.

"Yes! Thank you so much! I feel better for having spoken to you!"

And, indeed, Mrs Munro did look much happier. An unkind

thought occurred to me. *She's passed the problem on to someone else, and now she doesn't have to think about it anymore!*

★★★

Back in my bothy, the first thing I did was to phone Lyle. His phone was turned off. Of course, it was; it was his day off! So I tried Verity.

"*Hei*, Marie!" Her voice was a bit muffled. "Is everything all right?"

"Fine… well, actually, something's come up. Where are you?"

"Just east of Fyrtarn Fjell," Verity answered. "You'll need to speak up – the wind is incredible here!"

"Right!" I tried to speak loudly and clearly. "Freya Munro came over, looking for you," I explained. "And she told me something you really need to know – you and Lyle."

There was a muffled sound at the other end, then Lyle came on the phone. "We can't really hear you," he said. "I'm guessing it's important? Shall we come down to you? We can be there in… well, say, half an hour at the most!"

I walked down to the beach. I could see Duncan and Malcolm in the boat just round to the north of my bay, where my newly exposed rocks created a calmer patch of sea. They were sitting back-to-back in the little boat, both with rods in their hands. Even in the comparative shelter the boat seemed to me to be rocking wildly.

"Malcolm!" I shouted, as loudly as I could. "Duncan!"

Of course, they couldn't hear me. There were waves breaking against rocks and all the rushing and heaving sounds of sea in a strong wind. Then Duncan, who was facing more in my direction, saw me. He waved happily and said something to Malcolm. I saw him look over his shoulder and say something back. Then they reeled their lines in, picked up the oars and started rowing to the shore.

I watched them, feeling anxious although I had seen *bondii* manoeuvring these little boats countless times. They had to row out a bit to navigate round the rocky outcrop that had been deflecting the worst of the current, and I found myself holding my breath as the little boat rose and dipped in the swell. Then they were rowing in, Malcolm jumped out and pulled the boat up onto the pebbles, and Duncan climbed out.

"*Hei*, Mam! That was great!" he told me. "Although we didn't catch much! It's too early, really. Malcolm made me throw back the puny ones!"

Malcolm was pulling the little vessel further up the beach and turning her over in the grass. He took the oars – we would keep them in the storehouse – and Duncan carried their fishing rods and a bucket with a few rather sad-looking fish in the bottom.

"And what did our Freya Munro want?" Malcolm asked. "In trouble with her husband?"

"Not really." It was hard to talk while we climbed up to my bothy. "She came to tell me something pretty important, actually. I've phoned Verity – they're on their way."

"Good!" Duncan liked a bit of excitement. "A council of war!"

★★★

"But, once she had told me all that, she seemed much happier," I told everyone, as we sat round the range.

Lyle and Malcolm both looked grim. "I've heard of people lacking empathy," Malcolm exclaimed, "but to know that those people were over in the old airport for all that time, and to think that it was all right… I thought I'd come across a few fairly hard-hearted politicians in my time, but this…"

"It's not something I've ever understood," Lyle agreed. "We did a unit on human trafficking when I was training. It's as if the traffickers don't recognise that they're dealing with other human beings."

"They must have hated you four," Duncan commented, "when you enacted the thirteenth amendment!"

"Pardon?" Lyle looked confused.

"Freed the slaves!" Duncan told us, laughing.

"*Aja*," Malcolm agreed. "I don't think we realised what we'd done, to be honest. I'm glad we did it, of course, but now I realise we haven't finished the job. We can't have the refugees removed from En-Somi!"

The grin was wiped off Duncan's face at once. "*Nei*, we can't!" he agreed. "We've got to stop the *Oyrod*! Is it too late to go over to Storhaven tonight, for that meeting of theirs?"

Lyle glanced out of my west-facing window. It was another two hours at least before sunset, but the meeting was due to start an hour earlier than that, at seven. "We could make it easily," he calculated, "but is that the best plan? What would we do if we were there? Feelings are running high in Storhaven. If we start to speak in support of the refugees, it'll just cause more trouble. You haven't been over there recently, have you Marie?"

Duncan was looking deadly serious now. "I have!" he said. "Lyle's right. We need to find a different way of defeating the *harkrav*."

I looked across at my son and felt proud.

"Of course," commented Verity, "it would completely take the wind out of their sails if we found out who *is* responsible for the theft and the violence! In fact, that could solve half the problems on En-Somi!"

Lyle sighed. "You're right, my love," he agreed. "But neither Mirren nor I have any idea who's behind all this. We've been in and out of so many bothies in the last six weeks, and never seen any sign of stolen goods. And it's getting to the point that almost every islander is a victim. It doesn't leave anyone to be the villains except the newcomers, and they have nothing to gain and everything to lose – and, anyhow, we can be sure they haven't been in receipt of stolen goods!"

"We need to catch them at it!" suggested Duncan. "Whoever these thieves are."

"*Aja*, so we do," Malcolm agreed. "But how?"

"We could ask everyone to set a watch on their bothies and storehouses," I suggested, a bit lamely.

"But, Mam!" Duncan pointed out the obvious. "If we did that, the thief would know what we were doing!"

"And when Holti came across one of the villains, he was hit over the head," Lyle reminded us. "We could just be putting people in danger."

We were all silent, thinking over the problem.

"We'll have to do something," Verity said. "And we can't let people know about it. We could start watching bothies at night, couldn't we? We might catch the thief."

"It would just be pot luck," Duncan pointed out. "How many bothies are there on En-Somi? And we're spread out all over the moors!"

Suddenly an idea came to me. It was so obvious that I don't know why none of us had thought of it before. "We don't need to wait for the thief to strike!" I pointed out. "We just need to catch the person who's giving us food. They know where they're getting it from, after all!"

"*Aja*! Of course! Why didn't we think of that before?" Malcolm looked at me approvingly.

"I was hoping we could leave that person alone," Verity told us. "Whoever it is obviously doesn't want their generosity known about. I'd like to respect that."

"But they're giving us stolen food!" I pointed out.

"*Aja*, I know." Verity looked worried. "But that doesn't mean they're stealing it!"

"Or he or she," put in Duncan, unhelpfully. "We don't know it's a group of people!"

"If they're not stealing it, they can tell us where it's coming from!" said Malcolm. "We don't need to give whoever it is a hard time! After all, they've been pretty good to us! We just need to place a watch on the *fi'ilsted*, find out who this kind person is, promise them our silence in exchange for information about who the thief is, thank them warmly and let them go!"

"Easy-peasy," commented my son.

"Right!" Lyle sounded pleased. "So now we have a plan! If it's all right with you, I'll phone Mirren. And we'll need to talk to Malchi and Petter. But, other than that, let's keep this to ourselves."

"All of it?" Duncan sounded disappointed. "Even the bit about the *harkrav* knowing all along that there were slaves at the old airport?"

"All of it!" Malcolm said firmly. "For the time being."

CHAPTER 29

Petter saw the wisdom of our plan immediately but Malchi was reluctant to go along with it.

"Someone's playing Robin Hood," he told us. "We couldn't have fed people for the last couple of months or more without their help. They'd let us know who they are if they wanted us to know!"

"Not quite Robin Hood," I pointed out. "Didn't Robin Hood steal from the rich to give to the poor? This person's stealing from the poor too!"

"We don't know that they're the thief!" Malchi objected.

"Well, I think we do!" I pointed out. "Because we've found our own provisions returned to us!"

"There's another problem with the plan, though." Petter was leaning on the bar, frowning. "Do you remember the time we were given the duck? In those big catering tins? Well, after that I decided I wanted to find out who our benefactor was. You didn't want me to, did you, Malchi? But, anyhow, I stayed in the kitchen with the lights off, for two nights in a row. They just didn't turn up."

"*Nei*," Malchi sounded almost sulky. "Because they don't want to be discovered. The donations were left in the school porch that week."

Verity, ever the peacemaker, addressed Malchi's concerns. "But if we give you our word that we won't tell anyone who's donating the food, unless that person is happy for us to tell, would you object too much to us trying to catch them?"

"*Nei*, of course not, not really," agreed Malchi. Then the sulkiness was gone and he gave Petter one of those glowing smiles. "I know you won't hurt anyone!" Then he glanced around our circle and explained, "I broke a few laws to get here, to the UK, you know. There was no other way. So I sympathise with a fellow outlaw, if this is what they feel they have to do!"

"It's all sounding like Robin Hood again!" commented my irreverent son. "When do we start?"

★★★

Our anonymous food deliveries had always arrived on Wednesday or Thursday nights. We wondered if our Robin Hood knew that we weren't planning a meal for the Friday following Easter, but apparently whoever it was had good information. No food arrived.

Then the new term started and, with it, another meal was planned. Mirren came over on the afternoon of the Wednesday, planning to stay a couple of nights in Lyle's office and to help us in our efforts at catching our benefactor. Elise, who was still officially living at the *fi'ilsted*, was spending a lot of time down at Malcolm's bothy with Harris, so we had been able to keep the whole thing a secret from her. We agreed that we would station ourselves strategically around Hus. Lyle was to sit in his darkened bothy window, where he could see the track that runs through the middle of the village. From the office, Mirren could see down the hill towards the summer harbour. Petter was again in the *fi'ilsted* kitchen but Malchi was going to sit at one of the windows in the bar area. Malcolm waited until Sigrid's light went out, and then placed himself in the shadow of the school porch. Duncan and I hid in Shona's goat stable until the shop lights were all extinguished, then we waited behind the mound that separates the shop land from Bothan Ross.

We waited and we waited. I enjoyed having Duncan with me.

At first he was very excited, and seemed like a younger version of himself, but he calmed down, and gradually boredom set in. I am a good sleeper, which is a real blessing, but it also means it is more of a struggle to stay awake all night. In the end, when my head kept nodding forward, Duncan whispered, "Let's have watches, like seamen! I'll take the first watch and wake you at about two." After that I dozed, and dreamt about sitting in a cold bath, and woke with a stiff neck.

No food was delivered. We met up for breakfast and agreed to try again the next night, and then we all went to our beds and slept.

That Thursday night, I remember, was much colder. There were no clouds, and the temperatures drop quickly so far north. Duncan and I spent some time stargazing, nudging each other and pointing to one constellation or another. We saw a shooting star, or it may have been space debris, and Duncan wanted to look it up on his phone, but I was worried in case our anonymous benefactor saw the light and stayed away. If they did, not only would we have failed to find out who they were and where the food was coming from but we would also be on short rations for the Friday meal.

When we started to see dull, grey light in the sky over towards the fjell, I woke Duncan and we walked down the track to Lyle's. Malcolm was just emerging from the school porch, and we saw Malchi's face at the window of the *fi'ilsted*. We realised that once again we had caught nobody.

Verity was cooking breakfast. Their chickens were laying well, and plates of omelettes and hash browns went down well after a long, cold night, but our spirits were low.

"It isn't working, is it?" Verity said, pouring tea.

"It seems not." Malcolm looked disappointed rather than depressed.

"We can try again next week," suggested Duncan.

"We definitely need to do something," agreed Mirren. "The

situation in Storhaven is getting worse. Are you keeping an eye on social media?"

We were, and we knew what she meant. Some quite outrageous things had been posted, reports of incidents that Mirren and Lyle knew had not occurred. There was even a picture that purported to be a photo of a refugee breaking into the empty home of the *harkrav* man Duncan, who was at that time in prison on the mainland, but it only took Mirren half an hour and some clever technical research to show that it had been Photoshopped. The original, which 'Champion' had obviously worked from, was actually a photograph of Mirren checking the security of the empty property. Not that the anti-refugee lobby were going to believe that!

For a while we sat around talking but getting nowhere. After two nights keeping watch in the cold, I suppose we were all reluctant to make a move, however welcoming our beds would be when we reached them. I think we were feeling low, too. Since it seemed that no food had been delivered, how would we manage the evening meal? We heard the sounds of bairns on the track as they made their way to school, and agreed it might be better not to be seen emerging from the *nasyonihuss* so early in the morning. We didn't want to raise questions in people's minds. The track would probably be empty once the bairns were in their lessons.

And then there was a sudden hammering on Lyle's door.

"Oh dear!" exclaimed Lyle as he wearily got to his feet. "I suppose that'll be another theft!"

He took two strides and opened the bothy door.

Marigold and Christian were standing there, both neatly dressed for school and looking as gleeful as any two wee bairns could ever look. "Lyle! Lyle!" Marigold exclaimed. "The *huldufolk* have come in the night. Come and see!" And, in her impatience, Marigold grabbed his hand to pull him outside.

Lyle laughed despite his tiredness. "All right! All right!" he told them. "Just let me put on some boots!"

The rest of us looked at each other, surprised and bemused. "I have to see this!" Verity remarked, pulling on her own boots, so we all followed Lyle and the bairns.

They were walking up the track towards the shop. "We was just meeting up to go to school," Marigold was telling Lyle. "We always meets in the ruins what are next to my bothy. We tests each other on our tables."

"What a good idea," Lyle answered. "Which one of you is best at maths?"

"We're both good," Christian responded. "We're joint top for our age."

"My goodness!" Lyle sounded impressed. "I don't think I've ever been joint top in anything!"

"We's going to get married when we's grown up," Marigold confided. "Isn't we, Christian?"

"*Aja*," Christian confirmed. "And we're going to have six bairns!"

By now the little group at the front had passed the shop, and were outside Marigold's home, Bothan Ros, but they just kept going, skipping with excitement. They pulled Lyle into the ruins. "Look! Look!" we could hear.

It took only a minute or two to catch up, and then there we all were, standing round a neat pile of packages stacked on the floor of the ruin.

"See!" Marigold was exultant. "It's them *huldufolk*! They brung us our Friday night meal!"

"So it would seem!" agreed Lyle. "Well, that's something to be thankful for!"

"Marigold," Duncan said, teasing the bairn. "I thought you were going to marry me when you grew up!"

Marigold looked at him scornfully. "I wants to marry someone my own age!" she proclaimed. "Ain't got no time for older men!"

Duncan, Malcolm and I discussed the situation as we walked home.

"We were only one bothy away from those ruins!" Duncan pointed out. "How could we not have heard anyone depositing all that food?"

Malcolm was thoughtful. "There's never been food left there before, has there?"

"*Nei*. It's always been left at the *fi'ilsted*, except that one time when Sigrid found it in the school porch."

"So our Robin Hood knew we were on the lookout," persisted my partner.

"They must have done," I agreed. "This well-wisher of ours isn't going to be very easy to catch!"

CHAPTER 30

That the meal on Friday was another great success more or less goes without saying. Marigold and Christian were, naturally enough, full of their discovery when they arrived at school, and by break time not only did all the bairns knew of the latest *huldufolk* visit but so did most of the parents, having received excited texts and phone messages from their offspring. There was more good food, more entertainment from Olaf and Elin, an Easter bonnet competition organised by Sigrid, which was, if I remember correctly, won by the daughter of a family living up on the moors towards Fremdes Haven, and a general air of relief because the April tax bills had been settled.

On the other hand, I think it is fair to say that Lyle, Verity, Malcolm and I were worried. The news from over in Storhaven was not good. The *Oyrod* had held their first public meeting and it had been well attended by the group who drank at the Viking's Rest and quite a few other islanders. Mirren had reported back to Lyle that the atmosphere was, in her words, toxic. The kirk had only been half full but the meeting was very noisy and, according to the new *nasyoni*, words and sentiments were expressed that were not at all appropriate for a space dedicated to public worship.

"That Candy Williams…" Lyle passed on to us. "Apparently she stood at the front and told everyone that she was afraid to go out alone at night, and Blair Munro claimed that he had been over here, to Hus, on something he called a peace mission, and had been greeted with nothing but hostility!"

"And Ingrid told me that they're blaming us, in Gamla Hus, for causing most of the trouble," Verity added. "Malcolm, you were mentioned by name!"

"So what was the outcome?" Malcolm wanted to know. "What are they planning to do?"

"I think they're taking it one step at a time," Lyle told us. "So far, they're just stirring up as much trouble as they can. Later, I suppose, they'll call for a vote on the question of the newcomers, but not yet. Not until they're confident about the outcome."

"That fits with what Freya told me," I agreed.

"It fits in with what Jarvis told us," said Malcolm thoughtfully. "He was sure that there's trouble on the way."

Verity sighed. "How can people be so devious?" she wondered. "If only they would just think for a minute…"

"Mirren feels as if we're sitting on a powder keg," Lyle added. "It wouldn't take much to trigger off some real trouble. She's worried about this coming Friday, because a ferry's due in and there'll be a lot of people in Storhaven. She's asked me to go over."

"I was planning to meet that ferry," Malcolm told us. "And you wanted to pick up some wool that Fenna had dyed, didn't you, Marie?"

"We could all go over," suggested Verity.

"It might be better if you stayed at home," Malcolm told her sympathetically. "It's safer over here…"

"*Aja*," Lyle backed him up. "And, if Marie is with us, Sigrid might want some help setting up for the meal." He smiled tenderly at his young wife, and we all knew that this was just an excuse. That he would want to protect Verity was natural, however… I looked at Verity to see how she was taking it. I wasn't sure she was the sort of woman who wanted to be cosseted, but I intercepted such a look of warmth between the two of them that I looked away, almost embarrassed.

Of course, Duncan and Marigold wanted to come too, but

we pointed out that they were needed to help with the cooking, and they accepted with good grace.

★★★

Now that we had given up, for the time being, on trying to catch our elusive doner, the next food contributions were deposited in the *fi'ilsted* storeroom again, so we left that morning confident of a good meal awaiting us on our return. There were four of us in Malcolm's cart: Malcolm driving of course, Lyle, Yanni (who wanted to see his brother) and me.

It was a beautiful day. The sky was clear and blue and, although it wasn't warm, it felt like spring. There were daffodils growing on the lower slopes of the fjell and the red campions were just beginning to come into flower. The grass was a bright green and there was a bird with a red breast, definitely not a robin, singing its heart out on the wall someone had once built to keep the sheep away from the steep slope down to the burn. It was hard to believe that there could be anything to be worried about as we travelled towards the small town we knew so well, where friends lived, where Malcolm had been at school. Yet Lyle had a grim cast to his face, and Yanni looked edgy, as if he wasn't quite at peace with the world. Nobody was saying very much, and in the silence I held the situation in the light, asking that truth and love would prevail again on our lonely island.

I might not have described the atmosphere as toxic the way the new *nasyoni* had, although the description was apt. The dialect word Marigold had used came into my mind. *Vòldliggi* means wild or rough and is usually used to describe the weather when a storm is on the way. There was something about the way people were clustered in groups down by the harbour, the way they put their heads close together when they spoke as if they had secrets. It was uncomfortable when people stopped talking as Malcolm and I walked past them, and it felt as if their gazes were following us. Mirren was talking to Tom, who had already hooked up the chains to stop people falling into the harbour, although the ferry was not yet anywhere in sight. I guessed that he was worried in case there was some pushing and shoving, in case someone fell in not quite accidentally.

Fenna was there, talking to Ingrid Fraser and looking nervous. She came over to me as soon as she saw me.

"*Hei*, Marie!" she greeted me, but I noticed that she glanced over my shoulder. I followed the direction of her gaze and saw three men watching us, their expressions anything but benign. "I can't stay," Fenna added, sounding slightly panicky. "I've got a lot to do; I'm going straight home. Here's the wool – the green looks really good but I think the red has too much orange in it."

She handed over a cotton bag about the size of a pillow case, and turned to leave.

"Fenna's parents have been burgled twice," Ingrid told me, watching the departing woman. "The second time, the thief took all the cash they had saved up to pay their April taxes. They don't have a bank account, you see. Traditional *bondii*."

"That's tough," I agreed. What was our island coming to?

Lyle had stopped to talk to Mirren, exchanging just a few words and rather grim smiles, before the two officers parted to station themselves on two sides of the harbour, leaving Tom standing at his post where any passengers would disembark. Malcolm left me with Ingrid and strolled across to Tom, looking relaxed, as if nothing were amiss. The two men talked for a few minutes and Malcolm laughed about something, then they separated as Tom took a call on his phone. Yanni was standing with Dougie Fraser, but the two men weren't talking. They were looking out to sea in the direction from which the ferry would arrive. Four *harkrav* men were standing apart from everyone else. I recognised Fin Murray and the faces of the others seemed familiar, although I couldn't put names to them. As I watched, Candy Williams joined the group and the tall man with the tweed cap casually put an arm across her shoulders. *Ah!* I thought. *Mr Williams, no doubt!* There were other huddles of people, all familiar from my trips to Storhaven, all people I would normally have spoken to in passing, with simple greetings or nods of acknowledgement, but all of whom looked tense or even angry now.

"We had graffiti sprayed onto our door last night," Ingrid told me, almost casually. "'No blacks, no Irish, no refugees.'."

"Ha!" I remarked. "Not very original!"

"*Nei*," my friend agreed. "But not very pleasant either." Then she seemed to cheer up a bit. "But I'm glad those two young ones are over at Holti's," she added, thinking, no doubt, of Mo and Quincy. "They're much safer away from all this, and I hated to think of Holti on his own after that attack. Your Duncan did a good job persuading them to give it a try."

"It wasn't just Duncan," I reminded her.

"*Aja*, I heard," Ingrid replied. "I saw him with his friends when Malcolm drove them over. I'm guessing one of them is Shona and Patrick's lass? You can tell by that amazing blonde hair! And the wee one? Someone told me she's a Stewart, but I can't place her."

I laughed. "Therein lies a tale," I answered. "But yes, she's a Stewart sure enough!"

A general stir among several different groups told us that the ferry had appeared. My eyes were good back in those days but I squinted as I watched the little boat plough its way through the choppy seas towards us.

"Are you expecting anyone?" Ingrid wondered.

"*Nei*, but Malcolm's hoping there'll be a top-up of groceries from Lerwick. We're building up our stores ready for next winter. And, if his order of timber is on board, we can start building stabling for his ponies just up from my bothy, so that he doesn't have to keep going over to his place."

Ingrid smiled at me then. "It's going well, then, you and Malcolm?"

"*Aja!*" I grinned at her. "Very well."

There was a general move forward towards the quay as the little ship entered the harbour. We all watched as it manoeuvred and turned, and backed up to the two bollards where Tom would tie her up. Someone on board lowered a gang plank, and a couple of *En-Som-in-Fedii*, or islanders, with packs on their backs, walked gingerly towards solid ground. One had her arm in plaster; the other was assisting her. I guessed they had been to Shetland for some sort of medical treatment. Then Yanni's brother came on shore carrying a sack of mail, which he passed to Tom. He waved to his brother but went back on board to help with the unloading of the cargo.

A series of large boxes started to be brought to shore and piled neatly a few feet from the edge of the quay, and people gathered round, trying to find packages with their names on them. I saw the Williamses elbow their way through the small crowd to claim two sturdy cardboard containers. They interrupted Tom, who was talking to the woman with her arm in a sling, in order to sign for their orders, and then dragged the boxes away towards a waiting cart.

Tom was trying to sort the orders as they arrived. "There's something for you, Lyle!" he called across to where the *nasyoni* was standing. "*Nei!* Two boxes and a parcel."

I saw Lyle wave his hand in acknowledgement but he didn't come over. He was watching the crowd, alert for any trouble.

More packages and boxes were collected. Gradually the crowd dispersed. I saw the other *harkrav* men carrying away a crate of bottles, which was also loaded onto the Williamses' cart. Jeanie came down the cobbled track from the direction of her café accompanied by two of the Storhaven bairns. They made some sort of remark to Tom and claimed a wooden crate, which was carried back up the slope. Four *bondii* women, chatting in dialect, loaded grocery items into wheeled shopping bags and headed off towards the moors to the south-west. There was still a group of scowling men standing close to Mirren, but it looked to me as if the arrival of the ferry was going to pass without trouble.

Yanni said something to his brother, who shook his head negatively. It seemed the unloading was not quite complete. Both men went back on board and then Yanni appeared, carrying a huge bundle of building planks, tied together to make a secure load.

"*Hei*, Malcolm," called out Yanni. "The wood for your new stable is here!"

I saw Malcolm raise his hand to show that he had heard. He left Dougie – he had joined him a few minutes earlier – and started to make his way through the dwindling crowd to the quay.

And that's when it started.

"Stabling, my foot!" called out one of the scowling men. "He has stables already! That Malcolm McDough is building another home for refugees! He'd have the whole of En-Somi covered in bothies for strangers, given half a chance!"

"Then we need to stop him!" exclaimed one of his friends. "No blacks! No Irish! No refugees!"

"*Aja!*" cheered another man. "Stop him! No blacks! No Irish! No refugees!"

They surged forward. For a minute I thought that they were going to attack Malcolm. I stepped forward to join him, although what I could have done to help I haven't a clue. But quick as a flash both Lyle and Mirren had joined Tom by the offloaded cargo, and they stood there, all three of them, looking calmly and steadily at the advancing bullies.

The men stopped. They looked at each other, unsure what to do. Then, "Huh!" said the ringleader. "Friends in high places! But if they think they can stop us… Come on, let's go to the Vikings' Rest!"

They turned and headed back into the small town.

For a moment the small assembly of folk still left on the quay was quiet. Then Tom called out, "Will you bring your cart down here, Malcolm, to load this stuff?" That seemed to break the silence. People turned to their neighbours and resumed their conversations, and there was a palpable sense of relief in the air.

"That could have been worse," I commented to Ingrid.

She was looking in the direction of the men who had retreated. "It still could be," she answered grimly.

★★★

We had a light lunch at the Old Castle but also stopped off at Jeannie's. Tom had suggested that she might appreciate an invitation to a Friday dinner, which indeed she did, although she couldn't make it that week. It was after three when we finally left Storhaven – Malcolm, Yanni and me. Lyle was staying in the little town for a Zoom meeting with the sergeant on Lerwick, to whom the *nasyonii* answered on routine matters.

The days are long at that time of year. The sun wouldn't set until after nine and, even then, there'd be a long, lingering dusk. I seem to remember that we were feeling happy. Yanni had heard that his brother's wife was expecting another baby, and that his father, who was living on Wallis at that time, had been awarded a pension after a long and involved argument with some company he once worked for. We seemed to have survived the arrival of the ferry without the anticipated trouble, and we would be back in Hus before the community meal was over. Summer solstice celebrations were being planned. The temperature had risen after such a cool start to the day. Yanni raised his face to the warmth and closed his eyes. He was humming quietly, some ballad that Olaf had sung only a week earlier. I was reading a message from Duncan on my phone.

There's a part of the track, on the way towards Fyrtarn Fjell, where you can still see the higher houses of Storhaven behind you and the *fjell* in front. The road is relatively flat there and the land marshy. To the south is the ruined chapel, to the north a smaller track leads off to Fremdes Haven, where Lyle's parents lived. We were just approaching the turn when Malcolm, who was driving, drew on the reins and brought the ponies to a halt.

"What's happened here?" he asked of nobody in particular.

Yanni and I looked in the direction of Malcolm's gaze.

"Is it a person?" Yanni exclaimed, jumping down at once from the cart and crossing to what appeared to be a bundle of rags lying in the ditch.

"It is!" he called across to us. Malcolm was already down on the ground, and I jumped down after him. Yanni was kneeling by the prone figure, checking, I suppose, for a pulse.

"Who is it?" Malcolm asked, joining Yanni. "Is he injured?"

I was standing back a little. I could see no blood, no injuries of any sort. I thought it was one of the men who had wanted to attack Malcolm, but I wasn't sure. This man had a florid complexion. He didn't look ill. He looked just like a man lying beside the track with his eyes closed for no particular reason. Something wasn't right. They say that animals can scent danger. Well, so can humans, but I didn't recognise the sensation quickly enough.

One minute I was standing there looking down at the man, and at my partner and my friend trying to help him, and the next minute there was a wild screaming, like a war cry, issuing from the ruined chapel, and then we were joined by two more of those very same scowling men we had last seen down by the harbour.

The prone man sat up and in one fierce movement he punched Malcolm firmly on the nose. Malcolm reeled backwards and then it was him lying by the track and the man standing over him.

"Well done, laddie!" It was one of the other men, who now had Yanni held firmly with his hands behind his back. The third man grabbed my arm.

"You didn't think we meant it, did you?" hissed my captor. "No blacks, no Irish, and *no refugees!*"

"Don't hurt her!" groaned my partner, but the man standing over him just kicked Malcolm in response.

"So, you don't want us to hurt your wife?" Yanni's guard demanded. "But you've hurt us! It's our wives and our bairns that're suffering from these high taxes! You didn't think of that, did you, when you started to build bothies all over En-Somi to house perfect strangers?"

"It's always the same with these lefties!" claimed the man who was still holding on to me. "They don't think rationally! It's all 'let's help the down and outs' and never mind our neighbours!"

"The *Oyrod* told us as much at the last meeting," agreed the once-prone man. "They know what they're talking about!"

"So now," Yanni's captor said, glaring at me, "it's time we gave you some of your own medicine!"

"*Aja!*" The man who had been acting as injured had a grim smile on his face. "We're going to give you a little time to think over your actions. And we're going to relieve you of the contents of your cart!"

"This way!" demanded the man who was still gripping my arm, and he started to push me down the marshy track towards the ruined chapel.

"You too!" insisted the man holding Yanni.

"Get up!" ordered the third man, to Malcolm.

"I doesn't fink so!" came a fourth, and totally unexpected voice.

We all wheeled around. I don't know where he had been hiding, but there was Jarvis, Millwall football scarf around his neck, long coat flapping, bare feet slightly apart. And in his hands he was holding one of those two-pronged forks we use for turning hay, and he was pressing it up against the stomach of Malcolm's assailant.

I wish I had a photograph of the faces of those men at that moment. Jarvis was a wild sight, and I dare say that they had never laid eyes on him before. His hair was long, almost in dreadlocks, his face seemed to be sooty, and his expression was totally inscrutable. He looked neither angry nor concerned. He looked like a man just going about his everyday business, perhaps thinking vaguely about his dinner or some programme he had watched the night before. He looked like a man you wouldn't argue with, not because he was threatening but because it would be totally inappropriate, just as you wouldn't argue with the person who was in front of you in the bakery, buying a loaf of bread.

"I fink what it's time you was going back to that town," suggested Jarvis, and, as if to emphasise his point, he thrust the pitchfork a little more firmly against the well-upholstered gut of the man who had kicked Malcolm.

"All right! All right!" the man responded. "No need to get violent! We were only teaching these *sommy klingers* a lesson! No harm intended!"

"I doesn't like them words," Jarvis told our assailants. "I doesn't know what they means, but them's rude words. Say sorry!" And he prodded the man again.

"Oh, don't get so het up!" the man responded. "A bit of bad language between adults isn't a cause for violence!"

"Say sorry!" insisted Jarvis, sounding almost bored.

The man at the wrong end of the pitchfork sighed. "I'm sorry!" he proclaimed, sounding more indignant than sorrowful. "So there!"

"And now," Jarvis continued, "I fink it's time you went 'ome!"

By that point Malcolm and Yanni had stepped away from the men who had held them only a few minutes earlier, and were standing by Jarvis. Malcolm had a little blood around his nose but otherwise he looked fine. The man next to me had let go of my arm. "Better do as he says," he suggested.

"One more fing before you goes," Jarvis told them. "Take off them shoes!"

"You what?" The men couldn't believe Jarvis meant it.

He raised his pitchfork again. "Take off them shoes!" he

insisted quietly. "Put 'em 'ere!" And he indicated the ground at his feet. "Good!" he encouraged them, as one by one the men removed their footwear. "Now go 'ome!"

The three men looked at each other, confused, incredulous. "But…" the once-prone man complained.

Jarvis didn't reply. He just raised his pitchfork again in their general direction.

"What a fuss about a small prank!" muttered one of the men, as they turned to face Storhaven.

The four of us stood and watched them go. After a few minutes Malcolm said, "Yanni, I think you may not have met Jarvis, one of the refugees? Jarvis, this is Yanni. He lives over beyond Hus. You can usually recognise him by his curly ginger hair!"

"'Ello," Jarvis answered. "Yeah, I've seen you around. Well, I'll be on me way!"

"Hold it!" Malcolm was smiling at him. "We owe you a big thank you! You saved us from a rather tricky situation."

"Weren't no problem," Jarvis responded. "I were just passing by!"

"Come with us!" Malcolm invited. "Come and share some food with us! It's the least we can do, and there'll be people you know there—"

"Yeah, I knows," Jarvis replied. "Friday in that little school. Good food and music and laughing! But it ain't no place for me!"

And with that he turned down the track to Fremdes Haven, left it where a sheep track crosses the path, and headed up onto the moors.

We were all silent, watching him go. He didn't turn to look back at us. Malcolm sighed.

"I wonder if we'll still make it back in time for some food?" Yanni said, as we climbed back onto the bench seat at the front of the cart.

"Oh, probably!" Malcolm reassured us, and without further comment we set off for home.

CHAPTER 31

We nearly missed the food. The bairns were just going round offering second helpings when we walked into the school room, but Verity had saved us seats. Yanni, of course, joined his wife and baby Rionnag, who held out her wee arms to be picked up as soon as she saw her paps.

"So how was it?" Verity wanted to know. "As bad as Mirren had warned you? Lyle phoned – he said there was no real trouble, just angry looks and bad language. He's on his way home now."

"Well…" If Lyle was walking alone on the track where we had been waylaid, I didn't want to tell Verity what had happened. There was no point in worrying her. "It's pretty unpleasant over there." I looked around the crowded school room. "We don't realise how lucky we are on this side of the island."

★★★

It was about eleven in the morning, and the four bairns had met at my place to look at the new boat. It was a beautiful May morning, warm enough for all of us to be in short sleeves, sitting out on the slate patio overlooking the sea. I had already picked kale for dinner that evening, and dandelion leaves to dry to make tea. Marigold was tying the latter into bundles so that I could hang them under the eaves.

"You can make wine out of the dandelion heads," Duncan told us lazily. He was flat on his back, one arm under his head, staring up at the clear blue sky and chewing a piece of grass.

"I don't fancy that!" Alana was doubtful. "Wouldn't it be bitter?"

"*Nei*, Duncan's right," Andy said. "Paps has some in the storeroom. We drank a glass each last Christmas. It was sweet."

"You probably 'as to put sugar in it," Marigold remarked sagely, cutting another piece of string. "Like with dandelion tea." Then she changed the subject. "Malcolm, does your face 'urt?"

Malcolm grinned. He had cleaned himself up before we had entered the schoolroom the evening before, and nobody had commented, but in the bright sunlight a dark purple bruise was visible, stretching from his left eye over his nose.

"A wee bit," Malcolm told us. "Nothing to complain about, really."

"So, what happened?" Duncan was still looking up at the sky, his eyes screwed into slits against the brightness. "Obviously something did!"

Malcolm looked at me and gave a slight nod. It meant, *You tell them.*

Marigold put another bundle of leaves in the basket next to her. "I s'pose someone 'it you," she remarked, matter-of-factly. "Because you 'as 'elped us? And I s'pose Lyle arrested them?"

"Well, no, not quite!" I said, smiling.

"You're on the right track," Malcolm told the lassie. "But Lyle wasn't there."

"We were on our way home," I told the bairns, and described what had happened. "Then Jarvis walked off, onto the moors, and we came home!" I ended.

"Wow!" Duncan was sitting up, his knees under his chin, looking impressed. "I wish I'd been there!"

"That Jarvis is weird, isn't he?" Alana commented. "He's a bit frightening to look at. I think I'd rather have him my side than against me!"

"*Aja*," Marigold was in full agreement. "Bit it ain't – sorry, Marie, it *isn't* always easy to tell. Whether 'e's on your side or not, I mean."

Andy had been quite quiet until then. He was never a particularly healthy lad, and I thought he looked pale that morning. "I think he's on our side," he told us. "On the side of the *bondii*, I mean. He saved you yesterday, and he was worried in case we were hungry, that time that he saw us on the moors."

Marigold had finished with the leaves, and was busy making a daisy chain from flowers that grew next to my patio. "If we didn't already know what them *huldufolk* gave us the food for our feasts," she told us, "I'd guess it were Jarvis. 'E's all over En-Somi, watching what's going on; 'e doesn't miss nothing. And 'e likes us."

I was surprised. I thought that wee Marigold had completely bought into the story of the hidden people. Now I wasn't so sure.

Duncan was impressed. "Marigold!" he exclaimed. "You're brilliant!"

"Is I?" Marigold didn't seem too concerned. "Why?"

"Well, of course it's Jarvis who's giving us food? Why on the earth didn't we think of that before?"

"Well…" Marigold looped the completed daisy chain round her neck. "I suppose what we don't think about 'im much." She leant over to pick more flowers. "Does you want a daisy chain, Alana?" she asked. Then she added, "If it was Jarvis what was giving us food, where'd 'e get it? 'E lives over in that old airport and there weren't no food there when I was over there, when I ran away. Just a few tins of stuff… Mind you, I think what Jarvis would steal, if 'e felt like it. 'E stole a chicken once, when we was slaves. It were 'orrible!"

"Well," Duncan remarked thoughtfully, "whoever is giving us the food, they're getting it from somewhere, so the person must be a thief, don't you think? And I don't understand them taking from us and then giving it back. Some of our groceries have turned up in those food donations, haven't they, Mam?"

"*Aja*," I agreed, but an idea was occurring to me – more of a thought than an idea really. "Of course, the person responsible for the thefts might not be the same person who is donating the food…"

Malcolm suddenly sat forward on the bench where he was seated. "Do you remember, Marie, what Jarvis said when he came here?"

"Did Jarvis come 'ere?" Marigold was surprised. "'E ain't never been to our 'ouse!"

"Just once," Malcolm answered. "He was warning us that there might be trouble."

"*Aja*, he was," I agreed. "And you asked him who would make trouble, and he said it was always the same people who caused problems."

"And didn't he mention the bosses?" Malcolm queried. "I feel sure he did!"

Marigold was linking up the two ends of Alana's daisy chain. It was a tricky business. She had used all the flowers with the thickest stems on her own necklace, and the thin-stemmed daisies she was working with now kept splitting. For that reason, she didn't look up from her intricate task but seemed to address her handiwork. "So probably it's them bosses – the *'arkrav*, I means, what's stealing the food, and then Jarvis, 'e takes it back, and brings it over 'ere."

We all of us – except Marigold, of course – looked at each other, stunned.

"Marigold, you've proved my point!" Duncan told her. "You're a genius!"

"*Nei*," the bairn corrected my son. "I isn't no genius. Sigrid says what geniuses invent stuff, like rockets or medicines to cure people, or difficult maths that even Sigrid doesn't understand. I ain't never invented nothing. I's just got good common sense!"

"But why would the *harkrav* steal from us?" wondered Alana. "They're the rich ones, they don't need our food."

Andy was thinking it over. "Well," he pointed out. "Let's suppose that my paps is right. He thinks these new taxes are to make the *bondii* suffer, because we want the refugees to stay, and because we stood up to them."

"*Aja*," Alana agreed. "That what my mam and paps say."

"Well then," continued Andy, "they would want to make things as hard as they could for us, wouldn't they? So they raise the taxes and they take our food. That way we really suffer!"

"But haven't the *harkrav* had thefts too?" queried my son.

"So they say!" I was coming to believe that we had hit on the solution. "We don't have any evidence."

"Well, we do have evidence," pointed out Malcolm. "What about that food from the London store? That must have come from the storeroom of someone rich! So we have evidence, but it just doesn't amount to proof!"

"So 'ow does we get proof?" asked Marigold. "Marie, would you like a daisy chain too?"

CHAPTER 32

Marigold and Duncan were both disappointed when Malcolm and I insisted that we tell our theory to Lyle.

"Can't we just catch the thieves at it?" complained Duncan, "And then shop them to the *nasyonii*? After all, that's what you did, when you were freeing the refugees!"

"*Aja!*" Marigold was in a hundred per cent agreement with my son. "Then we'd be 'eroes and maybe win a reward, and my paps'd be so proud!"

"Well, we did have Lyle with us on our last adventure," Malcolm pointed out. "And it's the right thing to do."

Marigold sighed a world-weary sigh. "You's as bad as Mam!" she groaned. "Why does grown-ups 'ave to worry about *details* instead of just getting on wiv things?"

Andy and Alana, on the other hand, seemed pleased to pass on the business of catching thieves to other people. They had gone home that morning sworn to secrecy, and talking about the upcoming summer solstice picnic.

★★★

We took our evening meal down to the beach that day. Malcolm had phoned Lyle soon after Alana and Andy had left, and he and Verity had come over, bringing fried chicken. We sat on the rocks and watched the waves, discussing the theory we had come up with.

"All we 'as to do," Marigold pointed out enthusiastically, "is catch them *'arkrav* stealing from a bothy!"

"*Aja*." Lyle was patient with the bairn. "But how do we do that?"

It was, of course, the problem we had faced right from the start of all these thefts. We are a small island with an even smaller population, but we live scattered across the moors in secluded hollows and looking out over remote beaches. Where would we start?

"We 'as to think about a suspect!" Marigold suggested.

Duncan was tucking into a second leg of chicken. He was as thin as a rake in those days. Where did he put it all?

"Hail to thee, Sherlock Holmes!" he grinned.

"Actually," I said, "that's not a bad idea. If we're right, and the thief is *harkrav*, then that rules out more than half of the population of En-Somi…"

"More than three quarters, I'd say," Malcolm interjected.

"And we already know it isn't Freya Munro," I continued. "And some of the *harkrav* are on the mainland—"

"In prison!" chuckled my son.

"That still leaves a dozen or more people," pointed out Malcolm.

"P'raps we should ask Jarvis?" suggested Marigold. Then, apropos of nothing in particular, she added, "Christian won't eat chicken. 'E says it makes 'im feel sad, when he's seen it running around a few days earlier."

"Jarvis has been a bit cagey so far," I pointed out, "when it comes to naming names."

"That was when he was talking to you!" Duncan suggested. "He might tell Marigold."

"*Aja*, he might," agreed the bairn. "Is you a vegetarian if you doesn't eat chicken, or does you 'ave to give up all meat? What if a fly gets into your mouth? Can you eat fish?"

"You can certainly eat fish," Duncan told her.

"Then Christian ain't – isn't – a vegetarian!" the wee girl announced. "So shall we go and visit Jarvis?"

★★★

Of course, it wasn't that easy. If we *En-Som-in-Fedii*, or islanders, wanted to contact each other it was a straightforward enough business. Usually, unless a storm had brought down the internet for a while, we just phoned or messaged. Alternatively, we could pay a visit to someone in person. People rarely went far from their land, except perhaps during the summer or winter solstices or when the ferry came in. With Jarvis, though, it was different. Obviously, he didn't own a phone, and we weren't sure how much time he spent in the old airport.

"Can he read?" Lyle asked Marigold. "We could leave him a note in Malchi's storeroom, so that he'd see it on Thursday when he brings more food."

"I doesn't know." Marigold was staring out to sea and I thought she might be thinking back to her time as a slave. "We never talked about reading and writing, or nothing like that. And there weren't no books over there. I knows 'e knows 'is letters, 'cos 'e put a 'L' on Lavender's grave. But you learns your letters before you learns to read." She turned to me with a huge grin at that point. "Does you remember, Marie, when you started to teach me and my mam and paps, and I were so impressed what they knew their letters? And we 'ad fish and chips, 'ere, in your bothy?"

"Oh, *aja*, I remember!" And I smiled back. It wasn't so long ago, and so much had happened since then!

"But doesn't he sleep at the old airport, even if he wonders around the island when he's awake?" Duncan had been on Shetland when we had first encountered Marigold and her family, and he didn't share these memories.

"I think he must do," Verity told us. "That's where he keeps his supplies." Verity, of course, had spent several days over in St Matthew's Bay, where the old airport had fallen into ruins.

"Then let's go there, shall we? It seems like our best chance of finding him."

"We could go tomorrow!" Marigold was excited by the idea. "It'll be Sunday – no school!" Then she looked a little shyly at Lyle. "We could stop off at the cemetery and I could show Duncan Lavender's grave. Could we?" There was a note of pleading in her voice.

Duncan took matters into his own hands. He shuffled across to where Marigold was seated, and put his arm round her, for all the world like a big brother. "I would really like that, Marigold," he said.

So it was decided.

★★★

We had wondered whether Si and Rose would like to come too. They had a photo of Lavender's grave but they had never actually been there. However, Rose was a little under the weather and Si was planning to go out with Harry and Yanni, fishing. We were a large enough group as it was, for one cart and two sturdy but small ponies.

Lyle and the two bairns sat in the back, with a picnic basket, an old ice-cream container full of lamb casserole for Jarvis (a gift from Verity) and two plaid blankets. It was a beautiful morning, the beginning of the sort of day that gives the lie to the idea that we don't really have a summer this far north. The village was quiet when we left. Most islanders – well, anyhow, the *bondii*, tend to rise early. Animals still need to be cared for, even on Sundays! Nobody was out and about, though, and Shona's goats were bleating more than usual so I guessed that they were still waiting to be milked.

"I's going to learn to milk them – those – goats!" Marigold

announced. "Shona'll teach me. Then, when me and Christian's married, we's going to 'ave goats of our own."

"It's all settled then?" Duncan asked with a grin. "You and Christian?"

"*Aja*," the bairn replied. "But I 'asn't got a ring yet because we's too young. Mam says there's plenty of time for that sort of thing."

"True," agreed Duncan. "Can I give you away?"

"Don't be silly!" Marigold was scornful. "My paps'll do that!"

★★★

We stopped on top of the *fjell*, just because it was so beautiful. Looking back the way we had come we could see beyond the village to the sea, which was deep blue and sparkling. In the other direction we could see the cliffs by Fremdes Haven but not their beach, and over towards Frigg Moor we could see the top of Mac MacLoughlan's wind turbine, barely moving in the summer breeze.

"When I was a laddie," Malcolm told the bairns, "you would see little spirals of smoke rising all across the island. Except for a few of the *harkrav* who had generators, there was no electricity on the island. People still had peat fires in those days." He smiled, remembering. "My *pari-pari*, my grandfather, said the wind turbines would never catch on! But he had one before he died."

"Is 'e buried in the cemetery, too?" Marigold wanted to know.

"Oh, *aja*, all the best people are!" Malcolm told her, and I saw the wee one smile quietly to herself.

★★★

I was a little concerned about driving through Storhaven. We were not the most popular people on that side of the island, and I especially didn't want Marigold to be upset. However, there were not many people around. Jeanie was opening the wooden shutters of the café, but she just gave us a cheery wave, and Ingrid was making her way towards the kirk, and called out *"Morgoni*, everyone!" Then we were through the little town and onto the only track on the island ever to be paved, and heading towards the old airport.

Malcolm stopped at the foot of the track up to cemetery and we all climbed down.

"Come on, Duncan!" Marigold encouraged my son. "It's this way!" Then she raced up the slope.

The rest of us followed the bairns at an easier pace, so that, by the time we could see the grave, both bairns were kneeling beside it.

"Look what Jarvis 'as done!" Marigold called out as we walked past the crooked Celtic cross and the old, lichen-covered headstones of our ancestors.

Wee Lavender's grave had been made beautiful. When last I had seen it, it had been a small mound with the letter 'L' and a pattern in the shape of a heart, all made with pebbles. Those two things were still there, but the remainder of the grave was almost covered in sea glass – the rounded, coloured pieces of glass that are washed up onto our beaches, smoothed by the waves.

"I's going to take a photo of it, to show Mam and Paps!" Marigold announced, taking out her newly acquired mobile phone.

"How do you know Jarvis did this?" Duncan wondered.

"'O else would do it?" the bairn replied. "You reckon them *'arkrav* would come up 'ere to remember Lavender?" Then she set about making a daisy chain to add to the decorations, while Malcolm and Lyle wondered round the cemetery looking at the headstones of those who had gone before them, and Verity and I stood by the cliff wall and watched the gulls wheeling and diving over the calm sea.

It must have been mid-morning by the time we reached the

ruined airport buildings, and there were no signs of life. The makeshift corrugated-iron door had been pulled close, and no smoke issued from the hole in the roofing that served as a chimney.

"You lived *here*?" Duncan was dumbfounded, seeing the squalor for the first time.

"I were born 'ere," Marigold reminded my son. She stood looking at the broken tarmac of the landing strip. "It didn't seem so bad when we was 'ere," she said, thoughtfully. "There was things me and Lavender liked." She grabbed Duncan's hand and pulled him towards an old wooden picnic table. It had initials carved in it, and the bench seats were splintered. "This were our den!" she explained. "We 'ad this old blanket what we 'ung over it, and we pretended what it was a cave."

Duncan turned to look at me. He said nothing but his expression told me of his shock.

"There's a lovely beach over them sand 'ills!" continued Marigold, excited to be visiting such a familiar place. "We used to go 'unting for useful stuff over there. Come and see! It's bigger than Marie's beach!"

We all followed the bairns towards the sound of lazily breaking waves.

And there, standing in the shallows of an incoming tide, was Jarvis.

★★★

The man didn't look as shocked to see us as he might have been. It seemed that he recognised Marigold and Verity, who was indeed wearing the blue jacket by which Jarvis could identify her.

"'Ello!" he said. Then, to Verity, "You's the vicar!"

Verity laughed. "Well, I was!" she agreed. "And do you remember Lyle, who's the *nas—*" She stopped herself using the dialect word just in time. "He's the police officer."

"Yeah." Jarvis acknowledged Lyle. "But 'e ain't no real cop, not like they 'as in 'uver places!"

"And do you remember us?" I asked. "You came to see us at my bothy – I'm Marie and this is Malcolm."

"I knows you!" Jarvis told us. "I been watching you!"

Marigold was looking up and down the beach. "I *so* remember this!" she exclaimed. Then, to Duncan, "It's lovely, ain't it?"

Duncan smiled at her. "I'll race you to those rocks!" he challenged, and I watched as he let the wee girl win – but only by a little.

★★★

An hour or so later we were back on the beach with the rugs spread out and the picnic basket open. In the meantime, Marigold had shown Duncan around the old departure hall that had been her home, apparently unaware of my son's hastily disguised looks of horror, and Jarvis has poked his smouldering fire to bring it back to life, and made us some 'tea'. Verity's casserole was left for later, alongside a row of tins – Jarvis's food store, of course.

Marigold was showing off to Jarvis. "This 'ere cheese is goats' cheese, what Shona makes!" she explained. "And them tomatoes, they come from Andy's mam's garden. They's the first of this year's crop. And Marie made the bread."

Jarvis seemed to be enjoying his meal. "I fought you'd come," he told us. "But I never fought what you'd bring so much food!"

"Why did you think we'd come?" Lyle wanted to know.

Jarvis reached out for another sandwich, then looked to Verity as if for permission. When she said 'go ahead', he grabbed one and took a large mouthful, staring out to sea. Only when he had swallowed it did he reply.

"I reckoned it were time to put a stop to all this," he said obliquely.

"All what?" Duncan wanted clarification.

"It were one thing when they was just stirring up trouble – not really 'urting anyone, just taking their food. I seen what they was doing, and I knewd what I could sort that. But first they thumped that old codger, the one where Quincy and Mo is living, then they wanted to beat you up – them yobs on the road – and I knew enough were enough. I tried to warn you about them bosses but you didn't listen, so I fought what you didn't understand. So then I 'oped that per'aps you might come and ask me. You isn't daft. And 'ere you is!"

"I thought you'd know!" Marigold was exultant. "It were my idea to ask you!"

"So you know who's behind all this?" asked Lyle casually. He was trying not to sound as if he were interrogating the man.

"Yeah, I knows!" Jarvis agreed.

"So who is it?" Duncan asked.

"If you stays until this evening," he told us. "I'll show you!"

★★★

When the bairns realised that they were going to be right where the action was, that the plan was to catch the thief or thieves in the act, they couldn't have been more thrilled. We spent the afternoon down on the beach – it was a glorious day – and we texted Jeanie to ask her to let Si and Rose know where Marigold was, and that she was all right. It's almost impossible to phone Hus from St Matthew's Bay. Lyle made contact with Mirren too, and she joined us mid-evening. The sun had gone behind the moors by then, but it was still light. "We 'as to wait until it's dark," pointed out Jarvis. "They won't do nofing until then."

We made a fire on the beach and wee Marigold curled up with her head in my lap, and slept. She was accustomed to early bedtimes by then. Duncan was wide awake, his eyes sparkling, taking photos of us round the fire to show his friends later. Malcolm lay on his back with his hands behind his head.

"Did you know that the Quakers tell their members to live adventurously?" he enquired of no one in particular. "I think we're doing that, don't you?"

It was not quite pitch dark when Jarvis said, "Right then! Time to go!"

We woke Marigold, repacked the picnic basket, rolled up the blankets and stored everything in Malcolm's cart. Then, "Now, be quiet!" Jarvis instructed, and led the way.

At first, we walked along the track, south towards Storhaven. I noticed that there were more potholes than I remembered from the last time I had been there. Another winter had passed, and nobody was responsible for the paving. In a few years, I thought, you would never know that there had once been a smooth surface for carts and traps to drive along. The days of picking tourists up from the airport were long gone.

Then we turned west, up onto the moors. We were not following any recognisable track – at least, not as far as I could see. Jarvis was in the lead, almost springing from rock to rock, but the rest of us were less sure-footed. The going was hard, but we were fit and well, and our shoes were stout. I had walked these moors in bandaged feet in the past, and when the ground was soggy. Compared to that experience, following Jarvis's lead was easy. I was a little concerned for Verity because of her pregnancy, but Lyle was with her and, to be honest, she didn't look as if she was finding it hard work. Mirren was panting a little, but she was keeping up without apparent difficulty. She was an islander too, even if it was a different island!

I suppose we walked and climbed for about half an hour. The glow of late sunset to the west had gone when we saw a dark shape to the north. There were lights in the windows, and the door was open.

"A boss's bothy," whispered Marigold.

"*Aja*," Duncan answered softly. "We're on Floirean's Cnoc. No *bondii* live round here."

Lyle tapped Jarvis on the arm. "Do you know the names of the owners of this place?"

"I ain't no good at names and faces," Jarvis whispered. "'E is sort of tall and lanky and she 'as this long blonde 'air."

Mirren had caught up and we were standing in a tight circle, just beyond the stream of light that came from the nearest window.

"It's the Williamses' place," she hissed. "They called me over when they said they'd had a break-in."

"Duck!" whispered Duncan, and just in time we all squatted among the dark marshy hillocks as another person approached.

We watched as he moved towards the open door. "It's Blair Munro!" Lyle sounded almost satisfied with this discovery.

"Quiet!" demanded Jarvis. So we all crouched there, awaiting developments.

Sure enough, in only a couple of minutes Munro reappeared, along with the two Williamses. They all had torches.

"Where to this time?" enquired Mr Williams.

"What about that old man again?" suggested Candy Williams.

"No." Blair was adamant. "He's got those two young *sommy klingers* with him now. They might put up a fight."

"There's an old couple over by Fremdes Haven," Candy Williams pointed out. "We haven't paid them a visit yet!"

"Oh, good plan!" Blair Munro sounded happy. "I think they're the parents of that annoying young policeman!"

"Right then!" Mr Williams sounded decisive. "It's a bit of a walk, but it'll be worth it!"

I looked towards Lyle. Was he recording everything on his phone, as I had known him to do once before? He caught my eye and winked. "For now, we'll just follow them," he whispered. "We want to catch them in the act!"

So once again we were venturing over the moors by night. Marigold came and held my hand. She was almost bouncing from rock to rock, excited and energetic. Duncan caught my eye and grinned at me. Malcolm was walking with Mirren at the rear; Lyle was right behind Jarvis. Ahead we could see the torch light of the *harkrav* as they picked their way along sheep tracks and seldom-used footpaths. They were slower than *bondii* would normally be, less familiar with the moors, and it was easy to keep up.

We reached the point where the footpath crosses a burn. There is a sort of plank bridge there. It was, I realised, the place where Jarvis had once met our four bairns coming back from Lyle's parents. From there the path is clearer, more frequently used, and the three we were following started to speed up. We kept our distance.

There are three bothies in Fremdes Haven. Lyle's parents lived in the first one, if you approached as we did, from the east. Further along was another inhabited bothy. I can't remember who lived there then. And I think the third was more or less ruined at the time I am telling you about, although it's a pretty little place now – unusual because when it was renovated they only kept the westerly chimney.

There were no lights. It must have been midnight, and Lyle's parents never stayed up late. Their storehouse was attached to the western end of the neat little bothy, and it was in that direction that the three *harkrav* walked.

I saw Mirren and Lyle confer, then Mirren took out her phone. She was also recording events to serve as evidence later. Lyle turned to the rest of us and made hand signals, telling us to stay where we were. Then the two *nasyonii* crept forward, avoiding the rocks that jutted out of the soft turf.

Any of the Hus bairns would have known that using a torch limits how much a person can see at night. Within the circle of light everything is visible, but somehow the brightness makes the surroundings darker. The *harkrav* didn't see Mirren and Lyle as they approached.

One of the thieves – I think it may have been Candy Williams – started to saw the padlock so recently attached to the storehouse by Lyle's paps. The little saw was quiet; I could easily imagine how anyone asleep inside would not be disturbed. I expected Lyle or Mirren to step forward into the light to make an arrest, but they waited…

When the door was opened all three thieves shone their torches into the stone building.

"Quite a hoard!" I heard Blair Munro exclaim.

"Yes, they've started to stock up for next winter!" It must have been Mr Williams speaking.

"Can we carry it all?" wondered Candy Williams.

"Most of it," Blair told her. "We'll leave the potatoes."

"Have you got the new hiding place ready?" Mr Williams wanted to know. "It's a waste of effort to keep stealing from these peasants if someone steals it back!"

"No problem," reassured Blair Munro. "Whoever took all that stuff from your place, Candy – he'll never find it this time!"

The thieves started to empty Lyle's parents' storehouse then. They made a pile outside on the grass: tins and packets and two boxes of something. I was surprised, to be honest, at how far Lyle's mam and paps had got with their preparations for the coming winter. It wasn't summer solstice yet!

I suppose Mirren and Lyle had agreed a signal, because suddenly Lyle stepped forward and all three torches were suddenly shining on him as the startled trio of *harkrav* whirled around.

"Mr and Mrs Williams and Blair Munro, in the name of the *Oyrod* and the people of En-Somi, I am arresting you for criminal damage and for theft. You do not have to say anything, but it may harm your defence if you do not mention when questioned something which you later rely on in court. Anything you do say may be recorded or written down and given in evidence."

For a second or two there was a stunned silence. Then Blair Munro leapt forward towards Lyle, his torch held high ready to smash it over the head of the *nasyoni*. Lyle stepped back and Mirren stepped forward.

"I don't think you want to add assaulting a police officer to your list of crimes, do you?" she asked calmly.

By then, of course, Malcolm had joined them, and the two bairns had crept a lot closer.

"Do you need any help?" Malcolm suggested in his mild-mannered way. "I've got several other friends here."

Of course, the Williamses and Blair Munro didn't know that Malcolm's 'other friends' were two unarmed women and two bairns – and, anyhow, we would have stepped in if we had been needed! Mirren took out some handcuffs, and one by one the three *harkrav* villains were made to put their hands behind their backs, where they were firmly secured.

A light came on in the bothy and moments later Lyle's paps appeared at the door. He sounded, I thought, rather nervous.

"Who's out there?" he demanded. "I've called the *nasyonii!*"

"It's all right, Paps!" Lyle stepped up into the stream of light that issued from the open bothy door. "It's me! We've just caught our thieves – at last!"

After that there were a few minutes of chaos. Everyone was talking at the same time. Blair Munro was requesting that he see a solicitor at once, Candy Williams was trying to tell anyone who would listen that her husband had forced her to take part in the thefts. Duncan and Marigold were being warmly hugged by Lyle's mam, and Malcolm was looking over Mirren's shoulder as she played back – and immediately posted to the police in Lerwick – the very incriminating recording she had made. Then we all went inside and Lyle's mam fussed around Verity ('you shouldn't be out on the moors, hen, in your condition!') and some of us drank hot milk while others savoured some very good home brew. The *harkrav*, standing in the corner, were offered water.

It was only then that Marigold noticed who was missing.

"Where's Jarvis?" she wanted to know.

He wasn't there. Malcolm and I went back outside at once and called him. It was no good. He had gone.

EPILOGUE

The whole story only came out in bits and pieces. Jarvis became very elusive following the incidents I've just described, and he was really needed to fill in the parts we didn't know.

Gradually, though, our suspicions were borne out. We suspected that other *harkrav* had been involved but we could never prove it, nor did we ever discover who had masterminded the scheme. We did know, however, that the plan had been to cause so much trouble on En-Somi that the refugees would have to leave. The thefts from the *bondii* were designed to make our lives as hard as possible. Blair Munro's Edinburgh solicitor adamantly denied that Blair's motives had been to punish the *bondii* for daring to go against him and his friends, but nobody on the island believed that.

The difficult part was explaining Jarvis's role. We all understood that he had watched the *harkrav* and seen what they were up to, although to this day I doubt whether he understood why they were acting as they were. He had then stolen back from them, taking some of their supplies as well as the food removed from *bondii* storehouses. Then, when he saw what we were doing over in Gamla Hus, he donated the food for the Friday evening meals. A few tins, of course, he kept for himself. The man had to eat.

The problem was, there was no getting away from the fact that he, too, had stolen from others. His motives were good but he had broken the law, and he knew it. And he had no trust whatsoever in authority figures, or in any form of justice.

For months after these events very few of us saw Jarvis but, when Verity gave birth to little Joel, flowers appeared on their doorstep. I'm also fairly sure that Lyle went over to the old airport whenever he was over in Storhaven, taking gifts of food or other things a man might find useful. The two *nasyonii*, of course, never intended to report Jarvis, but I suppose he wasn't to know that.

Then Olaf wrote 'The Ballad of the Walking Man', which didn't mention Jarvis but which featured a barefooted man who kept watch over the poor and needy in a far-off land of trolls and spirits, and we all knew who he was really singing about. Gradually Jarvis became an island hero, a mystery man who was out there on the moors, keeping us safe.

Over in Storhaven it took time for things to calm down. We had to elect a new *Oyrod* because so many of the original members were now in prison. A proper doctor was recruited to work with our island nurse – Lyle and Verity's Joel was the first *En-Som-in-Fedi* she delivered.

It was years later, after he had that accident over in Caldbrae and broke his leg, that Jarvis finally moved to the other harbour cottage in Storhaven, just over from Tom. Initially it was just so that the doctor could keep an eye on him, but somehow or other he never moved out. He was, of course, a total recluse, but if we saw him at his window we always waved, and as often as not he waved back.

When Marigold learnt to knit, she created a scarf in Millwall colours, which she gave him as a winter solstice gift. He was wearing it still, all those years later, when we buried him.

THE BALLAD OF THE WALKING MAN

Over yonder, over there,
On the peat lands, in the air,
Hear the sound of bare feet moving,
See the tracks of silent roving.
Hold your breath and start believing
In the Walking Man.

Walking Man, silent one,
Secret friend to everyone,
Now you're here and now you're gone.
That's the Walking Man.

On the clifftops, by the shore,
Near the high stacks, on the moor.
Hear his breathing, slow and easy,
See his hands and feet so busy,
Tangled hair and face so grisly.
There's the Walking Man.

Friend of burns and trees and rocks,
Of Arctic hares and woolly flocks,
Of quiet harbours, churning lochs.
See the Walking Man.

He walks our land, he knows our ways,
Our crops and bothies, fields and bays.
We know his care and his protection,

His love for us, and his affection.
A shadow here, a strange reflection –
There goes the Walking Man.

Dark coat flapping in the gale,
Exploring every moor and dale,
He fights to make the evil fail.
That's our Walking Man.

Trolls and spirits, ghosts and thieves,
Tangled web around them weaves.
Hears the harms they plan unfolding,
In his heart our good he's holding,
All his powers for us he's wielding.
Our friend, the Walking Man.

Dark and lonely, foreign stranger,
Saving us from hidden danger,
Violence and harkrav anger
Thank you, Walking Man!

LOCAL DIALECT

aja	yes
bondi	peasant. Plural *bondii*
Bothan Ros	Rose Cottage
brenni	a ceremonial bonfire. Plural *brennii*
Caldbrae	Cold Hill (from Cauld Brae)
cludgie	loo. Plural *cludgii*
domstol	the court of the kirk elders (as in the elders' meeting)
En-Somi	Lonely Island
En-Som-fly-Kninger	refugees
En-Som-in-Fedi	an islander. Plural *En-Som-in-Fedii*
fi'ilsted	literally 'fish hearth', best translated as 'pub'. Plural *fi'ilstedi*
fjell	in English: fell. A high and barren landscape feature
frokost blomster	literally 'breakfast flowers'
Gamla Husmannsplass	'Old Homestead' – the village
Gamla Hus	abbreviation of Gamla Husmannsplass
gensi	a pullover jumper. Plural *gensii*
goddi morgoni	good morning. Often abbreviated to *morgoni*
gronnki sengi	kale beds
harkrav	from *har krav pa* – elites (literally 'entitled')
hei	hi or hello

huldufolk	elves (literally 'hidden people')
Hus	abbreviation of **Gamla Husmannsplass**
huss	'house' or 'building'. Plural *hussi*
jubel	Norwegian, meaning 'cheers!'
langspil	zither-like musical instrument
Liten Stein	Little Rock
mam	mum
mori-mori	grandmother
muckle scarf	cormorants
nasyoni	police officer. Plural *nasyonii*
neeps	swedes
nei	no
Oyrod	Island Council. Members of the *Oyrod* are *oyrodi*
papa (or paps)	father or dad
pari-pari	grandfather
Paske Ekstrom	Eastern Extreme
pylsa	the island version of hot dogs
saulė	sun
sól	sun
solstice-brenni	the fires lit to celebrate the winter solstice. Plural *solstice-brennii*
sommy klinger	corrupt and insulting form of *En-Som-fly-Kninger* or refugee
un-fed	outsider. Plural *un-fedii*
Vestrsear	Old Norse word for the sea west of Norway
voldliggi	wild, rough – relating to weather

This book is printed on paper from sustainable sources managed under the Forest Stewardship Council (FSC) scheme.

It has been printed in the UK to reduce transportation miles and their impact upon the environment.

For every new title that Troubador publishes, we plant a tree to offset CO_2, partnering with the More Trees scheme.

For more about how Troubador offsets its environmental impact, see www.troubador.co.uk/sustainability-and-community